I0563428

Advance Praise for *Settle Down*

With style, wit, and wisdom, and sly touch of the surreal, Ritt Deitz explores the mystery of home—the feeling, the identity, the story—but rather than solving any riddles for us, his unique and captivating novel *Settle Down* gifts us the questions to ponder for ourselves and leaves us dreaming of our own life journeys.

—John Galligan, author of *The Nail Knot* and *Bad Axe County*

Ritt Deitz has written a novel about how a place shapes a person's identity, their values, their politics, their language and even what they eat. His young characters are searching for a place to establish roots, aware that that first choice is like an opening paragraph that will give direction to the story of their lives. And Madison plays a starring role in his book. Local readers will recognize the street names, the bars and the theaters. Most importantly, a lot of Madisonians will see themselves in Deitz's book. Like his characters, on the way to someplace else, we settled down (but didn't "settle") right here.

—Dave Cieslewicz, former mayor of Madison, WI

Ritt Deitz's debut offers an irreverent and thoughtful examination of what it means to love a place—and how we communicate this love to others. With a keen eye and great empathy, he digs into matters of storytelling, history, and the geography of the human heart.

—Laura Anne Bird, award winning author of *Crossing the Pressure Line* and *Marvelous Jackson*

A playful, sensitive novel.

—François Leblanc, author of *Coyotes et alligators*

Ritt Deitz's debut novel is a thoroughly enjoyable romp, which will come as no surprise to anyone acquainted with his considerable gifts as a songwriter and storyteller. *Settle Down* is thoughtful, funny, imaginative and a pure pleasure to read.

—John Robinson, longtime Madisonian and raconteur

Deitz has imagined an American Heartland we can actually believe.

—Alain-Philippe Durand, Dorrance Dean for the College of Humanities, University of Arizona

SETTLE DOWN

a novel

Ritt Deitz

Settle Down

SC ISBN: 9781645386094
HC ISBN: 9781645386100
Settle Down
By Ritt Deitz

Cover design by Dana Breunig

Ten|16
PRESS

Published by Ten16 Press, an imprint of Orange Hat Publishing
www.orangehatpublishing.com
Wauwatosa, WI

This is a work of fiction. Names, characters, places and incidents are the products of the author's imagination or are used fictitiously. Characters in this book have no relation to anyone bearing the same name and are not based on anyone known or unknown to the author. Any resemblance to actual businesses or companies, organizations, events, locales, or persons, living or dead, is entirely coincidental.

For Truk, the real bear
of Willy Street

His voice had grown soft, and he had merged many accents and dialects into his own speech, so that his speech did not seem foreign anywhere.
—John Steinbeck, *East of Eden*

We live the given life, and not the planned.
-Wendell Berry

Madison, Wisconsin
1974

"It's quiet time, now," said Mrs. Brooking to the entire third-grade class. "No talking."

Kenny McLuher felt his cheeks flush, knowing his teacher was addressing him. He and his friend Kurt Lemke, who sat in the next row, had been giggling uncontrollably for a full minute over a ducklike creature Kenny had drawn on his spelling sheet and passed across the aisle. The creature looked a little like the two-headed Pushmi-Pullyu in *Doctor Dolittle*, except that it had bug eyes and wheels instead of legs. Kenny's older sister Kate, who was constantly drawing cartoons of her own, had shown him how to make what she called "action puffs," to indicate a speeding figure. Kurt had put them behind one side of the creature, then put a second set on the other side, puffing in the opposite direction. The creature looked startled, like it was rushing into itself.

"That's hilarious!" whispered Kurt. "That's a hilarious duck!" He was trying hard not to laugh, which made Kenny also want to laugh—and draw another imploding duck.

"No talking to our neighbors," repeated Mrs. Brooking, looking right at Kenny and Kurt this time. "We are here to work on our spelling, not entertain an audience." She glared a full two seconds longer, then turned back around and finished taping up the poster she had just unrolled against the blackboard. Next to it, an older poster showed a boy jumping off a fence to impress a little girl, under the red warning *Don't be a show-off!* The new addition, which Mrs. Brooking had brought in that very morning, was more modern-looking and, in the spirit of the times, more positive. It showed a little boy looking up at a star, his hand held toward it. *Reach for a star!* it urged, adding *Achieve your goals!*

"Achieve," whispered Kenny, to himself. The word looked cool. He was interested in words and had just discovered words that looked like this one. And that sounded like this one, too—Mrs.

Brooking had driven that point home by teaching the class, a few weeks earlier, to recite the rule *I before E, except after C.* Few of the pupils could understand this, let alone remember it, but to Kenny it sounded like a song. Maybe even the kind you could use as a soundtrack for a cartoon of a duck on wheels.

He looked back down at his spelling sheet. It had a column of typed words on the left side, with three identical columns of empty lines to the right. The students were to handwrite each word three times, from left to right, in those blanks. Kenny and Kurt had finished early; this is why they were doodling and giggling.

When she finished taping up the poster, Mrs. Brooking walked over to Kenny's side.

"You boys have finished early. Is that right?" Taller than most of the other Lowell Elementary teachers, she towered over him. But her voice was kind enough.

"Yes, Mrs. Brooking," replied Kenny.

"Did you want to write a little story, maybe practice a little?" she asked, gently. She had shifted gears, more carrot than stick. She knew both boys were interested in words, that they both liked stories.

Kenny lit up. "Yes, yes," he said, sitting up a little straighter in his seat.

"You may get your pads out," she said quietly. A row over, Darlene Gustafson lifted her head from her spelling sheet and glanced admiringly at Kenny, at this chance Kenny and Kurt had apparently earned to go farther, to do something more interesting. Kurt saw her and crossed his eyes at her, surreptitiously. She had already written an extra paragraph of her own on the back of the sheet, but no one had noticed. She grimaced at Kurt then turned the sheet back over and began making extra copies of the word *circus*, the dot above the *i* a generous round circle.

Kenny took out his pad and wrote a little story:

Great, Great, Great Uncle
by Kenny McLuher, Age 8

During the Civil War, my grandmother's grandmother's great, great, great uncle shook hands with Aberham Lincoln. When my grandmother told me that, I was about three, and I thought I was related to him. I also have the same birthday Febuary 12fth. He achieved a lot of goals. "Good old Abe's part of our family!" I cried, "No, not exactly," said Grandmother. I was crushed.

The next day, I woke up early in the morning and said, "I wonder why he doesn't live here anyway?" Grandmother had been listening outside my room and couldn't stand it any longer. The door flew open. "He got shot and killed by John Wilks Booth!" I burst into tears. Yep, that was the way it was in 1969, when I was three.

When he finished the last sentence, he looked over at Kurt, who was still writing. Kenny sat back and looked at his own pad, comparing his story with the ones he had seen in the books he had been reading, or which had been read to him. A title, a space between paragraphs, some good words in there. *A little suspense*, as his mother sometimes said when she and their dad would refuse to tell Kenny and his sister where they were going for a special occasion, like a birthday dinner. Especially satisfied that he had found a way to use *achieve*, he thought for a minute about spelling. That was down deep in the words, and sometimes you had to guess, based on the way you said things. But the suspense, the *action*, was in the way they flowed one after the other. Also, it was good if you could get yourself into the story somehow.

Up at her desk, Mrs. Brooking seemed to be waiting for the class to finish. She looked up at the clock on the wall, then over at the new poster. Sighing a little, she took a small mirror and some lipstick out of her purse, then looked nervously at the class for a second. She quickly re-applied the makeup, snapped the mirror closed, and put both tools back in her purse before looking back at the clock. Kenny knew what this series of movements meant: in a minute or two, Mrs. Brooking would announce that it was time for everyone to finish their spelling sheets.

Darlene was resting her head on the desk. Having finished her work, she seemed to have fallen completely asleep. What had made her so tired? Just a minute earlier, she had been looking over at Kenny, making faces at Kurt. Now she was just dozing away on her spelling sheet. Maybe she had just gone to bed too late.

Kenny made a mental note of her position in the room and about how far she was across the aisle from him. It looked like five feet or so. The floor tiles had scuffs on them, but they were dark and shiny. Everything felt like it belonged right there where it was. A slight burst of adrenaline spread out into Kenny's limbs. He looked back down at the last line of the story he had just made.

"I'm the narrator," he thought.

Charlottesville, Virginia
(1987-88)

Birdwood Pavilion

After almost four years of college, Kenny was pretty sure he could identify what was Southern about things. In this case, it was the bow tie. A lot of middle-aged men wore them around here, and not just historians, either.

It wasn't just the fact of the tie, so well-kempt and silky, all Virginia blue-and-orange. It was something about how it lay against the neck of its wearer, a biographer of some renown. Crisply knotted yet also somehow relaxed, the tie drew Kenny's attention to the man's jowls, which jiggled slightly to the rhythmic *clink-clink* of the ice in his otherwise empty lowball glass, even in those rare moments when he wasn't talking. The small hors d'oeuvres tray in one hand, Kenny put his other hand in his pocket to avoid nervously scratching his chin. He had enjoyed a bong hit with Wayne at the beginning of the shift and was still a little high.

Knox Chiffonier IV stood in a dull half-circle of handlers who had been marshalled by the reception's organizer, Dr. Burton of the Alumni Association. Whatever energy had been generated by the lightly-attended talk on Chiffonier's latest book, *Mr. Jefferson: Our Shadow and Our Light,* had dissipated. Clearly uninterested in anything these people might do or say next, the biographer turned to Kenny, who was standing close to him, holding the hors d'oeuvres.

"So what are you *may*-joring in, young man?" asked Chiffonier, twirling a toothpick from which he had just liberated a sausage ball.

"History," said Kenny. Chiffonier's face stopped moving for a second or two.

"Hm, well." Chiffonier laid the toothpick down onto the dish in his hand and picked up a fresh sausage ball, his jowls having gently resumed their quivering. "A more than reasonable choice."

He paused, oration still fragrant upon him. "The University of Virginia." Another pause. "Our university. And Mr. Jefferson's lifelong dream." He popped the meatball into his mouth. A Mississippian by birth and upbringing but sure he was really a Virginian in the deepest part of his soul, Chiffonier pronounced it *Vuh-gin-yuh*. As a young man keen on professing, he had cherished this pronunciation, already indigenous to him and members of his family. But he really emphasized it, purposefully slowing it down to a rate not even Hollywood actors playing Southerners would be coached to use in films.

"Yes, sir," Kenny replied, as he had suspected a younger man in Virginia was supposed to say in this kind of situation, but he was just one of the caterers. Was this what majoring in history was for?

Chiffonier ate a third meatball with unusual speed, then half-whispered "Indeed"—less in response to Kenny than to his own sage pronouncement from three seconds prior. His plate now empty, Chiffonier looked wearily over at Dr. Burton and the rest of his group, who were still standing between the buffet table and entrance to a second, smaller room. He smiled weakly, gave Kenny two little pats on the shoulder, and walked unceremoniously toward the other door, which led to the foyer and outside. His gait half small-town tourist crossing a big-city intersection, half bewhiskered British officer about to thump his swagger stick onto the chest of a new recruit, Knox Chiffonier IV exited the building as if it were his sole purpose.

Dr. Burton watched the author leave. Sighing discreetly, he turned back around and sniffed, Don Knotts-like, then adjusted his belt with his free hand. His other hand gripped an empty cocktail plate, which he pointed at the buffet table.

"You should bring some more sausages out," he said curtly.

He made no eye contact. It was less an actual request than the resigned demi-chirp of a man who had understood for some time that he would never be able to make things happen with his words.

* * * * *

Back in the kitchen, Wayne stared red-eyed at the grassy expanse outside the window.

"Man, the view sure is pretty out onto that golf course."

Wayne was not a student at UVA. Hailing from Waynesboro, a few miles to the west of Charlottesville, the full-time cook always noted this when introducing himself to new student workers at University Catering. "The name's Wayne... and I'm from Waynesboro," he'd say, with the same sly grin every time. "No comment!" He had the best weed in Charlottesville.

"Hey, Wayne," asked Kenny, sliding a fresh metal bin of sausage balls out of the Cambro, "who gave Birdwood to UVA?"

"How should I know, man? Some family, I guess," said Wayne, still looking dreamily out the window. It was very green outside Birdwood Pavilion. "Man, I sure do love golf though."

Kenny went back out into the main room and dumped the sausage balls into the chafing dish. Burton was gone. In fact, the room was just about empty, but for three people. Two elderly ladies chatted near the podium, and over by the buffet table, a mousy younger man in a blue sports coat, probably Dr. Burton's assistant, seemed to be waiting for someone. Or maybe just something: when the half-load of meat nuggets arrived, he speared ten chunks, one after another, onto his cocktail plate. He smiled weakly at Kenny.

"Good meatballs," he said. He sounded like he was from that part of the Midwest where, when you think *I get treated like a moron in this job, and I can't wait to quit*, you say something like "Good meatballs."

"Yes," replied Kenny, an Upper Midwesterner himself. "They're pretty good." It had been a vaguely comforting Midwestern exchange, here in faraway Central Virginia. Kenny picked two used cocktail napkins off the buffet table and returned to the kitchen.

Twenty or thirty seconds later, Logan came into the kitchen and plopped down on a stool next to the big metal serving table. Also a history major—and, like Kenny, a fervent fan of Wayne's weed—Logan was the other student caterer at this particular event. Kenny was supervising the event, at least officially. Logan was pouring the booze.

"Bar action?" asked Kenny.

"Dead," said Logan, who Kenny just realized had been chewing gum at the bar. Logan dropped his head onto the table, then lifted it again slowly. "I'm super bored, dude."

Kenny looked at the clock above the stove. "They're wandering away. Let's wrap it up."

"What did you think of his reading, though?" asked Logan.

Kenny began consolidating platters into a pile on the table. "Well, first: how about the guy's name?" he said. "Knox Chiffonier? The *Fourth*?"

Logan seemed not to have heard. "I liked the lecture," he said. He chewed his gum open-mouthed now, smacking a little as he spoke. "That whole part about Jefferson's relationship with John Adams? He seemed to be making some point about Northern liberals today, don't you think?"

Kenny looked up, familiar with Logan's politics and his mostly friendly jabs at Wisconsin, which he imagined as full of liberals.

"I mean," Logan continued, "I don't think UVA students appreciate the importance of Jefferson biographies."

"Wait, what? You don't think we have enough 'Mr. Jefferson' fed to us in the dorms first year? You don't think they pay enough homage to him in every last building, event, or whatever?"

"Come on, man. That's not just a Founding Father you're talking about there. It's the Founder of the University." This order of importance struck Kenny as particularly Virginian.

"Dag," said Wayne, still looking dreamily out the window. "I'd sure like to play me some on that course out there."

Kenny exhaled fast through his nose then issued a crisp *hmph* at Logan. He set down a plate. "You know, I notice that when people like this fop, or even the Monticello guides, like at that event we did up there last spring, they never mention Sally Hemings. They still don't mention her."

Logan's face began to pinken. He stopped chewing, and his mouth gathered tightly in the half-pout his lips would form when anyone he had just smoked pot with started to say negative things about Reagan or the American financial system.

"There's no proof of that, man. That's just political correctness."

"Relax, dude. This is 1987. It's probably okay for us to acknowledge that a very famous, long-widowed Founding Father was probably sleeping with this younger woman who lived in his house in a place where, you know, dudes like him were allowed to legally own other people."

"Oh right, it's always about slavery."

Kenny picked up a new plate. Twelve years of public school in Madison, Wisconsin, had very earnestly suggested to him that everything in the South was, in fact, primarily about slavery. "It might be a little bit possible, Logan. You think? In 1820, in Virginia? Like, on a slave plantation?"

"Mmm," they heard Wayne say to himself. "Golf."

"Whatever," chirped Logan, "fucking facile liberal bullshit."

Normally, Logan's second use of the word *liberal* would have worked as bait, but Kenny was suddenly distracted by a strange feeling just behind his navel. It didn't hurt; it was just like a slight vibration or a hum that only he could hear. Like an itch but inside, somewhere in his entrails. He looked over at Wayne, who was still staring out at the golf course, and then back at Logan, who had begun to chew his gum again, open-mouthed and defiant. Instead of rage or even irritation, Kenny just felt this strong urge to tell Logan a story.

"All right, man, whatever. Hey, you know who Brer Rabbit was?"

Logan gave a start. "What? Uncle Remus? Are you fucking with me?"

Undeterred, Kenny began to tell the story, in the voice his own father had used when tucking him and his sister in at night. Kenny was from Madison, but Kenny's dad had grown up and spent most of his youth in Central Kentucky. His dad was also just over four years in the ground.

"Mm-hm! Brer Rabbit. Cuttin' capers out dere in de woods with all dem udder crittuhs..." This was the Stepin-Fetchit-y language from the big book accompanying Disney's *Song of the South*, which Kenny's dad had read to him and his sister a lot when they were kids, at bedtime. Walt Disney's dream machine had taken Joel Chandler Harris's "original" rendition of Georgia slave dialect and smoothed it out for nationwide consumption, mostly by white people. Whatever it was, however stale or offensive it was now, it had always completely entranced little Kenny, and his sister, too.

"You see, heah, ol' Brer Rabbit, Logan—he weren't no reg'lar rabbit. Naw, suh."

Logan looked confused, as if he were trying to decide if

Kenny was mocking him, testing to see if he was a racist, or having a stroke. But neither of them moved.

"No suh, dat Brer Rabbit was a *quick* one. He was smartuh'n dem other crittuhs by a *country* mile." Kenny was speaking as low as possible, in what sounded like it wanted to be a smooth Confederacy-Apologist drawl but was really, underneath the exaggerated phonemes and diphthongs, just his dad's voice, boilerplate Central-Kentucky country-storyteller timbre.

"One day, ole Brer Rabbit, he was just a-skippin' down de lane, cuttin' capers like no critter in the woods could cut 'em. Dat sun was sho' shinin' down, like it usually do in de summertime, out in dem woods whey de critters lived..."

"Whoa, Kenny, that sounds kinda weird, man," said Wayne, who had just swiveled around from his position at the window and was smiling uncomfortably. "I don't know if people really talk that way. You know, like nobody I know really does." Deferring to the college kids a little, as always, Wayne was nonetheless registering a gentle complaint.

Why was Wayne so bothered by this? Logan had himself been the target of a similar complaint the day before, registered by Tracy the Vegetarian (a Women's Studies major and fellow caterer), after he had criticized the recent film adaptation of *The Color Purple.* He could understand that kind of thing coming from a fellow student and Northern Virginian suburbanite, but this cultural sensitivity in Waynesboro Wayne surprised him.

"I mean," said Logan, his gaze fixed on Kenny, "you are kinda doing an old, like, blackface kinda voice, dude. I mean, it's a little..."

"Heh heh," chortled Kenny, elsewhere, his eyes closed serenely. His voice got deeper. He looked possessed. "Heh, heh, old Logan done got hisself wrapped up in de tale!"

By this late-October day in 1987, most people within earshot of Kenny would have found his storytelling a crude and embarrassing imitation, at best. At worst, it was a full-bodied ethnic slur, but this was the farthest concern from Kenny's mind. He was even swaying a little, as if in a trance.

Logan, on the other hand, was now fighting just to stay awake. The deep Hollywood-Sambo voice was morphine to him. Wayne's half-protest acknowledged, Kenny's performance was now free to do what it had apparently been designed to do in the first place: put Logan softly to sleep.

"Why don't you say nuffin', Tar Baby, when peoples greets ye?" chanted Kenny, sauntering through the part where the trickster hare is getting angry at the mannequin-trap that will soon have him struggling in goo. Logan's head tilted forward, as if he were losing most of his neck strength.

Keeping the same accent, as if to maintain regional integrity, Kenny had now switched to a tinny, nasal voice: the nefarious Brer Fox was explaining to Brer Bear how he had made the Tar Baby so sticky. Brer Bear replied with the deepest voice yet—a standard *Of Mice and Men* Lenny, but in that same idiom Kenny had kept since the beginning of his trance. For a full minute, Kenny gave life to a full-bodied exchange between Brers Fox and Bear, who were watching from behind a tree. He alternated between the high-voiced hunter and the low-voiced accomplice, as the angry little canine explained melodramatically to the dumb ursine how Brer Rabbit, so long on top of things, was finally about to get his comeuppance.

Logan teetered slightly, his hand on the counter.

"What did Brer Rabbit..." he whispered slowly, like a child about to fade during a bedtime story, "what... did the... smart rabbit... do *then*?"

"He got hisself all *caught up*," Kenny said, still fully in the voice. Angry that this stranger would not return his neighborly hellos, Brer Rabbit—as we all know—began to strike the Tar Baby, eventually getting so stuck in all the tar that he found himself ensnared. And likely to be eaten, at long last, by Brers Fox and Bear.

Logan jerked spasmodically, in a vain attempt to maintain

consciousness.

"Get out, Brer Rabbit... Get out! They're gonna... eat you..."

Before Kenny could get to the denouement, in which Brer Rabbit tricks his assailants into sending him into the briar patch and thus escapes yet again, Logan's eyes closed completely. A moment later, still sitting on the stool, he dropped his head on the metal table, deep in slumber. His hands lay motionless at his sides. The gum rolled out of his open mouth, and he began to snore.

Kenny's head cleared. It was like his forehead had unzipped or been cleaved open, but without any pain at all. No longer high at all, maybe even the total opposite of high, he felt like his brain could taste the kitchen air. It was like no feeling he had experienced before. It wasn't like the romantic renditions you might see on *Oprah Winfrey* or *The Phil Donahue Show*, by people who have been "born again" or had some kind of important life epiphany. It was just a kind of total clarity, but Kenny didn't have the slightest idea where the feeling had come from or what had preceded it.

Wayne stood motionless by the window, his mouth and eyes a little more open than they had been a minute before. He also, suddenly, no longer looked high, but he was alert and still smiling unnaturally. He seemed keen to hear the next thing Kenny was about to say.

As refreshed as he was, Kenny had no urge to speak. He just knew it was time to pack up the catering gear and go.

Couch

On Sunday, Kenny stared bleary-eyed at the University Catering time clock, gathering what little energy he had before punching in. 8:32 a.m. He had stayed out too late the night before, dancing spasmodically in a basement nightclub after his shift at Birdwood earlier in the day. He had gone with his roommate Chris and some other caterers to hear a very loud band fronted by a tireless behemoth with two saxophones dangling off his chest. When the guy wasn't singing or yelling, he would put both horns to his mouth and blow long simultaneous duets at the roomful of delighted drunks. All the players wore skinny ties.

"Punch on, bro," said Logan, who arrived brandishing his own timecard. "This lunch is not going to cater itself." Kenny nodded but stayed quiet, still waking up. Neither of them said anything about the odd hypnotic-storytelling incident at Birdwood, probably because neither of them could remember it at all.

They walked into the servery, a big open kitchen with refrigerators, a small counter, an industrial gas stove on one side, and a service elevator on the other. In the corner, a small couch sat next to a big office desk. In the middle of the area stood a large stainless-steel table, by night an important center of activity: whoever arrived first each day would hit the lights, sending legions of cockroaches skittering across its surface to darker, safer places. The servery itself could be quiet, but—like most places where work produced food—it was a place of constant transformation.

Wayne was by the stove, working on a marinade for Catering's warhorse, the London Broil. Standard flank steak, always marinated, always in copious amounts. Wayne always disposed of leftover meat by sending piles of it home with the student caterers at the end of a shift, and there was always leftover London Broil at University Catering.

"You done prepping that garlic, honey?" said Wayne, over his shoulder, to Tracy the Vegetarian. Like Logan, Tracy came from Northern Virginia, where she had grown up learning about math, field hockey, and man's inhumanity to man at a place called the Torydon School.

"Yes, I am," said Tracy as she scraped the aromatic choppings onto a plate. "And I'm not your honey."

Wayne grinned, taking the plate. "I call my mama honey, honey," he said, winking at Logan.

"I'm not your mama either, dickhead," said Tracy. "Do you call your *mama* honey, though? I don't get the analogy. And stop winking at each other, you male chauvinist swine."

Wayne winked again at Logan and Kenny. "Swine? I could use a big glass of swine right now. Maybe some fine *French* swine, heh heh."

"Did you just say 'male chauvinist swine'?" asked Logan. He talked over Wayne, designating Tracy as his adversary. His urge to prod didn't really stem from his longstanding discomfort with intelligent women. It came from his desire to goad liberal students of both sexes into pronouncing dramatic statements that would reveal privileged childhoods. When Tracy had decried the "Salvadoran penchant for death-squad murder," during a political argument with Logan a few weeks earlier, she had pronounced the word *penchant* in a French accent.

"Okay, Gloria Steinem," said Logan, side-eying Kenny. "Did you just get back from taking a Tab break with Mary Tyler Moore?" He leaned over, his hand ready for a fraternal hand-slap of approval. Having never joined a fraternity, Kenny could not discern whether the remark had been clever enough to warrant a hand-slap.

Kenny's hesitation was brief but had distracted Logan, who did not notice Tracy dipping her wound-up garlic rag in a glass of water. With lightning speed, she rounded the corner of the table and snapped the towel in the air, very near Logan's face. "I stand by my slur!" she whispered, play-menacingly.

Kenny and Wayne both laughed. Logan jerked his head back.

"Fiend!" yelled Tracy. She snapped the towel again, this time dangerously close to Logan's cheek. His head jerked back again. Tracy's words were playful, but her strength was in her physical game.

"The fuck, man!" His gaiety had ebbed significantly.

Wayne looked up from his marinade, his eyes all lit up. "Cat fight!" he said, unhampered by questions of gender or the mixing of metaphors. "Locker room style!"

Tracy snapped the towel again, this time grazing Logan's cheek. Kenny was chuckling outright, and Tracy was bobbing up and down slightly, like a boxer after the bell. Logan was angry now.

"What the hell, man?" he barked. "You hit my cheek!"

Tracy put the towel down and made the kind of face you make when talking to a baby. "Aww, widdle Wogan is getting *angwy*." She stroked his cheek maternally. "Does somebody need a nap?"

Logan yanked his head back in disgust. He reminded Kenny of a teenager recoiling cross-armed in a restaurant booth, freshly chastised by a parent.

"Heh heh," chuckled Wayne, back at his marinade. "Cat fight."

"Come on, Wayne, you about done?" snapped Logan, apparently trying to change the subject. He rubbed his cheek, his eyebrows furrowed and tense-looking.

Tracy's snapping arm loosened and dropped to her side. "I was just joking, Logan."

"Whatever," said Logan, still massaging his cheek.

Tracy looked over at Kenny and silently mouthed the word *whatever*, her head rocking slightly back and forth with each imagined syllable. Logan hadn't seen her imitation. Kenny grinned and started folding napkins. Tracy pushed a handful of curly hair behind her left ear and resumed her parsley-chopping.

"What's with all the drama, anyway, Tracy?" asked Logan. He wasn't ready to be bested this way, at least not in front of other caterers. He was going to strike back a little, or at least save some face. "You cut your armpits trying to work the hacksaw this morning?"

Tracy ignored him. She pushed the chopped parsley into a little pile, then grabbed another handful of spears and began chopping again.

"Okay, Logan," said Kenny, no longer grinning.

"No, seriously," said Logan, trying another door. "Your women's studies girlfriends head to the protest meeting and forget to invite you?"

Kenny felt that twinge again, right behind his belly. If he had been able to remember it, he would have compared it to a vague vibration or a humming. This one felt just like a little spot—a *place*, as his Kentucky grandparents would have called it—a minuscule but foreboding location, embedded somewhere between the front of his stomach, the organ itself, and whatever fat buffeted that organ from the outside world. Less a thing with mass or weight or size, more of a *process*, like the beginning of a flu bug, but without the dread of an impending vomit.

Tracy stopped chopping and glared.

"Fuck you, Logan."

Logan was still angry, though. Maybe angrier. "What's your problem with me, Tracy?"

Kenny stood up and looked oddly above Tracy's head, into an imagined distance. Logan was still sitting, leaning back as if relaxed but obviously ready to argue. He noticed Kenny's weird stance but, like Kenny, had no memory of the unusual event that had taken place at Birdwood the day before.

"You're the one with the problem," said Tracy. She had put her knife and parsley down and turned her torso toward Logan, her body designating him as an opponent. It was a move as old as time. Logan stretched and stood up, as if in response. If he was aiming for masculine confidence, he missed his mark, but it worked as a basic signal of deeper engagement. Wayne wondered if they were about to wrestle.

Kenny's eyes, however, were still fixed on an imaginary horizon, over his fellow caterers' heads. He looked like a candidate for office practicing for a speech he was about to give on a factory floor. He was in a trance again.

"Once upon a time," he said, slowly, his eyes far away.

"What?" said Tracy, looking back at Kenny, her nose a question mark. "What?"

"In a small village," continued Kenny, stretching his arm out like a beauty contest emcee, "along a little river at the foot of Mount Hemlock, there lived a little old man who could never tell whether it was day or night." His voice stayed deep, and his accent had changed considerably. He sounded like Tennessee Ernie Ford.

Logan crinkled his own nose a little now. Tracy looked at him, then back at Kenny. Wayne stopped stirring the marinade and looked up to see what was going on.

Kenny's gaze turned to Logan, who he now addressed directly.

"Day or night, you ask? Why, they're as different from one another as a pop gun and a dollhouse." His deep Southern Appalachian accent flowing uninterrupted, he was now also starting to sound like the narrator of a 1960s educational filmstrip about state capitals or the free enterprise system.

Tracy's tensed nose tightened more dramatically, and her mouth opened so you could see both rows of teeth. "What are you talking about, Kenny?" she asked. She executed a very long yawn. "Why are you talking like that?"

Logan sat back down suddenly. He rubbed his temples but didn't say anything.

"You see," continued Kenny, his voice sweetly didactic, "Mount Hemlock had long been a mystery to the old man, even though he had spent his entire life by the river that ran along its valley."

Tracy yawned again, staring right at Kenny. It was like she was pointing the yawn at him.

"Where *is* Mount Hemlock, Kenny?" she asked, her voice soft and downy all of a sudden. "It's in North Carolina, isn't it?" She leaned against the table. The palm of her hand hit the cutting board, which slid a foot or so across the table toward Kenny. Tracy righted herself with a little start at the midsection, like someone who has just realized she has had too much to drink, then shook her head a little. "North Carolina? Like, by Black Mountain or, like, by Asheville maybe. Like, around there?" She was slowing down considerably. She yawned again. "Like, around that part?" she repeated, through a gaping, third yawn.

Kenny raised his gaze back up toward what, if the little catering servery had been an auditorium, would have been its last row of seats.

"For you see," he continued, dropping his intonation even more on the word *see* and pausing for effect, "Mount Hemlock was a place of magic." He paused again, then looked directly at Tracy. "Magic. And mysterious journeys of discovery."

"Whoa," said Wayne, transfixed. Unlike the others in the room, he was fully awake.

Logan, however, had collapsed onto the servery couch in a fetal position and was snoring, completely asleep.

"What... kind of... journeys?" said Tracy, yawning hard a fourth time. The words rolled slowly out of her mouth, which she kept wide open. Her eyelids drooped. For a moment, there was total silence. Kenny just smiled, the strange narrator he had become dominating his facial expression, as if he were waiting for something.

Tracy turned her head slowly toward Logan on the couch, then closed her eyes, like she was bracing herself for who knew what. She opened her left eye again, first raising her eyebrow along with it, as if both operations required immense effort and maybe even created a small jab of pain. A full second later, her right eye opened—this time without the accompanying eyebrow lift—and she rubbed her mouth, shaking her head gently once. Her eyes fixed on Logan and the couch, as if they shared a singular purpose, then hesitated. She turned her head to Kenny for a second or two.

"The magic," intoned Kenny, still in that same voice and looking right at Tracy. "The journey home."

Tracy gave her head one more little shake and sat down slowly on the floor. Her gaze back on Logan and the couch, she leaned forward and let out a soft but exhausted-sounding groan, as if to say *I can do it, just a couple more yards*, then pulled herself up on all fours.

She advanced cautiously, her somnolent stare trained on Logan. One knee at a time, one hand after the other, she moved forward. She moved like someone imitating a sloth. Wayne began to stir the marinade again but kept watching Kenny—who, in turn, continued to stare off at that far-flung point most dramatic orators in the educational filmstrip era would have been expected to stare off at.

After what to any other unaffected witness, of whom there were none, would have felt like a very long time—probably two full minutes, across six or seven feet of servery floor—Tracy arrived at the couch and lifted her front end off the floor, grabbing Logan's right foot to steady herself. Logan issued a delicate grunt, his unconscious breathing momentarily interrupted, then shifted a little and returned to a deep slumber. Holding on to the foot, Tracy mustered enough energy to pull herself up to a low squat, then rolled slowly onto the couch next to Logan's rear end. He was on his side, facing outward. She assumed a similar shape, behind him, her left shoulder nesting down into the space behind Logan's buttocks, settling as comfortably as she could. She draped her arm over his right thigh and knee and pulled her own legs up as Logan had, on her own end of the couch, her black Chuck Taylors coming gently to rest against the inside of the couch's armrest, completing the two-person tableau.

Wayne, still stirring the marinade, realized that Kenny had grown completely silent. He removed the spoon from the bowl and set it down, then looked at the S-shaped two-person creature on the server couch. He whistled softly and said, "Whoa, look at that," to no one in particular.

The Sixteenth President of the United States

"Of course you'll have realized, by this point in your study of history, that not long before I was born, Kentucky was part of the Commonwealth of Virginia."

As was usually the case in his dreams, Kenny couldn't tell if he was there or just watching. Or, in this case, listening.

"I was born in 1809," the voice continued. It was higher pitched than one would imagine, thought Kenny, even though he had read about Lincoln's voice in a book, or maybe heard about it from his father. Where was President Lincoln, anyway? Kenny could hear him, but he couldn't see him.

Things began to feel more tangible to Kenny. He was walking down a hallway, maybe at his grandparents' house. It was dark, like the small hallway that led from the living room into the den his grandfather had built onto the house in the fifties, but this ceiling was unusually high, and the hallway was much longer than the real one. Abraham Lincoln came into view at the end of the hallway.

"Come on down here, son, a little closer," said the president, almost in a whisper.

Kenny stood still.

"What are you waiting for, son?" asked a different voice, to Kenny's left, in the living room. It was Harlan, Kenny's father. Everyone within range was calling him *son.* He was definitely in Kentucky.

"Dad?"

"I know, how unoriginal. Visited by a ghost." He laughed and lit a cigarette. It was a Pall Mall.

"Come on in here," said the president. "I have something to share with you."

Kenny looked back at his dad, who raised his eyebrows and cocked his head in a combination of exclamation point and question mark. "Son, go on. That's *Abraham Lincoln.*"

Harlan took Kenny's hand, as he had when Kenny was a child. He didn't mind. His father's hand was covered with age spots and smelled like cigarettes. It felt like he was holding his own hand, but it was warmer. The hallway seemed to expand a little as they walked down toward Lincoln. Somewhere in the hallway, Harlan dropped Kenny's hand.

As they emerged into what would have been, in real life, his Grandpa Maesby's Northern Kentucky den, Kenny understood that they were now outside and in a completely different part of the state—the eastern part—looking out over some mountains.

"Bell County," said the president, still looking right at Kenny. "That's Cumberland Gap. Sixteen hundred seventy-seven feet."

They considered the view. "My daddy called that pass *the navel of Kentucky,*" said Harlan, his gaze unbroken. Had Kenny been having what people were calling a "lucid dream," he'd have been hard-pressed to define what they were all standing on as they looked across at the mountain pass, but things were otherwise realistic enough. Maybe they were just floating.

"The navel, yes, the navel," said the president, like he hadn't heard this before. "Daniel Boone came through there in 1775."

"Shawnee," said Harlan, suddenly a child.

"And Cherokee," said the president. "None too friendly with one another."

Lincoln turned slowly toward Kenny, who became aware of the light across the president's cheek. He could pick out some gray hairs in Lincoln's beard, and his cheeks were lined and leathery. His skin seemed a little dark—less from sun than from his Kentucky origins. Kenny had seen that famous, tired photo of Lincoln from late in his presidency. Older than his years, and anyone looking at that picture now knew what was coming for him at Ford's Theater.

"You and I share a birthday," said the president. "And there's the Cumberland Gap." He pointed.

Kenny had grown up hearing stories—telling them, too—so his dreams were often the kind of thing you could talk about coherently. But this? What was the thread here? Usually there was some kind of language thing in a dream like this one—a quote he'd remember when he woke up, even a rhyme. Especially when the dream took place in Kentucky, as they often did since his father died. A few months earlier, he had dreamt he was being held hostage by some elderly hooligans in an abandoned Stuckey's, just off an I-71 exit ramp. The hooligans had him tied to a chair. Everything felt imminent and dangerous, but the only thing Kenny could remember when he woke up was a sentence the main hostage-taker had said to him, as if quoting a poem:

They'll lie like the trash will
Down in Nashville

This dream was more coherent though, and it seemed important. Lincoln! This dream was bound to be more memorable than most.

"You aren't going to remember this dream," said the president.

Kenny kept noticing his father, whose unbroken gaze remained on Lincoln.

"I was the one who caused you to tell those stories," said the president. "I want you to know that."

As he dreamed, Kenny saw the Birdwood Pavilion kitchen, then the Catering servery, where he had put other caterers to sleep on two different occasions. The face of an elderly-looking Black man appeared nearby, floating, but it wasn't anyone Kenny knew. The man wasn't looking at the mountains, Kenny, or even at the president; he was just looking straight ahead. You couldn't tell what was on his mind. He just looked pained and exhausted, like he felt this way all the time, as long as he could remember. Some white children's faces appeared, somewhere. They looked up at him, like they wanted a story, but the old man gave no sign of wanting to say anything. He didn't seem to notice them.

Harlan, his gaze still trained vigilantly on Lincoln, seemed to know about his son's recent trance. "Why the Uncle Remus story?" he asked Lincoln. "Why *The Tar Baby*?"

"Why not?" replied Lincoln.

"Why that particular way he was speaking?" asked Harlan, even more urgently. "I used to use that voice when I would tell that story to the kids. His voice sounded just like mine. Why that one?"

"It's how Joel Chandler Harris imagined it," replied Lincoln.

"I'm not prejudiced," said Harlan. Kenny didn't know if his dad was talking to Lincoln or to the exhausted old man floating near them. "I'm really not." The old man looked on, still exhausted. Still quiet. He didn't know anything about Joel Chandler Harris or about the storytelling at Catering.

Harlan was definitely talking to the president. "How do you know about Joel Chandler Harris? He was still a kid when you died. Are you omnipotent?"

"I consult the Lord in prayer, but He has given me no powers any more special than the ones He gave you."

"But you are the Great Emancipator."

Lincoln smiled. He looked tired. He was beginning to resemble the exhausted-looking man floating nearby, but the president was clearly used to being addressed reverently. The floating man had never been anything but yelled at or talked down to, you could tell.

"There was a lot of compromise involved," said Lincoln. "It wasn't entirely my idea, especially at the beginning. I had to compromise."

The old man nearby leaned forward, straining. Maybe he wanted to hear more.

"Hodgenville!" yelled Harlan, excited. "You were born in that cabin! I've been there so many times. It's like a shrine."

Harlan looked over at Kenny. His hair was fuller than Kenny had remembered. He looked very young all of a sudden, in spite of his aged hands.

"I was born in Kentucky," intoned the president, the chanting voice of a bona fide ghost. He was addressing Kenny directly again. "You and I share a birthday."

The Cumberland Gap had faded from view, and now—as is often the case in dreams—there were only the characters. The subjects. The actors, the ones about to do something—or, in the case of the old man, the ones just watching in silence. The president spoke again, resuming a more conversational style.

"I can't tell you why you had that power. I'm no hypnotist, even if I have been known to mesmerize a crowd or two." He grinned subtly.

Kenny had read that the real Lincoln had been funny. He had been known for this, said some historians. His biographers made it sound like Lincoln always knew exactly what he was doing. But why the hypnotic power?

"I directed what happened to you," said the president, "but only at the beginning. You were getting out of joint. Somebody was out of joint." For the first time, Lincoln looked a little confused. He was looking down at his hands, touching his fingers one after another, as if he were trying to remember a series of things in a particular order. Kenny looked at his father, who was still unusually young and watching Lincoln like a hawk.

"You were in Virginia, as you still are," continued Lincoln, sounding presidential again. "And there, for a short while yet, you shall remain. But you are not fully there, really, and it's not where you are meant to be."

"Virginia!" yelled Harlan, urgently. He had been dead four years now, and it was like he had some unfinished business but knew he was about to return to wherever he had come from. Kenny was expecting a question about the war, or something about Robert E. Lee or treason, but Harlan said no more.

"We share a birthday, you and I," intoned Lincoln. "I left Kentucky."

"You did!" said Harlan. "So did I! I came north."

"Northwest, as did I," said the president, turning to Harlan now. "First, Indiana, as you know. But you know the real place for me was Illinois."

Kenny could see that his father found this fact both painful and intriguing.

"This will happen to you again," said the president, looking at Kenny again. "One more time, when you know you are home."

Am I like Scrooge? thought Kenny. Even in a dream, one could think things like this without saying them. *I'm the narrator,* Kenny had once realized as a child. Dreams sometimes felt this way. If he was the narrator now, however, President Lincoln was most likely the protagonist. Or was he the author? Either way, compared with Abraham Lincoln, the rest of us are pretty small. Even the narrators.

"When he is home?" asked Harlan.

"Home," replied the President, turning to Kenny, "and you are not Scrooge. This is not Dickens. You are in real life." The Cumberland Gap came into view again, and Kenny was sure Lake Mendota would leap from its loins, flowing out from southeastern Kentucky and directly into Madison, Wisconsin.

"You aren't going to remember this dream," Lincoln said again. "At least, not yet."

There Goes the Neighborhood

A lot of children, when they first learn to walk by themselves, do this thing where they point at an object and then jabber a statement of some kind. The adults find it cute, but the speaker usually doesn't; he obviously has a sense of purpose in crossing the room, indicating a thing, and telling others what it means. Sometimes the adults assume it's the crossing the child is talking about, that the pointing finger is just an exclamatory gesture, but they can never be totally sure of that. One thing adults do sometimes notice is that these young narrators are most ambulatory right after they awaken from a deep sleep. It makes one wonder if talking, walking around and dreaming aren't just different versions of the same thing sometimes.

Already a "morning person," Kenny hopped right up out of bed after his Lincoln dream, fresher than usual. Like an energized child, he was brimming with words, likely a result of the vividness of the dream. Problem was, he had already forgotten every detail of the story, and he had no one to tell it to anyway. So, with no obligation until his first class later in the afternoon, he threw some clothes on and decided that, if he couldn't talk, he would walk. Downtown would be good—he could get away from the university for a few hours, wander around parts of town he still didn't know all too well, and hopefully recover a few remnants of the dream along the way.

On West Main Street, just a few blocks from the university, he passed a young family getting into their car. "Home again, home again, jiggety-jig," said the father, strapping a seat belt around a wriggly daughter. The scene unlocked something in Kenny, who suddenly remembered that his dad had been in his dream. In the year or so following his death, Harlan had appeared regularly in Kenny's dreams, but not much since then.

Kenny walked another block, death now on his mind, then remembered Abraham Lincoln. Had Kenny and his dad done something or been somewhere important with the president in the dream, or had they just sort of thought about him, talked about him? Something about a gap or a mountain? He often woke up with the urge to write down his dreams but usually didn't—mainly because, until he had come to college, he could always count on there being someone at the breakfast table who wanted to talk about dreams. "So what happened last night?" his dad would often ask, as if the recently-awakened listener had just returned from a real, physical location. Most people were bored by hearing about someone else's dreams, but not Harlan. He often told Kenny and his sister that, if they were lucky, dreams would allow them to see into the future. "Maybe that's just a Kentucky superstition," he would add, hoping to imprint a little bit of Appalachia onto his Wisconsin children.

As Kenny crossed the overpass near Eighth Street, he saw the Amtrak Cardinal pull into the station below. The Cardinal, which came through only three times a week and ran between DC and Chicago, was the train he sometimes took to get home. He promptly forgot about the dream and began to worry about what he would do after graduation. It was getting closer, and Kenny thought about it more and more often. *I could start a restaurant around here,* he would say to himself. *Local bands could play in it, and there would be art, and regulars, and poetry readings.* Then he'd remember Catering, and all the business stuff he knew nothing about. *Maybe a nightclub, then.* Was he seriously imagining he might stay in Charlottesville?

When Kenny got distracted like this, he'd move through his thoughts like he was hopping across a creek on the flattest rocks, picking them as he came to them. One thing would lead to another. Then he'd find himself three or four blocks further down his actual path, with little or no memory of the corners he'd crossed or even where he actually was, in time or space.

This dawned on him, so he decided to take stock of recent events. An inventory of sorts would give the walk more purpose. Other than the dream, what else had he just done? Two shifts that weekend: one at Birdwood on Saturday evening, and a lunch event on Sunday, with the basement nightclub show wedged in between them on Saturday night.

All he could remember about the Birdwood event, other than a dull encounter with the historian who had given the lecture, was a feeling that something *odd* had happened in the kitchen. His shift the next day had also been a little weird, as they were setting up in the servery for a lunch event. Kenny had stepped out to get bar fruit, or maybe to gather some plates from the rack down by the dishwasher area; when he got back, he found his fellow caterers Logan and Tracy curled up together on the couch. Wayne was in a weird mood, too. A good one. He was humming the 1975 Starbuck hit "Moonlight (Feels Right)" but substituting the words *cat fight in sight* for the title words of the song. Kenny just supposed he was high, but he had to wake Logan and Tracy up so they could load the Cambros and coolers into the van. They had been sassing each other when Kenny left—they sniped at each other a lot, usually about Central America or women's salaries compared to men's or how hypocritical drug policy was, but things usually resolved with drinking or bong hits after the shift. Never with a nap.

Kenny passed the Blue Moon Diner, not really taking notice of where he was. He moved in an imaginary current, as if he were floating down the Lower Wisconsin River, past Arena or Spring Green, in a canoe with his friend Kurt. Paddle laying across the gunwales, looking at the sky, wondering about things.

Reeeeeeekkkkkk! A driver leaned on his horn as Kenny wandered across Seventh Street by the First Baptist Church. "Whoa!" he gasp-muttered to himself. An urge to look down at his hands came over him, then passed. He rubbed his ear then walked a few more blocks, onto the Downtown Mall.

Kenny had only discovered downtown in his second year, when his German TA Gaby had invited him to an ironic Tupperware party thrown by mushroom-gobbling MFA students affecting approximate British accents. Other than that, he had only been all the way downtown three times: to look for used books with a girl named Kylie, to watch *Children of a Lesser God* at an arthouse cinema with a girl named Catherine, and to drink his first legal Virginia beer in a bar with a fellow caterer named Nora. It occurred to Kenny that his attraction to women may have been the only reason he had ever gone downtown at all.

As he ambled along the mall, he looked off onto a side street and saw a barber pole, lit up and turning. *BURGIE SHIFFLETTE BARBER SHOP* was hand-painted on the window. Here was what his walk had led him to: a good old-fashioned haircut. It would provide a little purpose. Plus, Kenny thought, the place looked really authentic. Yes, authenticity would bring him down to earth.

A little bell attached to the top of the door tinkled limply as he stepped into the shop. A middle-aged barber, surely Burgie

Shifflette or maybe his offspring, sat smoking a Pall Mall in the barber's chair, conversing with a customer in a chair next to the coat rack. The customer looked like a retired farmer, the kind Kenny's grandparents said "eventually just moved into town." Both inside and out, this barber shop looked like it had been here for a long time. The cigarette's aroma put Kenny at ease.

"Are you taking customers?" was all he could think to say, politely as he could.

"You bet, son," said the barber, extinguishing the cigarette in an ashtray by the mirror. He stood up and brushed off his apron in a habitual sweep of the hand. "Just chewing the fat some. Have a seat." He gestured toward the chair.

"Complaining about politics, mostly," the customer chortled. "Course, in here, it's always Burgie doing the complaining. Ain't that right, Burgie?"

"You the one complaining, Lamar," said the barber, as he draped the barber's cape around Kenny, who had just sat down. "You'd complain with a steak in your mouth." Lamar chortled again, the same chortle.

Kenny smiled uncomfortably. It was one of those moments when he felt like he had just interrupted people in their native element, people who had known each other a long time. *Interloper* wasn't exactly the word—Kenny was a customer after all, and welcome in that sense. But even though he'd have enjoyed being part of a community like this little one he sensed in the shop, he knew he was just a passing part of these people's day. He was the current, they were a settled little house on the shore.

"You go to the university?" the barber asked, bringing the apron around all the way.

"Yeah, just about done, actually."

"Is that right," said the barber. "I think it's great, all y'all UVA students coming down patronizing my business. I been gettin' more students here, some reason." He pushed two plastic buttons together behind Kenny's neck and gave the plastic cape one final adjustment.

The customer by the window grinned. "Y'ask me, they's all just like a bunch of twenty-dollar bills walking around with legs on 'em."

The barber chuckled. "There's a Southern gentleman for you, son." Lamar chuckled back and opened the *Daily Progress* he had been reading. Sports section.

They can tell I'm not from here, thought Kenny, forcing a little laugh, feeling suddenly very young and a little defensive. *They think I'm just a college kid and a Yankee. They probably say "Yankee" on purpose, to get a rise out of people. They will for sure, after I leave.*

Kenny noticed a working miniature train moving along the top of the wall. The little train ran the circumference of the shop, along a narrow plywood shelf installed ten or so inches below the ceiling. The shelf was rounded off at the corners to accommodate the curve of the metal tracks. The train circled endlessly above the barbering action. *He must have it on all day*, thought Kenny.

"I like your train," said Kenny, awkwardly.

"Thank you, son. I bought it for my boy. He lost interest 'fore long, so I set it up here. Years ago."

"My daddy worked on the C and O," said Lamar, without looking up from the sports section. "Yardmaster for a long time." He paused without looking up. "Long time," he said again.

The barber eyed up Kenny's ears and neck. "What kind of cut you looking for, son?" He said *son* with the same intonation as Kenny's dad. Other parts of his speech, though, had a Tidewater ring to them: *oat and aboat,* sort of, like Canadians, but Southern.

"Just about a half-inch off, I guess."

"All around?"

"Sure. Maybe closer on the sides."

Burgie Shifflette fitted a Number Two clipper guard onto his electric trimmer and turned it on. The trimmer buzzed as it burrowed smoothly into the scruff along Kenny's left temple. No one spoke for a full minute.

"You headed anywhere for Thanksgiving?" asked Kenny, his intonation rising a little higher and faster than he had expected. This was something students asked each other.

"Headed anywhere?" asked Lamar, rhetorically, without looking up from his *Daily Progress*. "Shoot, old Burgie don't ever travel nowhere for turkey 'less they's a tom and he's standing in a field behind some corn he thew out there to bait 'em."

Burgie let out a chuckle that sounded more like offense than defense. "You'd know about bait, Lamar."

Lamar's smile disappeared, and he looked down lower onto the sports page. He stopped talking, and his face got a little red. Some things had obviously happened between these two people, and probably over quite a long period of time.

"What about you, son? You going to see your people somewhere?"

Kenny liked the barber's use of *people* to refer to his family. Both his parents and his Kentucky grandparents would have called this *country talk.* Kenny brightened: had he seemed Southern enough to have "people"?

"Yes, I'm going to see my people," he replied. Immediately, it sounded wrong. His Midwestern accent and all.

Lamar chuckled. "Your *people*? Are you Moses? Are you Sitting Bull?"

Shit, I pronounced it wrong, he thought.

"Heh heh, yeah, no, you know, my *family*," he stammered. "Who are, coincidentally, people. Heh heh." Kenny was the one with the red cheeks now.

"I's just kidding, boy," said Lamar, returning to the sports page. "Just pulling your leg."

"No, I know," said Kenny, feeling about six years old. Six years old and immobilized, here in this foreign barber chair, wearing a nylon cape, his cheeks still a little pink. He began to hope that Burgie Shifflette would make another allusion to Lamar's embarrassing past, so that Kenny could enjoy what was left of this haircut.

"Well, Lamar's right, I don't travel much this time of year," said the barber, exchanging his clipper for a pair of scissors. "Even for turkey hunting, anymore," he added. He started trimming around Kenny's ears.

"Aha," Kenny said, as he often did when in situations where he was unsure what one was supposed to say next.

"Plus, we're fixin' to sell our house 'fore long, got to get it ready," the barber said. *Fixin'*. That sounded like something Kenny's Kentucky grandma would say, which made him a little more relaxed.

"So you live around here?" was all he could think to say.

Lamar laughed and looked up. From a mirror on the side wall, Kenny could see the barber grin a little.

"Only my whole life. Which, given the neighborhood, is way, way too long."

"Now, Burgie, be nice," said Lamar.

I see, thought Kenny, his ears reddening. *He's a bigot. He's talking about Black neighbors moving in. I get it. You see this kind of shit all the time in the South. Working class people are the same as the rich ones this way. I can't wait to get out of here.*

"I am being nice, Lamar," replied the barber, a playful lilt in his voice, "people like you and Faye's just about as nice a neighbors as a man could ask for. Even with that Chevy y'all drive." He grinned and snipped a lock of hair just above Kenny's ear.

"Shee-it, Burgie. You come down from Pantops with that new German mon-stru-osity, and *I'm* the one should be saying *there goes the neighborhood*. Shee-it."

Burgie leaned in a little. "Some people jealous of success, my friend," he said to Kenny, with a conspiratorial glance.

"A goddam BMW. Son, you ever met a barber drove a BMW?"

Kenny didn't know quite how to respond. Maybe this "neighborhood" thing wasn't what he thought. Were they actually just talking about *cars*?

"Heh heh, Beemer, yeah," said Kenny, a touch too loudly given the size of the room.

The barber paused, a little embarrassed for the young man. "Yes, they do call them that sometimes."

Clip, clip, clip. The barber was all business now, working his scissors around Kenny's left cowlick. There was no more talk of cars.

Taylor Makes a Phone Call

The small stone house that Kenny lived in with his fellow caterer Chris was divided into two apartments—one upstairs, the other downstairs. It sat on the shadier end of a curvy little lane called Valley Road, a block or two down the hill from Grounds, tucked back into the crepe myrtle, pin oaks, silver maple, and a bunch of other trees you could only identify during those few months of the year when they weren't covered with kudzu. For most of its life, it had been a single-family home, probably neat as could be, but by the time Kenny and Chris moved into the place, it possessed that comfortable shagginess that rentals in that neighborhood acquired naturally over time. Part of what Kenny liked about the house was the abandoned old Saab in the front yard. Parked up against a tree near the porch, the old sedan's rusting doors and hood were covered with hand-painted cartoon telephones.

The only actual phone in Kenny's apartment was in the living room, next to the futon. Chris had wanted to get a phone for every room, which Kenny found strange. "There are only three rooms in this apartment," he had said, after which Chris had shrugged and started an unrelated conversation about how rare roller rinks seemed these days. He never brought up phones again.

Kenny was still feeling anxious about his imminent graduation from college, so he decided to read. He had finally immersed himself in a book about the First World War for his "Europe and Modernism" class when the phone in question rang. This was not unusual on Sundays, when Kenny would "check in" with his mother, his sister, Kate, and—once or twice a month—his Kentucky grandparents, Grandma and Grandpa Maesby. Long-distance costing what it did, it was usually his family who made the call.

"Hello?"

There was an unusual silence on the other end. Kenny could hear what sounded like a fork hitting a plate, or maybe a ballpoint pen tapping a bowl.

"Hello?" he said again, rubbing his newly shorn head.

"I don't know if it's him," said a small voice on the other end of the line, away from the receiver.

"Taylor?"

"Go ahead, honey. You can say hello," said a voice in the room on the other end. It was Kate. Suddenly the small voice returned, very close to the receiver but only as a slow, deep breath.

"Hello, Taylor? This is Uncle Kenny."

After another long breath, "Oh, hello, Uncle Kenny," said the little voice. A pause. Then, "What are you doing right now?"

"That's good, honey, ask him some more questions," said Kate from several feet away. It sounded like the first phone call Taylor had made by herself.

"Well, right now, I'm sitting on the couch," said Kenny.

"I'm sitting on a chair. I'm watching Mommy do the dishes."

A half-second later, he heard a loud crash in the background, followed by a partly stifled, frustrated yell. "Dammit!" shouted Kate. "Sorry, Taylor. Mommy dropped a plate."

"Really she threw it," said Taylor into the phone, dryly. "But I think it was on accident." Kenny imagined his sister's graceless rubberiness, an arm moving too fast, a slapstick release of plate against wall. Kate was the least coordinated person he knew. Once, at a party in high school, Kenny had watched his older sister sweep her hair behind her ear and laugh flirtatiously in front of a boy she had a crush on, after which she walked immediately into a closed sliding-glass door.

"So what are *you* doing, Taylor?" asked Kenny, always a little unsure how to converse with his five-year-old niece.

"I'm making a picture of Wisconsin." Kenny could imagine his niece's facial expressions as she spoke. "Miss T is teaching us all the things in Wisconsin."

Taylor's teacher's actual last name was something like Teodorowski or Tischdoskowicz, so she had instructed the kids to call her Miss T.

"Things in Wisconsin? Like what?"

"Like we learned there's a bird."

"The *state* bird," said Kate in the background. Kenny could hear cleanup sounds. "The official *state* bird."

"The official state bird," repeated Taylor. "It's a robin."

"Oh, I like robins," said Kenny. He actually did kind of like them. Their arrival meant spring had come.

"We're supposed to ask somebody we know in a different state what their state bird is," she said, "and you're from Virginia, so you're supposed to help me."

"I'm not from Virginia, Taylor. I'm from Wisconsin, like you are. From Madison, like your mom, too."

"But you live in Virginia, so you're from there, too."

"No, I'm not, Taylor. I just go to college here."

Taylor found this uninteresting.

"What birds are in the college?"

Kenny had no idea what the state bird of Virginia was.

"Grandma said the Kentucky bird is the cardinal," said Taylor. Which, as it turned out, was also the state bird of Virginia and every other state between it and the Wisconsin state line, but Kenny had never learned those either. "And the tree is a coffee tree."

"What? A *coffee tree*? Can you walk up to it with a cup and just pour yourself some, right off the branches?"

"No, you can't," she replied with startling professionalism. "It doesn't even make coffee. It's just called a coffee tree. Grandma told me."

Bested by a child, he abandoned his jovial tone. "So, what did you think about dialing the telephone for the very first time, Taylor?"

"Grandma told me the trees in Kentucky are the same as the ones on our street," she replied, continuing on her own terms. "Some of the trees are different, though, but we went on a walk and she showed me the one she likes the most. She says they are all over the place in Kentucky. By creeks and stuff, because they like to drink. They're called sycamores. There's one in our neighborhood. We walked by it."

A sycamore that Kenny knew flashed in his mind's eye, a big one at the corner of Fourth and Winnebago. He used to walk by it on the way to school in the morning. The day he sprinted home from East, after the secretary had interrupted his French Two class and announced in front of everyone that Kenny's dad had "been in a terrible car accident," Kenny stopped suddenly at that sycamore and just leaned against it for a minute. He didn't know why. He wasn't even that winded yet. He just felt the need to stand with that tree for a second. Its smooth elephantine bark was almost like a skin, but cool. He felt it for a second, against his arm, then his face. After what seemed like a long time but was probably only a few seconds, he ran home and into the whirlwind of events that inevitably follow an unexpected death.

He had also recently learned a few facts about sycamores from Chris, who was from Southern Indiana, where they abound. "I like those trees," Kenny said to Taylor. "You know they don't grow as well where we live. The ones in Madison are about as far north as you'll see them."

"I have a uterus," replied Taylor.

"Aha," said Kenny.

"Mommy was talking about hers, and she told me I have one, too. You don't have one, Uncle Kenny."

"Aha," Kenny repeated, then cleared his throat. "You are right about that, Taylor."

"Who tucks you in where you live?"

"Well," began Kenny, "most times, when adults go to sleep, no one tucks us in."

"Then how do you go to sleep?" She sounded almost indignant.

"Well, you just close your eyes. Then you wait."

"What are you waiting for? Is there a sound?"

Kenny had no idea what this meant. Like most five-year-olds, Taylor periodically asked things that completely perplexed Kenny, things like "How long does it take to kick down a barn?" or "What time did Jesus go to school?"

"Aha," he said, for the third time. "A sound. Aha. Not really, it's mostly like you kind of just slide slowly into a place."

"Are there sounds there?" she asked again.

"Sometimes," said Kenny, feeling himself taking the question more seriously. Talking to Taylor was like a puzzle, keeping him on his toes. He had no idea where she would go next.

"When you dream," he added.

"I dream all the time," said Taylor. Now she was following, if just for a second. Kenny felt like he had a small part in the conversation, at last.

"When we saw the tree yesterday, Grandma said trees like that one are nice because you can daydream about them."

Kenny thought again about the day of his dad's accident, and *dreamlike* was definitely a way to describe that run home from school. After a few weeks, when the shock had settled down and he had resumed something like a routine, he would make sure he passed that sycamore every time he came home from school. He'd cross Fourth Street to walk by it, stopping to touch it for a few seconds before continuing home. His Grandma Maesby had once told him she thought church "overdid ritual" sometimes, robbing the gesture of its true spiritual value, and maybe that's what had started to happen on his daily visits to the sycamore. But he did feel something almost religious about the need to touch it on the way home. Maybe he would daydream some more about that tree when he got off the phone.

"I can throw a rock into the creek," Taylor added, after a second. "I miss when you tuck me in sometimes."

"Well, I miss you, too," he said. He had only tucked her in a couple of times, most recently at the end of the summer, before he left for school. Both times, she asked him to invent stories, and she had seemed to grow more energetic with every narrative turn or new tale, just as Kenny had felt his own energy draining away. Was it like this for his sister every single night? He assumed Taylor found something special about his own storytelling style because she didn't have a dad—or had never met him anyway. Plus, Kenny was only seventeen when she was born, so he had always felt a little more like a big brother than an uncle.

"I'm going to hang up now," said Taylor. Then she did.

A couple of minutes later, Kenny's phone rang again.

"Hello?"

"Sorry, Kenny," said Kate, "we're still working on that last part."

"She did pretty well. Was that her first time calling someone?"

Kate laughed. "It was. You got the honor."

"And the privilege," said Kenny, drawling what he thought was a Virginia accent.

Kate ignored it. "Yes, I was doing dishes, and she just suddenly goes, 'I wonder what Uncle Kenny is up to right now. I think I'll drop him a line'."

"*Drop him a line*? She said that?"

"I know. I didn't correct her. I don't know where she gets stuff. It seemed like pretty serious business."

"Can she hear you?" asked Kenny, suddenly aware they were talking about a person, maybe in her presence.

"No, she's in her room. She practically ran right in there after she hung up. I think it may have surprised her, how loud it sounded when the receiver came down. She jumped a little, but I also think she may have squealed. You have made her day."

"So what's up with you?"

"Living the dream. Paying the bills." Kate had been working at Magenta Manor, a nursing home a couple of miles up the road from her apartment on Milwaukee Street, since she was nineteen. Going on six years now. She had been promoted from "aide" to "activities coordinator" and was doing a pretty good job of it, from what their mom had told Kenny. Kate was always good at getting along in the present moment, or, at the very least, taking steps as they came.

Taylor was the result of one of these steps, a youthful indiscretion of Kate's in August of 1982. Nineteen years old and defaulting her way through classes at the technical college, Kate had ended up one Friday night at her friend Becky's parents' house. The parents were somewhere else, Becky had some pot, there was a bottle or two of André. Some other friends trickled in, Becky put on a Styx album, *The Grand Illusion.* More friends, a little more smoking and drinking. More André.

For Kate, the party ended in a noisy coital interlude under a basement ping-pong table, with Kev, the visiting cousin of somebody at the party. Immediately following the proceedings, Kev crawled quickly and shamefully to the couch—then, his jeans mostly on, out to his Camaro—and drove away.

Kate had to do a considerable amount of work to locate Kev. She finally found his number and called him at the trailer he shared with his older brother Jim outside Des Moines.

"Whoa, that sucks," he replied. He took an audible drag on a cigarette and also sounded like he was chewing something. "What are you gonna do?"

"Become a mom, I guess," she had said, oddly relieved by his relinquishment of duty. "Take care, man." And that was that. She never heard from him again.

"Mom is doing pretty well," said Kate, changing to their other usual subject. "She still hasn't talked about dating or men or anything, just school and coworkers and Grandma and Grandpa. She's been down to Taylor Mill a couple of times since you were here in August."

"How are they?" asked Kenny, a little worried that his mom had been to see her parents twice in a span of seven or eight weeks. They weren't that old, but still.

"They're fine," said Kate. He heard a plate or an empty cup hit what sounded like a fairly hard surface. "Damn it."

"Was something going on in Northern Kentucky?" he asked.

"No, she just missed them, I think. She invited me and Taylor to come, but I had to work. She took Taylor that first time, September something. It was just a long weekend."

For some reason, the thought of his mom and Taylor in a car bound for Kentucky reminded Kenny of Madison. They were all going to meet in Taylor Mill for the holidays anyway, and he looked forward to being at his grandparents' house, but he couldn't get the idea of his own home out of his head.

He could also see the end of college itself, a few months away, and he still had no idea what he was going to do for a living. Also, had he even learned anything about life in the South? He had overshot Kentucky on purpose, coming to UVA in part to learn more about what might be Southern about his parents, his family, his roots. He had been spinning a lot of wheels trying to make sense of the place, but all he seemed to have gathered was a casual appreciation. Maybe that's because he knew he had only been a guest here. And how much time did one have to spend in a place to understand its story anyway?

North Sea Oil

A couple of weeks after Christmas break, which Kenny spent with his family in Northern Kentucky, it snowed a little in Charlottesville. In his first year, a fellow student had warned him that "up here in the mountains it can get really cold." This had proven true to some extent that first winter, but Kenny was from the Upper Midwest. This kind of talk reminded him of what he'd sometimes hear in Kentucky. *Wes-con-sin? It's cold up there!* Kenny may have liked Charlottesville a lot and identified closely with his Kentucky roots, but whenever he heard pronouncements in those places about snow, cold, or winter, he remained a polite but very dubious Northerner.

It was during this last week of January, in his final semester at UVA, that Kenny had his second Lincoln dream. This time most of it stayed with him, including how it began.

He was walking along the Lawn, that central green space that rolls out from Jefferson's Rotunda and cascades gently down past a statue of Homer, to Old Cabell Hall, the building that closes the rectangle on the Lawn's other side. Bordering the rectangle are the East and West Ranges, with their Pavilions housing important deans and faculty members, between which are single dormitory rooms, designed originally for all students but now home to the cream of the crop, fourth-year and graduate student politicos who sit relaxing in the old cane rocking chairs provided by the University and which allow them to imagine that, had *they* been here when it happened, there is no way they would have agreed that young Edgar Allan Poe should be tossed out for ungentlemanly behavior.

In waking life, the Lawn was one of the many things about UVA that were both historically interesting and completely foreign to Kenny. He could never enjoy the Lawn, as beautiful as he found it. In his dream, however, the place felt much more like home. The Lawn, deep in snow, was littered with ice fishing shanties, half of them emblazoned with hand-painted Green Bay Packers logos and big green-and-gold flags. Home.

"C'mon, try it," yelled one ice fisherman, from the upturned white *Farm and Fleet* bucket he was perched on. Kenny hadn't seen a Farm and Fleet anywhere outside Madison before, and they definitely didn't have them in Virginia. The ice fisherman's Wisconsin accent was strong. Kenny's Virginian friends would have heard *c'mahn.* He didn't say *Milwaukee*, but if he had, even in the dream, it would have been a two-syllable word. The dream Lawn was a frozen lake, filled with feisty yellow perch.

"Over here," said a high-pitched voice that Kenny recognized immediately. President Lincoln was sitting in one of the classic Lawn rocking chairs, wrapped in a wool blanket. He pulled deeply on his pipe, and a small light-blue cloud gently encircled his tired-looking head.

"This is Jefferson's domain. I have already done what I needed to for Virginia," Lincoln said.

Kenny wondered if Jefferson could hear them and if he would find Lincoln's comment rude or presumptuous. Kenny had read enough to know that, for some people around here, what Lincoln had done was less *for* Virginia than *to* it.

At that moment, Kenny heard a bell tolling in the distance. No, wait—it was a foghorn. It sounded just like the warning blast you could hear from Kenny's East Side neighborhood in the summer, from all the way over on Lake Mendota. Each evening, the university lake safety people alerted sailing club members that it was time to come back to shore or that a storm was coming. And that the lake was bigger than some of them thought.

"Look over there, on that hill," said the president, rocking slowly and taking another pull on his pipe.

This time, Kenny had his wits more about him. He understood what was happening. For example, he knew that there was no big, bare hill right behind the actual Rotunda. In waking life, yes, lots of hills around Charlottesville, but this was a large, bald surface that went up about a hundred yards, sloping steeply and treeless, even on the top. It looked like it would make a good sledding hill. Very little snow on it, though.

"Look closely," said the president.

Kenny squinted. On the hill was a solitary figure, carrying a backpack, walking in a straight line, up, up, up to the top.

"That's Orion," said Lincoln.

No, it isn't, thought Kenny. *That's my dad.*

It was Harlan McLuher, in fact. But, as things often go in dreams, the characters seem to agree to refer one way to things, all the while knowing full well that those things are something else entirely.

Kenny knew a little bit about Orion, but if he was being honest, to him it was just the first line in the chorus of a Jethro Tull song by the same name. Say *Orion,* and Kenny was as likely as not to imagine the unusual five-four time signature of "North Sea Oil," another song from the Tull album.

"Orion is the Hunter," said the president, knowing full well that Kenny was distracted. "He's up there," he added, pointing his pipe. "You find his belt first, then you can imagine him with his bow and arrow, crossing the sky."

"What is he hunting?"

"Zeus put him there, as a constellation. For us, a winter constellation."

You may be our Zeus, thought Kenny. He noticed Lincoln's frail shoulders beneath the blanket. Kenny looked over again at his father. Harlan was in the distance, about where he had been on the hill when the president first pointed him out, climbing and straining upward, headed for some kind of task.

"His backpack has books in it, doesn't it?" asked Kenny.

Lincoln disregarded the question. "Orion is astronomy as much as he is legend, but really he's just a legend." Then, the president became quiet for a little while.

I'm the narrator, Kenny had once realized as a child, after he had written one of his many stories. In your dream—and later, if you remember most of it, you *are* the narrator. You tell it, as it is telling you. Then, if you remember much of it when you wake up, you tell it again, to real people around you. Was it superstitious to think it might let you see a little into the future, even if its meaning was still so blurry?

It definitely allowed something of a glimpse into the past. Kenny looked more closely at his father. As far away as Harlan was, Kenny could tell that he was in a hurry and that he was laboring a little. It being a dream, Kenny knew the contents of his father's backpack. There were three books, all having to do with the man sitting near him in that rocking chair. All were hardbound, which suggested why Harlan might be laboring so. There was Carl Sandburg, *Abraham Lincoln.* This was one Harlan would mention sometimes, especially once Kenny had arrived in about fourth grade and was writing stories all the time. Harlan wanted him to learn a little about the man he shared a birthday with. There was also Gore Vidal's historical novel *Lincoln.*

The book Kenny could see best, though, was a biography of the president for older children: Ingri and Edgar Parin d'Aulaire's *Abraham Lincoln*, published in 1940 and focusing on the future president as a young man. The cover showed a young Lincoln, probably a year or two after his voice had changed, sitting on a fence rail, a yellow sun behind him sending rays out from a spot just behind him. It was as if the sun were contained in the boy's heart.

Lincoln shifted in his rocking chair and grinned. "They made me a little bit into a myth."

Zeus, but splitting a rail. Kenny cleared his throat, also a little uncomfortable. "Mr. President, wasn't that part of your strategy, a little bit?"

Lincoln heard the word *strategy* in a mid-nineteenth century way, but he knew Kenny was only talking about the public image part.

"I allowed it to happen," he said, looking off toward Harlan in the dream-distance behind the Rotunda. "It's part of what led me to Virginia at this point in history, comfortable knowing that we're all in the same country."

Kenny felt silent and oddly reverent for a moment. "That's my dad over there," he said.

"Orion," said Lincoln, not making eye contact. "Watch him climb."

Kenny felt a lump in the pit of his stomach. He couldn't shake it. "He won't be back," he said to Lincoln.

"Orion returns every single night, even in the summer when you can only see him in other parts of the world. He hunts, and he returns. He moves, yet he is true to his place."

"But my dad," said Kenny, feeling a stammer coming and a lump in his gut. *Be afraid,* the lump suggested. *You know what's about to happen.* "He's going to die."

"Orion never dies. He always returns," said Lincoln, as if to reassure Kenny. "Anyway, he's a legend."

Afar, Harlan turned as Kenny strained to see him. Now Kenny was feeling intensely sad, even in his dream he could feel it. His father had passed away four years earlier. The insurance money was what was paying for this entire college adventure. All this reading, all this history, and all so far away.

Harlan waved back toward the Lawn, to Kenny, or maybe to Lincoln.

Harlan didn't see the Madison Public Library Bookmobile rumbling across the hillside toward him, but Kenny could. The driver, a young librarian who had just been hired, had pushed her curly red hair behind her ear and slipped a cassette into the boombox on the passenger seat. For at least five seconds she was looking down as the great vehicle surged blindly forward. Of course, the song was Jethro Tull, "North Sea Oil," with its odd time signature. Kenny knew, in just a second or two, the van would hit his father, erasing him from waking life forever.

Waynesboro

Go West, young man. Kenny had been up over Afton Mountain several times, usually in someone else's car. Unless he was taking the train, I-64 was the first leg of the trip home.

The view across that valley was pretty stunning. Even Wayne said so once, and he had grown up there. Afton Mountain always reminded Kenny of a particular stretch of Richardson Road, a much smaller Northern Kentucky highway not far from his grandparents' house. It was steep—his uncle Bill had been in two separate car wrecks on that hill in high school. It ran along a modest but pretty little valley sprinkled with houses, a couple of outbuildings, and an unfinished basement project always surrounded by old cars. There was a trailer or two. At the top was a farmhouse looking down on the rest.

There was no such house at the top of Afton Mountain, just an interstate exit onto Skyline Drive and a lot more valley to look down at. When you got there, you were at the top of your run—and, depending on what kind of car you were in, that run could be dicey. Once Kenny limped up that hill with a grad student he had met on the university ride board, in a banged-up 1965 VW Beetle. The other cars flew by as they climbed the slope. By the time they got to the top, they were going fifteen miles an hour.

Waynesboro lay on the other side of this climb. For Kenny, Waynesboro was just a highway sign, a name on a road atlas, a benchmark. Today it was an actual destination.

Kenny pulled the borrowed Pontiac along the side of the road in front of Wayne's house. He checked the address on the handwritten map Wayne had made for him, then looked up again at the place. Halfway down a little residential street not far off the interstate, the house sat back behind a maple tree and a chain-link fence. A small house, well cared for. A single story, a couple of bedrooms, maybe a dining room half in the kitchen, like his grandparents had. There was a trailer next door—a mobile home somebody kept nice and clean. The flowers in the decorative tractor tire out front were reminiscent of his grandparents' neighborhood in Taylor Mill. Here, though, the houses were a little closer to the road, and in the distance there were mountains. *The Blue Ridge,* thought Kenny. *They really do look blue.*

"Hey, man!" Wayne came out the front door. He was wearing a homemade cape. "Nice wheels!"

Kenny got out of the car. "Hey, Wayne."

"That Chris's Grand Prix?" Wayne had come around the opening in the fence and ran his hand along the front fender of the large car. He was wearing eyeliner, which he seemed also to have applied to parts of his mustache, most likely with a toothbrush. He looked vaguely marsupial, an effect enhanced by his tendency to raise his eyebrows regularly when he talked.

"1972, baby. Even with the rust, pretty cool, pretty cool. What'd you burn in gas from Charlottesville, about four hundred gallons? Heh heh. Come on in. We have *serious work* to do."

They were going to play "Dungeon Lord," a game Wayne had invented based on some limited experience with a much more famous game with a strikingly similar name. The main difference was that Dungeon Lord allowed the game master, which Wayne called "the Chief Lord," to interpret dice rolls however he liked. An absolutist vision of the role-playing game, a narrator in complete control whenever he wanted it. This may have been what made Wayne want to wear the cape.

"Plus," added Wayne, "there shall perchance be *wizardry* afoot."

He led Kenny through the front door and into a small living room. Between a couch and a rocking chair, a man in his late fifties sat on a green recliner, watching a rerun of *The Gong Show*. He was wearing a white t-shirt and jeans, both streaked with dirt, and house slippers.

"Kenny, this is my dad," said Wayne, in a less sprightly voice.

"How you doing, Ken?" said Wayne's dad, who showed no sign of getting up. After a second, he leaned forward, stood up, and turned off the TV. "Jim Halard." He held his hand out. Kenny shook it, a little formally.

"Nice to meet you, Mr. Halard."

"Jim."

Kenny smiled politely. "Nice to meet you, Jim."

"Sorry about the dirt. A little gardening break. Y'all fellas dressin' up for your game?"

Wayne winced. "Dad, come on, it's part of the whole thing."

"That's what they said about the Hindenburg, Wayne, and look what happened to them Germans." He grinned. Kenny detected a little bit of Wayne in his style.

Wayne rolled his eyes then walked into the small hallway, pausing in an open doorway. "Come on, man, we're set up downstairs."

"Good to meet you, Ken."

Jim strolled into the kitchen. "Break's over, I guess. I'm gonna be out in the yard," he yelled toward the door. It sounded to

Kenny like *Amo be oaten the yoard.* "Your mom's at the store. She'll be home 'fore long."

"Okay, Dad," came Wayne's voice from the stairwell. He had left the room in some haste. "We'll be down here," he added, repeating a just-said fact like Kenny's relatives in Kentucky always did.

Kenny walked through the basement door, where Wayne had gone. Long rectangles of shop-grit sandpaper ran along the edge of each step, a homemade safety precaution. The staircase and handrail were painted dark gray. It was all pretty crisp for an area most visitors weren't likely to see. Kenny's own dad could get this way about house projects. His mother, too.

The stairway opened onto a medium-sized room, not really "finished" in the way a suburban basement rec room or den might be, but tidy in an older way. The concrete walls were lined with stacks of boxes reading things like *Scarfs, Christmas,* and *Nancy Crafts,* handwritten neatly in black marker. A furnace and water heater sat off to the left. In the middle of the far wall was a door, through which Kenny could see part of an unmade bed and a poster for the rock band Triumph.

In the middle of the room, at a card table beneath a fluorescent overhead light, sat another guy in a Jethro Tull t-shirt a size too small for him. He was reading a sheet of paper.

"Kenny, this is Fats Trustell. He's a buddy from a long time."

"Hey man," said the guy at the table, looking up from his reading and nodding. Kenny noted that he was Black, then immediately felt bad for noticing this. Fats leaned over and shook Kenny's hand awkwardly, like he was practicing. Something about him reminded Kenny a little of his best childhood friend Kurt Lemke. "You work with Wayne."

"Yeah, we work at Catering," said Kenny. "At the university," he said, unsure why he had felt the need to add that.

"Yeah, Charlottesville," said Fats unnecessarily, maybe also a little unsure of what to say.

"So, yeah, um," said Kenny, not yet sure if he should sit down, "you guys known each other for a while, then, um...?" He was unsure if he had heard the guy's name right.

"Fats," said Fats.

"Yeah, um. *Fats*," said Kenny, shifting in his chair.

"I know," said Fats, grinning. "It's kind of a funny name, for a dude my age at least. Kind of like a older guy's name."

"I guess that's true," said Kenny.

The introductions done with, Wayne sat down to his duties. Installed on a folding chair, he began doing something with dice and paper, behind a black cardboard screen decorated with a Van Halen logo that looked like a salvaged tenth-grade art project.

"I rolled your character, Kenny. For the rest of the game, you are Gawain Deathslayer, fighter-wizard of Berg Krocken. Fats's character is Nor-Fer, Ring Thief. Also of Berg Krocken."

"*Gawain* and *Nor-Fer*," said Kenny, slowly, testing the pronunciation of the names.

"It's actually a *honor*, Wayne," said Fats, his head tilting a little sideways. "Fats Domino. Minnesota Fats. Think about it. Like, musicians, and probably your gangster here and there, too. You know, in the past."

Wayne rolled a die methodically behind the screen, "If I was a gangster, they's no way I'd call myself Fats. It's like saying, *Hey, y'all should chase me down and catch me after we rob this bank, 'cause I'm fat and slow.*"

"You don't get it, man. It's like a honor."

"You already done said that."

"That's 'cause you didn't grasp it the first time."

Wayne remained focused on whatever he was working on behind the Van Halen screen. He rolled another die.

Kenny was unsure what was supposed to happen next. "Do I get some kind of sheet to study, or refer to, or whatever?"

"What about Baby Face Nelson then?" said Fats, looking up from his sheet of paper at Wayne.

"Yes, Sir Knight," said Wayne, ceremoniously, to Kenny. He looked at Fats. "You mean Baby Face *Wilson*, dumbass."

Fats frowned, ignoring the error. "He was a badass, and he *wanted* people to call him Baby Face. It's not like, after the bank robbery, the cops is gonna chase some actual *baby* out into the street." He sounded prickly, like a younger sibling holding onto a lost argument.

Wayne looked up from his Chief Lord work and grinned. Kenny could see that Wayne and Fats argued every time they were together.

"So do I need that piece of paper, or...?" said Kenny.

Fats looked closely at his character sheet, then back up again. The argument had come and gone. "Frickin' Dungeon Lord," he said, tenting his fingers. "Let's do it, y'all."

Wayne handed Kenny a sheet of paper over the Van Halen screen, moving with even more delicacy than he used when slicing a London Broil. Handwritten on a piece of college-ruled notepaper, with vertical lines drawn on to create four columns, the sheet read *Gawain Deathslayer, fighter-wizard of Berg Krocken.* Below that were several lists of numbers, showing the character's levels of strength, intelligence, and so on. Kenny had tried to play Dungeons and Dragons a few times in high school but had quickly lost interest, the other kids in the game having been so involved in the math-and-numbers part of things. Kenny had just wanted to imagine a world in which he could explore, make decisions, be part of a group with others on an adventure.

"Unto you I speak this truth," said Wayne, his voice deepened slightly, sitting up unusually straight in his chair. "You have wandered into the Ruins of Starb-Loring, Lair of Trellmander, Frost King of the Gnome Killers." He appeared to be reading some notes he was holding low behind the Van Halen screen. Kenny glanced over at Fats, who was watching Wayne's eyes intently, as if already working on some kind of strategy. His eyes betrayed an earnest hunger, suggesting some war wisdom he might reveal momentarily in the gloom of this imaginary place.

"Remember, men," said Wayne, looking up from his notes and making direct eye contact with Kenny. "*Battle* need not to be the only fight moves you make here in the Ruins. You might, perchance, use your hypnosis skills." He grinned conspiratorially at Kenny, a single eyebrow arched just a tad.

Kenny looked down at his sheet, for a sign of what this might mean. He didn't see any "hypnosis" category or any word like it anywhere. In spite of the four columns, there wasn't much information on the page beyond the name and description of the character and his basic characteristics.

Wayne cleared his throat, still looking at Kenny. "You know, *hypnosis*." He raised the other eyebrow. "Or any other kind of sleep magic you might have. Either one of you."

"Hold on a second," said Fats, leaning away from the card table and temporarily leaving the game's imaginary world. "You that guy at work who did that sleep thing on that dude?"

Yes, a couple of caterers had fallen asleep, weirdly, at the past couple of functions Kenny had worked, but beyond that he had no idea what Fats was talking about.

"What do you mean?"

Fats was looking at Kenny with some interest. "That thing, where you told that story and those guys went right to sleep?" He smiled and shook his head once, for emphasis. "And—Uncle *Remus*? Like, realistic-sounding, the *Tar Baby* and shit?"

Already confused, Kenny was now also startled. Wayne hadn't said anything, but he looked about to.

"The *Tar Baby*?" asked Kenny, still on guard but relaxing a little. Fats seemed friendly. "I loved that story. My dad used to read it to us all the time, doing a... a *country* voice and everything." He said *a country voice* instead of *a Black guy voice*, which is what he really meant but didn't want to say. "Except, uh, my dad's not, like, racist or anything, not like, making fun of how people talk, like Uncle Remus, he just came from Kentucky, you know, it wasn't so weird for them..."

"Yeah, *zippety do dah, zippety yay,*" laughed Fats, unworried. "Like some kind of *Gone with the Wind* cartoon, you know what I'm talking about? But that story's pretty good."

Kenny was adrift. What were they talking about, and how did they get into this thing about stereotypes and voices? How did you talk about this kind of thing?

Fats laughed again. "That thing where the fox and the bear are trying to kill Bur Rabbit and eat him. We loved that shit, with my little brother and me all doing the voices at bedtime and shit." A boyish enthusiasm had overtaken him. He seemed nowhere near the Ruins of Starb-Loring. He also seemed completely unaware of Kenny's embarrassment.

"But, so, like—how does it work? The hypnotizing thing? I saw a guy do it at a school assembly once, in like fifth grade. He got Larry Verness to say all kinds of hilarious shit on stage. We was bustin' a gut."

"I have no idea what you guys are talking about," said Kenny, a little frustrated now. He really did have no idea what they meant.

"You weren't just hypnotizing 'em," said Wayne. "You were like, in a trance *yourself*, man. Telling them stories while Logan and Tracy—well, Logan two times—they just started dozing off, little by little. Or even real fast."

"What?"

Wayne looked at Fats. "I'm telling you, man. It was wild."

Kenny felt a slight rush of something. A head rush. He put his hands to his temples and took a breath.

"You aight, man?" said Fats, putting down his character sheet.

Kenny nodded but moved his head from side to side a couple of times, breathing deeply for a second as if to get more oxygen into his bloodstream. Everything seemed to come into focus at once: Wayne's confused face behind the screen, the Van Halen logo, Fats's equally concerned look, the card table, the four dice sitting outside Wayne's screen. For a moment, all he could think about was a misty castle scene, the kind Boris Karloff might wander into in one of his 1940s monster roles, in black and white: the place Wayne was bringing to life as Chief Lord. Kenny could see Wayne's lips moving, but for a second or two, he couldn't hear anything. Then he couldn't imagine the castle yard anymore, or anything having to do with his character or the world they were supposed to have in their heads. All he could see was himself and these two other guys sitting at this table in a Virginia basement.

"Sorry, guys. I get these migraines sometimes," he lied.

"You want a drink of water or something?"

"No, I'm all right, thanks."

Just then, Wayne's dad came down the stairs into the basement.

"How's your game coming along, boys?" His voice was jolly. It sounded to Kenny like he was talking to middle-schoolers at a sleepover. He winked and patted Wayne affectionately on the shoulder. Irritated, Wayne reached across his chest and readjusted his cape so it sat more squarely on his shoulder again.

"I's just coming down to get something I left down here." He walked over to a box marked *Goodwill*, reached in, and pulled out a small garden trowel. "Here it is. I thought I'd maybe put this in here. Snatched back from charity, just in time." He winked again, toward the group. "No comment!" he added, then walked back up the stairs.

"Well," said Wayne, scooting his chair an inch or so closer to the table, to mark a new chapter. "Let's get this show back on the road, shall we?"

As they played, Wayne became more and more animated behind his screen, looking from one player to another as he conjured up visual scenes for the game: a forest clearing, the bank of a small brook, the tumbledown opening in a wall that had once been part of a castle. His voice underwent theatrical changes he had never used before, at least as far as Kenny could recall. Kenny and Fats took turns rolling dice, respectively saying what their character would do at this or that moment, often stopping to consult after Wayne had thrown them for a loop. ("Suddenly, a elf-dragon appears from behind a rock!" or "Light fills the air, and neither of you know what to do for fourteen seconds!")

Fats seemed to be on some kind of wavelength with Wayne, in his Chief Lord role, but Kenny found everything increasingly difficult to see in his mind's eye. All he could imagine was the basement they were sitting in. Yet here was Wayne, exultant in his own voice, speaking a new world into existence. A place parallel to this real spot just off the highway in Central Virginia, while outside his father loosened soil and spread mulch around the little house where Wayne had grown up so unusual and imaginative.

Memorial

Kenny walked along the reflecting pool with Logan and Tracy. The sun was low in the sky, and it was comfortably warm. They had come up from Charlottesville to see the Red Hot Chili Peppers, but Kenny had been adamant about visiting the Lincoln Memorial first.

"How could you never have been here?" asked Tracy as they strolled toward the monument. "Four years at UVA, and no trips to DC?"

"I don't know," replied Kenny. "In my family, we have this tradition of not really thinking of the obvious thing."

"Charlottesville isn't that far, man," said Logan. "What's your family have to do with it, anyway?"

Jabs like this one usually bothered Kenny, but the low sun and the reflecting pool had him in a pensive mood. For a minute, they walked in silence. Tracy even took Kenny's hand for a full minute, still without a word, as the trio strolled along the water.

"I have a dream!" yelled Logan as they approached the monument.

"Look up over the colonnade," said Tracy, ignoring Logan's tasteless attempt at a joke. Her hand had naturally fallen away. "You'll see the names of the states."

Logan glanced at his watch. It was scuffed up but looked like it had cost a pretty penny. "The states in the Union when they built the building," he said, correcting her.

They walked around so that Kenny could see Wisconsin, its birth certificate reading *MDCCCXLVIII.*

"There it is," said Logan, "All the cheese you ever desired."

"A little respect, Logan," said Kenny, his gaze on the words unbroken.

"Whoa, Dairy," said Logan, his tone unchanged. He wandered ahead, into the building.

"Somebody's in a mood," said Tracy. She took Kenny's hand again for a second then dropped it, just as gently. They walked around some more until Kenny could see Virginia, then Kentucky, on the frieze. He was relieved that Logan, who had rejoined the group, didn't call Kentucky "just a big county that left Virginia," as he had once remarked at a Catering function.

As they strolled closer to Lincoln, the space otherwise empty of people, Kenny imagined huge joyous crowds—Martin Luther King's speech, Marian Anderson singing "He's Got the Whole World in His Hands," the sermonizing, and the impending change. The place also conjured assassinations, Vietnam, all that other violence in black and white in Kenny's young mind. Open as it was, the place had something of the mausoleum about it.

"You a alien, man," came a voice, surprisingly close. Kenny turned around.

"You a alien," said the man. He looked homeless and was probably crazy, but he seemed calm enough.

"Aha," said Kenny.

"All right, man," said Logan, who called lots of people *man.* They all did, with seemingly everyone their age, but Logan used it a lot with Black men. "Hey, man," he had once said to a very old custodian outside the servery in Newcomb Hall, "would you mind taking a look at the loading dock before you head out? There's a bunch of stuff down there that usually isn't there, you know. It probably needs to be cleaned up."

"You a alien," the man repeated.

"All right, man," Logan said again.

"You a alien," said the man again, as if Kenny were the only one there.

"Aha," said Kenny, looking at Tracy.

"Yes, yes," said Tracy, in a helping-professional voice, "we're aliens. It's okay."

"It's cool," said Kenny, very unsure.

"No, you not aliens, *you* a alien." He poked Kenny gently in the chest.

"Yeah, it's cool," added Logan.

The man looked up at the president and said, without shouting but directly at Lincoln himself, "And *you* a alien. You a alien."

He looked up at the monument ceiling, then back at Kenny and smiled. "You know Orion," he said. For a second, Kenny thought he had said *You know Ryan,* and he wondered who Ryan was. Then, as if to make it clearer, the man said it again, more slowly. "You... know... Orion." Like in Kenny's dream.

Tracy and Logan looked at each other, but Kenny kept his eyes on the man.

"You know Orion," he said. "You a alien."

Everyone was quiet, then the man suddenly raised his hands in the air.

"Jefferson!" he yelled. "It's my name! My name *Jefferson!*" He dropped his hands, and his mouth made a straight line. "Thomas Jefferson was my people, he done spread out all over creation and back again. His statue ain't real, though, not like *this* one. He spread himself out way too thin, you know what I'm saying?"

He grinned again a little and moved closer to Kenny. "You," he said, almost in a whisper, "you a *alien.*" Then he backed away, turned, and ran down the steps and out of view.

Logan looked at Kenny for a second more then let out a sigh of relief.

Kenny looked out over the pool, unsure what he had expected from this little pilgrimage. His parents had come here once in college, and it had seemed important to them. Kenny had wanted it to mean something to him, too. Sure, the homeless guy would be memorable, and the Orion thing was weirdly coincidental. And there sat Lincoln, belonging to the ages. But when he imagined the president asking him *What are you doing here?*, Kenny couldn't think of any answer at all.

Commencement

Only one bookshelf still needed cleaning out, but it did contain three shelves full of books Kenny had acquired since his first year in college. A banged-up little piece of furniture, it had occupied the spot beneath the biggest window in the apartment ever since he and his roommate Chris had moved in.

He had picked up three boxes at a liquor store, lined them up in a row, intent on filling them systematically, by size. As he began to pull them off the shelf, however, he found himself lingering on the Jefferson books. Most of them he had found at yard sales or bookstores, and his interest in them stemmed more from a vague urge to collect things than it did to document the life of the third president. But now that he was loading them up, one after the other, into a box originally intended to transport bottles of bourbon, he had to admit that he was glad to be returning to Wisconsin with something uniquely Virginian. Besides his four-year education, that is.

He hadn't read any of them yet but intended to. The books were all cut from what felt like the same cloth: all written by men, probably all Southerners; all bearing titles that seemed to call out for some kind of background music. The first one he pulled off the shelf was called *The Father of the University*, by an author named Culciver Broadlake. Each time he took one out to pack, he'd look at the publication date. This one was from 1967. The next one was William Deckerforth's *Our Dear Friend Jefferson* (1972). Then Standiford Burnington's strangely haunted-sounding *Mr. Jefferson, the Renaissance Wizard of Albemarle* (1970). After that, a smaller volume bearing a title that sounded as if he had been translated from Chinese: *Jefferson, Ingenious Progenitor of the American Wine Industry.*

The last book, he realized, he had completely forgotten about. It was by Knox Chiffonier IV, the writer who had spoken at the Birdwood catering event. Its title reminded Kenny of the way its author made conversation, or even the affected way he ate meatballs: *A Quietude Above the Fray: Jefferson and the Mists of Monticello* (1982). Kenny's mother had given this book to him as a Christmas gift during his first big trip home from UVA. He opened the cover and reread the inscription:

> *For Kenny, the first Virginian in our group. This book probably takes itself pretty seriously, but it looked like it had some interesting stories in it about Jefferson. Your Dad would have eaten this right up. Merry Christmas 1984, and Wa-Wa-Hoo! -Mom*

Every time he came home, at some point, Kenny's mother would shout what she thought was the official chant of loyalty to the University of Virginia, but it was never quite right. "Waha-Hoo!" she would yell, a glass of wine in one hand and the other shooting up in the air in a faux-cheerleader gesture. Or "Hoo-Wa-Wah!" Or even once, when they were watching the Cavaliers play in the nationally televised Peach Bowl, a totally unironic and genuinely excited "Hoo-Hee-Wah-Wah!"

"You're a teacher," Kenny had said. "It can't be that hard to remember *Wahoo-wa.*"

Not about to be lectured by her own child, Linda had raised both hands, in the touchdown gesture she often did when excited, and yelled "Wah-Waddley-Hoo-Hoo!" Kenny rolled his eyes, determined not to cede territory. His mother joked with her full body, like his sister dropped plates or ran into telephone poles, but with a great deal more control.

He slid the Chiffonier book into the cardboard box, then grabbed his backpack and keys. He had left a couple of things over at the servery, after his final shifts two weeks before, and wanted to pick them up before his family got here for commencement. That was in two days. He slipped out the door and walked up the hill toward Grounds.

* * * * *

When he got to the servery, Kenny took a minute to remove his Catering key from the key ring on the carabiner hanging off his belt. He went to put his key in the door but found it ajar.

"Hey, anybody here?" he asked, into what looked like an empty room.

"In the walk-in," came a voice from around the corner.

"Hey," said Kenny to the voice. "Just getting some stuff I left."

Tracy came around the corner. "Kenny, old man!" she said playfully, lowering her voice to do some kind of preppy character Kenny imagined wearing madras slacks and hoisting a gin and tonic. He had been at UVA long enough now to have at least glimpsed such people. Tracy's own dad probably talked like this. She had played field hockey at a place called the Torydon School, after all.

"Hey," replied Kenny.

"You ready for the Lawn?" asked Tracy, her eyes surprisingly bright.

"Just got my cap and gown. I'm oddly psyched for it."

"Yeah, it's weird. I'm not even leaving town, but it feels like something you don't want to miss."

"Totally."

"So you're headed back to Wisconsin, pretty much right away," she said/asked, her hand gliding nervously to the back of her neck, massaging it a little once it landed.

"Yeah, with my folks. Well," he corrected, "my mom and sister, and her kid. They want us to go to Williamsburg, then we'll all drive back to Madison. So I'll leave in like a week or so."

"Tricorne hats for the road," said Tracy. Kenny noticed freckles on her nose, which he hadn't seen before.

"Aha," he said, then grinned. "Yeah, actually never been."

Tracy walked casually behind the couch, across from where Kenny was standing, like she needed to be a little closer to hear him when he talked.

"Did you hear the news about Steelmark Services?" she asked.

"What's Steelmark Services?"

"It's the corporate scumbags that the university just farmed Catering out to, starting in a month or so. Sold us off."

"That sucks." Kenny hadn't heard anything about this. For most of them, Catering was just a student job, a way to pay for at least part of what college cost you, but it also provided a community of co-traveling weirdos who enjoyed each other's company and might not have otherwise rubbed elbows—not to mention a lot of leftover London Broil and a little "extra" bourbon after work. Kenny had to admit he had come to enjoy the white glove-level kind of service the Catering style took when setting up lunches, dinners, mixers, receptions. He had never done any kind of management, just supervising—which meant regular serving, with an extra level of responsibility for what his grandpa would have called "time-motion work." Getting things back into their place at the end of the night and such. Catering itself, at least according to the older caterers, had never been something the university had looked to for profit. The whole service was just something the school had in its pocket to lubricate the larger wheels that made it run.

"I thought UVA was flush with cash," said Kenny.

Tracy shrugged her shoulders. "I'm going to stay in Charlottesville for a while," she said. A lot of his Catering friends graduating with humanities majors had said this lately. "I gave my two weeks' notice yesterday. I got a job waiting tables at Etta's."

There must be a run on restaurant jobs every spring, he thought.

Etta's was a storied little café off the Corner, across from the Rotunda, with a brick patio outside, lights strung up around the front yard, and a couple of indoor rooms full of unmatched old kitchen chairs around tables here and there. They had a liquor license and served dinner, too. Kenny had been there a bunch of times, and it had always made him think of the East Side of Madison—at least in the summertime.

Maybe I could open some kind of place like Etta's in Madison, Kenny thought. His vaguely entrepreneurial fantasies had recently begun to unspool in Madison, even though, so far, they all stemmed from experiences he had had in Charlottesville. As if he knew the first thing about starting a business.

"Cool," was all he could say. "What about Wayne?"

"I guess he'll keep working here. I don't know."

"It's a shame that Catering's about to get all corporate," he said. "It's been my favorite job."

"Yeah, I guess."

"It would be cool to find something like this back home," added Kenny, looking away for a second. "Charlottesville's all right, but it never really took with me."

"*Took?*" said Tracy, raising an eyebrow. "You just came here for college. You're not colonizing the moon." She had a point but was keeping it light. She was chiding him for being too intense, or maybe for trying to be more than just a kid away from home for a few years. Something inside Kenny's gut tugged at him, gently but noticeably.

"That thing at the Lincoln Memorial was wild," she said, moving closer. Like how she had taken his hand that day on the Mall, but more purposefully now. Kenny's tug felt slightly more taut. "It was funny how that guy came up to you and just started saying that thing about you being from another planet." She was breathing audibly.

"Yeah," said Kenny. "*You a alien.*"

Tracy didn't laugh. Her eyes locked on Kenny, who realized the tautness he had been feeling in his stomach was occurring in a different organ, a few inches below. He did his best to return this new romantic gaze, in part because, well, *why not*, but mostly because his previously loose Bermuda shorts were now pointing unambiguously at Tracy and it felt urgent that she not look down.

Tracy moved closer now. Kenny moved back a tad, up against the rear of the couch. He wondered if he might hyperventilate.

"Maybe we're the only ones in here," she whispered. "There's nothing booked for today. I let myself in."

Kenny's heart began to race. He lowered his eyelids in an attempt to look suave.

Tracy noticed and moved back an inch or two. It seemed inevitable that she would glimpse the clownish bulge in his shorts, so Kenny decided to act. He pulled Tracy toward him and kissed her on the mouth. After a second or two, he rotated his face counter-clockwise, then clockwise back again. Kenny's experience making out with girls had taught him the universality of this move, which signaled the kisser's feverish passion and, at the same time, his sincerity.

Tracy moaned, a little louder than Kenny found natural. But given his state of arousal, who cared? Her hand wandered to the back of his neck—as if to confirm that this business was now very compelling. They continued to neck, rotating their faces back and forth a few times, emitting sounds like *mmh* and *nngh*.

Tracy unsuctioned her face, which produced a light popping sound.

"Oh Kenny," she hummed. Her hand dropped to Kenny's left buttock, where it remained.

"Yoo-hoo, any y'all chickens in the house?" yelled a voice from around the corner.

"Shit!" whispered Kenny, sending a strong enough burst of air into Tracy's face that she blinked.

"Okay!" replied Tracy, like she had just heard her first fire drill bell. The spell had unraveled. She stood frozen, facing Kenny, apparently unable to decide where to place her body for the imminent arrival of a third party.

Wayne sauntered around the corner.

"Hey," he said, immediately noticing his coworkers standing oddly close to each other next to the couch. He continued, slowly and more interrogatively, "Hey... Kenny? Hey... Tracy?"

In that exact same second, Tracy twirled to her left, as if dancing or ice skating. Landing almost perfectly abreast of Kenny, as Wayne was finishing saying her name, she tilted her head as if she were the most relaxed person in the room, moving her right hand over to lean against the back part of the couch.

The problem was that the place where she put her hand was several inches past where the couch ended. Because she was turning so fast, she continued to spin and fell sideways into the empty space next to the couch.

"Aah," she gasped, grasping at air then finding the top of Kenny's Bermuda shorts. The vestment in question being so loose, Kenny's defensive instinct was stronger than anything Virginia had taught him about gentlemanliness; as soon as he felt Tracy's hand on the fabric shielding his lower dignities, he grabbed her hand and yanked it unceremoniously away.

"Aah!" she yelled again, repeating the sound she had made a half-second earlier, and disappeared next to the couch with a thud.

"Well," said Wayne. "Well."

"Hey Wayne," said Kenny again, smoothing his hair back with the hand that had just released Tracy to the floor. "Hey."

"Hey Wayne," said Tracy, gathering herself to stand upright again.

* * * * *

It was a warm May afternoon on the Lawn. The faculty and law students and other groups proceeded regally down from the Rotunda, toward Old Cabell Hall, and to their places in rows of folding chairs. The Blue Ridge off in the background. The sun already high. Kenny in his cap and gown, Logan and Tracy and a few other fellow caterers sitting in his row. The speaker, a Supreme Court justice whose remarks no one could hear. The turning of the tassel, and everyone pulling out their bottles of champagne. Pop, a drink, caps in the air.

Tracy and Kenny exchanged a glance just before they tossed their caps. A warm glance, it felt like a conclusion. Logan was looking somewhere else. Linda and Kate were visible, for a few moments, on the edge of the crowd, Taylor having briefly appeared on her mother's shoulders. Grandma and Grandpa Maesby were there; Kenny just couldn't see them. So were his Talmadge Street neighbors Glenn and Mary, who had sold them their house before Kenny was born and who had been so kind to the McLuhers, especially since Harlan died. Wayne had come, too, for the first time, to watch his fellow caterers graduate. But he stayed near the back, and none of them knew he was there.

The sun was high. Kenny did in fact recognize, maybe for the first time, how alien he really was here. The Mr. Jefferson who had approached him at the Lincoln Memorial had been right about that. The place wasn't foreign; he was.

He saw, for the first time, that his foreignness had no effect on the place itself. The Lawn sat comfortably, where it had been for so long and where it intended to stay, signifying its curious ideals of democracy, a backdrop for generations of Virginians, poets, and future real estate barons and others—students, janitors, spouses, slaves—headed for marriage or careers or a long drowning in depression or alcoholism. And for all the non-Virginians, too, part of that same parade and larger ones to come. Everyone there had some kind of role to play there, didn't they? Except for Kenny, who felt unnecessary to anything the University of Virginia would ever mean to anyone but him. All of a sudden, he felt blank. It was a merciful feeling.

They turned their tassels, tossed their caps, popped the corks on their bottles of champagne. And college was over, just like that. Time to scatter.

Madison, Wisconsin
(1988)

The Willy Bear

The woman in the back booth took a sip of her Huber, then began writing in her notebook again. Like most East Side taverns, the Willy Bear was pretty dark once you got a few feet away from the bar area—at least if you were trying to write something. This could be important in an otherwise working-class dive like the Willy Bear, since a number of its patrons were old hippies who had come to the university in the sixties, stuck around the East Side, and settled into jobs in carpentry or driving cabs or even carrying the mail. There were always a handful around who wrote plays or novels on the side.

In the afternoon, the back booth was often the one where the aspiring writers usually sat. The window in the rear of the long, skinny room usually allowed in what little natural light could be had, even though that window was rarely washed, faced north, and looked onto an overgrown weed patch. On nights when there was live music, that mildewy little yard became a makeshift backstage area for the musicians and their friends. A weedy, overgrown haven to smoke a doobie in, with the drummer or the one who thought she might be his girlfriend.

The woman in the booth put her pen down and took another sip of beer. Once in a while, she'd look up, but just for a second or two, as if she were testing out a new thought. Her hair was long and curly and appeared to be red. She had tied most of it up in the back. When the occasional long strand tumbled down in front of her face, she would tuck it behind an ear, without ever looking up from whatever it was she was working on.

Kurt finished drying the lowball he had in his hand, then held it up to the light, searching for traces of moisture. He looked back at the woman in the booth the same way he inspected glasses: checking the perimeter, tucking in the corners. Keeping the ship from listing. In short, working. He turned back to Kenny, who nursed his own bottle of Huber across the bar.

"So how's the hotel business?"

Kenny sipped then nodded. "Pretty good—so far, anyway. They pay well, and the work's not too different from what I was doing in Charlottesville."

"How so?" asked Kurt. He had once been an employee of the Pinckney Plaza, one of the workhorse downtown hotels whose eternal humming resulted from a fortunate proximity to the lakes, the university, and Capitol Square.

"The supervisors are just caterers, too, like they were at UVA. More storage, too."

"Yes, storage options," replied Kurt, who genuinely appreciated such things.

"The 'crewmen' thing is new. Having all the furniture set up and taken down for every function creates some extra time, but I'm not sure it's really necessary."

Kurt wiped a new glass dry. "Is PJ still the lead crewman?"

"I haven't met anybody named PJ yet."

"What about Lori DeKampf?" asked Kurt, with a quick grimace.

"Yeah, she's my boss."

"Of course she is. She's everybody's boss."

Lori DeKampf was the prompt and slightly gangly hotel employee who interviewed Kenny on the day he put in his application. She managed the catering operation and offered him a job on the spot. Kenny was struck by her last name—the *p* right before the *f*—and so immediately thought of her by both names together, almost like *Mary Jane* or *Peggy Sue.* "I'm looking forward to working with Kenny," she had said brightly, welcoming him aboard with a practiced and very firm handshake.

An energetic talker, Lori DeKampf would show up inexplicably when caterers were scrambling to put the final touches on an event. She always had a clipboard. Although no one ever saw her writing on it, she gestured with it when asking questions or suggesting improvements. Though not strictly necessary, it seemed a robust management tool Kenny had not yet experienced in his limited tenure as a caterer. Yet it was the sheer physical drama of her arrivals and departures that impressed Kenny the most. The way she swooped into the servery or dining room just before a meal went out, combined with her height and her forward lean, reminded him of a wading bird landing or taking flight.

"How's the coworker situation?" asked Kurt, pushing the visor of his *TRAFFIC SIGNAL* baseball cap back an inch or so.

"What's *Traffic Signal*?" asked Kenny, "A band?"

"I don't know," said Kurt. He picked up another lowball glass and began to dry it with a towel. It was about three-thirty, and things in the bar were slow.

"Everyone's pretty cool, so far," said Kenny. "This other new guy Gordon just wiped all the silver down with tonic water the other day. Said it was a 'folk remedy' he had learned from his grandmother."

Kurt snickered hospitably, like he might have once made a similar mistake. "Sticky forks. Back to the drawing board."

"I think the big difference really is that everything is in the building. In Charlottesville, most of the functions happened around Grounds or in town or even out in the country sometimes."

"Ah," said Kurt. "*Grounds.*"

"I know," replied Kenny. He had always found the term a little embarrassing, having adopted it just because everyone else around him in Charlottesville had. For most people, a university's property was just a *campus.*

Kurt finished the lowball and rinsed a fresh glass, the towel now over his shoulder.

"So what's different?"

Kenny sipped his Huber and set it down on the bar. "I don't know. Not much, I guess. It's easier. You don't have loading docks and vans and all this stuff to move in and out of them, Cambros and racks of glasses and all that. I mean, you have those things, but everything's nearby, kind of backstage, behind some doors. Like a temporary restaurant, I guess, except that it's a wedding or some kind of meeting or whatever."

"I remember," said Kurt, who had worked in food service since the summer before tenth grade. He must have washed dishes in half the restaurants on the East Side, including the food court at East Towne Mall. He had been in so many kitchens and basements and walk-in coolers that Kenny was surprised Kurt didn't run his own restaurant by now. Kenny had worked, too, but so much less. Four years in college had made him feel a little behind.

"At UVA, part of the thing was, I don't know, the *unity* of it. Even with all the stress you had sometimes. Like you had to get all this stuff done in one time frame, pack up, head out, drive somewhere, then unpack and set everything back up and, I don't know, *stage* the thing. Doing it as a group gave it more purpose. Maybe that's just how it feels now that I'm away from it."

"I can see that," said Kurt, less romantic about work generally.

Kenny looked around. It was calm. There was one other guy, seven or eight stools down, drinking and staring straight ahead, at the rows of bottles along the wall. He might have been looking at himself through them, in the mirror. He didn't seem like a drunk. Maybe he was one of the cab-driving novelists or playwrights Kurt joked about, the ones who hung out at the Willy Bear.

"When do things pick up?" asked Kenny.

"What is it, now, about three?" Kurt looked over at the clock. "In about an hour, usually. That's when Greasy Time starts." He gave the towel an abrupt twist in the highball, punctuating his cleverness. *Greasy Time* apparently meant that there would be lots of action for Kurt at the bar: drinks and food ordered, delivered and removed, advice dispensed, relationships weighed in on. "Greasy Time," he said again, chanting Gregorian-style.

The woman in the rear booth was still working in her notebook, but for a little while she had been looking up periodically in Kenny's direction, then dropping back down suddenly to her scribbling. Kurt caught one of these movements out of the corner of his eye but stayed focused on drying glasses.

"Don't look now, but I think Red back there is checking you out a little."

Kenny shot a sideways glance toward the rear of the Willy Bear, but without turning his head.

"You look like you're trying not to look, captain," said Kurt. He had started calling Kenny *Captain* in middle school, during a window of time in which they and their circle of friends began experimenting with nicknames inspired by *Star Trek* reruns.

Kenny let out a nervous laugh. "I don't think so."

"I *do* think so," said Kurt. "Back home after college, you a bachelor. And here is a woman of *mystery*," he added, slowing down and adopting a slight hiss in his voice. Like a lot of people who have known each other for a long time, they would sometimes lapse into weird accents or tones of voice, without need for explanation.

"Speaking of Greasy Time," said Kurt, "I had a girl from down in your neck of the woods come in here a couple of weeks ago, a real Southern Belle."

"My 'neck of the woods'?" said Kenny.

"Whatever, man, you know what I mean." He looked dramatically off toward an imagined horizon. "The *South*," he droned, as if imitating someone, maybe on a television show. "She said she was from Georgia. She was in town for some university thing. I have no idea what she was doing on the East Side." Kurt put the highball up on the shelf with its companions and rinsed out the last one next to his sink. "She was with this other girl, who didn't really talk, so I'm not sure if she was from Georgia too, or whatnot, but she asked me about food. 'I can make you a burger,' I tell her, 'with fries or onion rings.' She looks at her friend and asks if we have *salad*." Kurt shot Kenny a look. Kenny knew the only offering resembling salad at the Willy Bear was a pickle spear. "She decides she doesn't want the burger and asks if we have 'chicken chests'."

Kenny immediately thought of a girl he had known in his dorm who might have said something like this. Her earnestness had charmed him, although it could also have been her smile. "Ah, the human comedy," he said, raising his Huber.

"I got that, captain," said Kurt, clinking Kenny's beer with the highball he had just dried. Kurt often said *I got that,* for some reason, to mean something like *Word* or *I heard that.* He was the only one Kenny knew who said *I got that* in this fashion.

Kurt changed his glass-drying move into a robotic one-two twist, as if to draw attention to his hands. "Bad, bad chickens," he said, in some kind of voice that sounded as if he meant it to be European.

Bob Marley was playing over the house stereo, but they both heard the thud in the back of the room. The redhaired woman's head had dropped onto her notebook.

“Is she okay, you think?” asked Kenny.

“Maybe she’s sleeping,” said Kurt. He put the dry glass up on the shelf with the other highballs. “Hold on, I’ll be right back.” He walked out from behind the bar and went quickly back to the booth, where the redhaired woman was slowly raising her head up from the notebook.

“Hey, are you all right?” he asked.

The woman wiped her mouth with her forearm, as if she had been napping for an hour and thought she might have been drooling. “No, it’s just, I...” she stammered in a low voice, looking at Kurt for a second before averting her eyes. “I’m okay, just a little sleepy for a second. I get migraines, and... you know.” She waved her hand in a way that suggested she didn’t wave her hand a lot when she talked. “I’m fine.” Still no more eye contact.

“I’m glad. Do you want a glass of water?” He noticed that her Huber was still about a third full, after at least an hour with it.

“No, no,” she said, “Thank you, though. I’m fine.” She took her pen and began writing again, her eyes on the pad.

“Okay,” said Kurt, and walked back to the bar.

“Whoa,” said Kenny upon Kurt’s return. “Kinda weird.” He took another sip from his Huber. Kurt started gearing up the grill area, since soon he’d be serving food alongside the beer and other drinks he’d be slinging soon.

“Is Doug working tonight?” asked Kenny. Doug Stacy was another old schoolmate of theirs, also an East Sider, and for the past few months the second bartender at the Willy Bear.

“Yeah, he starts at four, or close to it,” said Kurt, reaching for something in the drying rack.

Out of the corner of his eye, Kenny saw the other guy at the bar lean back oddly on his stool, like he was trying to look relaxed. He was staring back at the redhaired woman in the booth. At this point, he did look a little like a drunk.

“So I ain’t seen you around here before. Are you, like, writing a book or a letter or something?” asked the enstooled inquisitor.

The woman looked up, over her reading glasses, and stared at him for about two seconds, in a way that seemed to Kenny both cool and shy. Kenny averted his own gaze, so as not to appear to be rubbernecking.

"Okay, okay," said the stool guy. "Not much of a talker, I see." He turned back to his beer and sipped it twice. He looked at himself, or at the bottles along the bar, then turned back around. "So you, like, a college student, or...?" he asked casually.

She looked up again, then back down, and resumed writing. The man shot a glance at Kenny, who looked back at his own beer. He didn't feel like getting winked at or thumbs-upped by this person, even at a distance.

The woman in the booth got up suddenly and went into the bathroom. Kurt, who had just gone back to get some meat from the walk-in, noticed that she had dropped her notebook onto the floor. He leaned over to pick it up, figuring he'd just put it back on the table where she had been writing on it. That way, when she came back, she could resume whatever she was working on.

He looked down at the page it was open to. It looked like a poem. Kurt looked a little more closely; it was just a two-word line, copied six times.

Forgive me

Forgive me

Forgive me

Forgive me

Forgive me

Forgive me

Self-conscious, he swept the notebook up and laid it on the table, then went into the room where the walk-in cooler was. The guy on the stool belched lightly.

"Ope!" he said, "My bad. Guess it's time to head back to the old home base."

Go Cougars

"Behind you," said Kenny as he came through the service door into Ballroom B, where the Wisconsin Association for the Study of Sleep and Consciousness was hosting an awards dinner. He carried the tray to a stand on the perimeter of the large hall, which must have had twenty tables full of doctors and other health professionals. The crewmen had arranged the tables a little more carefully than they usually did. Kenny found their symmetry appealing, given the time-sensitive tasks he would have to complete.

"I hope you enjoyed the delicious dinner," said the speaker, bespectacled in a grandfatherly way. "I think we are about ready to get underway." The din softened as the room directed its attention to the podium. Kenny moved quietly around his two tables, slipping plated triangles of cherry pie in front of the seated guests.

"For those of you who don't know me, my name is Dr. John Deverick, and it is my pleasure as Executive Director Emeritus of the WASSC to present the awards this year." He had pronounced the group's acronym *wahssock.* For a second, Kenny wondered why they didn't pronounce it *whask.* Mild applause rippled across the room.

"As many of you may know, this is my twenty-fifth year as a member of WASSC, which began in a humble lab on the campus of the University of Wisconsin in the summer of 1963." More applause, lighter now. No one at Kenny's tables seemed to be clapping, but a few of them turned to neighbors and smiled politely. Two of them looked a little worried. "Back in sixty-three," continued Dr. Deverick, "we didn't know the half of what we know now about sleep."

Kenny's diners remained silent, like the rest of the room appeared to be. One of Kenny's diners shifted uncomfortably, and another looked discreetly at his wristwatch.

"Sleep, ah, sleep," continued Deverick, raising his hand as if about to pronounce something important. On its way up, his hand brushed the microphone, knocking it to the side and sending out a loud bumping sound through the PA system. "My apologies," said Deverick, readjusting the microphone, then assuming his former facial expression. "Sleep, yes, sleep."

He paused for a long second then resumed, his voice more stentorian. "Where do you lead us, O Hypnos? Where, upon the ruins of Rome, should we gaze, O Somnus?" He stood back for a second, then surveyed the room, from right to left, beaming oddly at the audience.

Kenny decided that the diners at his two tables would be the best barometer for whatever weirdness might ultimately characterize this shift. Rather than retiring quietly to the servery for the duration of the award, he decided to stand back, servant-like, to see what would happen next.

"Or be you Morpheus?" asked Deverick, looking skyward now.

A diner at one of Kenny's tables began to nod off. A colleague sitting next to him gently touched him on the shoulder. A woman across the table from the two looked at them in quiet alarm.

A long pause at the podium. Deverick continued to stare at a spot above the heads of his audience, as if practicing a technique for conquering stage fright.

"The place was special," continued Deverick, looking back down, to the evident relief of most diners within Kenny's view. "That little lab, with its side area, that little couch..." He looked toward a table in the front, at two attendees about his age. "Gene, you remember that little couch, eh? Ha ha. Barbara, the couch?" He laughed again, and Barbara and Gene laughed, too, uncomfortably. It felt like an amateur standup act at a professional event where attendance was mandatory.

"Okay, thank you, John," said a woman who had appeared out of nowhere, clearly part of the WASSC leadership. Deverick broke the gaze he had fixed on Barbara and Gene and jerked backward a little, as if coming out of a trance.

"Ah," he said, gathering himself. "Ah. Yes."

The woman put her arm gently around Deverick. *They're giving him the hook,* thought Kenny. The woman didn't remove Deverick from the stage, however. She just stayed next to him, moving the microphone tactfully over toward her own face. "Let's take a minute to enjoy that delicious pie our servers have brought out for us, shall we? After which—let's have those awards!" She clapped demonstratively, as an encouragement to the audience. Deverick began clapping loudly next to her, and the rest of the room followed. After a few seconds and a flurry of surreptitious glances, normal conversation resumed.

"Kenny," said a voice from behind Kenny, a little urgently. He turned to see Lori DeKampf, standing next to him now, clipboard in hand. The servery door was still swinging a little on its hinges. As always, she had come through it fast and furtively.

"Things under control here, captain?" she said with a slight grin. Kenny felt an inner wince. Kurt was the only person who ever called him *captain*. He hadn't realized that one might feel protective of a term of endearment, but he guessed there were worse things than your new boss sidling up to you with a friendly nickname.

"Hey Lori. Yeah, they're all set until we clear dessert. Looks like they're waiting now a few more minutes until their presentation."

"Can you come with me? I need you for something. I'll ask Evan to clear your table if you're not back in time." Kenny looked over at his coworker at the next tray stand. Evan looked bored.

"Yeah, sure, yeah. Should I bring something?"

"No, no," she replied, shaking her head crisply as if she had practiced it. The gesture reminded Kenny of his job interview. "No, Kenny, just bring yourself. We'll go back out through the servery."

He followed her through the door, to the elevator in the hallway. Lori DeKampf's office was on the third floor, in a hallway full of guest rooms. You could see part of the lake out her window. This was where she convened smaller meetings or asked individual caterers or crewmen to see her for special instructions. The catering and crewmen schedules were also in her office, on the wall next to the door, so that when you checked the schedule for the coming two-week period, she could see you from her desk and say hello or ask you a question. This approach had likely been laid out in *Make Them Come to You:The Fire Outside the Box*, a popular management book she kept prominently on her desk.

When they got to the office, Lori DeKampf walked to her desk, which was in the middle of the room. It was a strangely large and empty-feeling room. Kenny didn't know exactly where to position himself in the vast area, nor how exactly to stand in a way that signified professional attention. He had only been working here a few weeks now and was just starting to get oriented to the spaces and how to move in them.

When she got to the area right beside her office chair, she swiveled quickly around to face Kenny. She brushed her hair aside, as if to imply a combination of pride and certainty in what she was about to say.

"Do you like your work so far, Kenny?"

Kenny swallowed. Was he already about to be fired?

"Yes, Lori, definitely. I definitely like it. I like catering."

"Don't you feel a little, um, *overqualified* sometimes?" she asked, leaning forward onto her desk like a soap opera character about to announce that she would be taking control of the family company.

"I'm not sure what you mean."

"Well, you did go to college," she said, "in West Virginia. Kinda fancy."

Kenny nodded. A lot of people here had a pretty vague sense of where he had gone to college. "Well, I did major in history," he said, grinning somewhat, as if to remind her that he was realistic about his career prospects.

"Studying history could have its merits," she said. She was looking at him as if history were part of a performance review. Was this a performance review? "Its merits," she repeated, walking slowly around the desk, her index finger tracing a little line along the surface of the desk as she walked, "and its drawbacks." She left her mouth open after she said *drawbacks*.

"Yes," he said. "Ha ha. It's not exactly a job machine."

Lori DeKampf had walked into the yawning space between her desk and the bulletin board, an area she never occupied when employees were in the room. Normally, she stayed behind her desk, her clipboard visibly within reach. Now that she was nearer to Kenny, he could see that she was six full inches taller than he was. Casually, she slipped off her shoes.

"A 'job machine'—I like that idea," she purred, placing a hand on her hip. She tilted her body a little, her nervous angles softening somewhat. She laughed. "That's so silly."

Suddenly, she raised both arms straight up on either side of her body. She turned her head to the right, then faced forward again, staring robotically. It reminded Kenny of cheerleading. She dropped her hands back to her sides. Kenny realized that the stone-washed jeans he thought she was wearing were actually stretchy-looking tights of some kind.

"You want to see me do the splits?" she asked.

"Aha," said Kenny. "Ah um, yeah, sure. I know it's pretty hard. I have an older sister who..."

"We got the *power*!" she barked, looking straight forward. "Cougars can't be beat!"

"Aha, I..."

"We rock the tower, so get on your *feet*!"

As surprising as it was, the eruption was relatively restrained and even graceful in a way. But the cheer wasn't complete yet. As soon as she had landed the final rhyme, Lori DeKampf executed a Pete Townsend-like windmill move with both of her arms, jerked her face upward (perhaps to thank God for the Cougars), then lurched forward, her long right leg shooting out toward Kenny as she went down.

"Okay," said Kenny, stepping back instinctively, as if to protect himself from the protruding leg.

As she went down, Lori DeKampf gazed intently at what lay before her—the future, victory, the final buzzer—apparently all floating virtually around Kenny's person. As she descended into the splits, her left leg remained behind her, in a perfect line with her leading front member. *She must practice every day*, he thought, *like stretching or jogging.*

She smiled, her hands held high in the air as she maintained her pose for two or three seconds. Kenny felt like he should clap or make a noise of some kind.

"Well," he finally said. "All right, Lori. That's awesome!"

Lori DeKampf rolled to her left and stood up, assumed a

professional pose once again, then re-established eye contact with her employee.

"Brackhorn Cougars," she said, brushing off her slacks at the knee. "They'll never know what they missed."

She looked over at the desk for a second. "Cindy and Megan." She made a face and lowered her voice. "Bitches. *Too tall.* Whatever."

Kenny wondered what to look at. He did notice that, after she had let out the word *bitches,* ostensibly aiming it at the invisible yet formidable Cindy and Megan, Lori DeKampf was invigorated. She adjusted her hair and looked coyly back at Kenny. He wondered if this repertoire of exaggerated movements had come from a chapter of *Make Them Come to You*.

Her eyes softened again, her eyelids drooping suggestively.

"Ha ha, I guess you think I'm a little competitive," she said, looking down at the ground coquettishly. Kenny again noticed her height and remembered her long legs reaching forward for glory, just minutes earlier.

"You probably just assumed I was a varsity cheerleader. At Brackhorn."

He had no idea where Brackhorn was.

"But then you probably don't even know where Brackhorn is," she said, in a voice she would have used if Brooke Shields had been playing her role and had just whispered, to Kenny's character, *I know you better than you know yourself.* "You went to college down in Tennessee and you come back here to Madison, where you grew up, no big deal, here in the action."

The action? What action?

"The hotel business may not be 'a job machine,' as you put it, you goofball, ha ha," she said. "But we have plans here at the Pinckney. Plans that start here. In catering."

She began staring at Kenny again.

"*My* plans."

Lori DeKampf stepped a foot closer to Kenny, bringing her left foot up next to her right foot with a military-like snap. Then, almost as if to congratulate herself, she relaxed visibly. She lifted her hand to her face and covered her closed mouth with two fingers, as if she had just been caught digging in the cookie jar but didn't want anyone to tell the adults.

"Oops," she said smokily. "Looks like I just came up a little close to you, Kenny." Her eyelids drooped again, and she bent her hip suggestively and put her hand on it. Then she smiled, her lips opening a little wider than she probably intended. Her teeth were large and shiny. She licked them once.

I'm being propositioned, thought Kenny. *Propositioned* was a term he had heard once as a child, after he walked into a conversation his Grandpa Maesby and uncle Bill were having about an "Irish secretary" who had "presented her rear." His grandfather, who rightly understood that young Kenny's excitement about rears was of a different character than his own, was forthcoming. "I was surprised at being propositioned, right there in my office," he told the boy.

"Speaking of job machines," Lori DeKampf whispered, "sometimes history teaches us that we have to listen to a new kind of job machine, Kenny. A machine called the *human heart*." She undid the top two buttons of her shirt.

In Kenny's sex life, like most young men, he had usually been the one to initiate. As far as he could tell, he had only been the object of two attempts at seduction, and both had occurred in the past month or so. Both had taken place in or near catering facilities. Neither had been too subtle, but both had taken him longer to understand than he wanted to admit. One might have worked had it not been interrupted by a coworker. The other, currently in progress, had begun with a call for victory on the gridiron.

Yet, unlike the Brackhorn Cougars, Kenny was indecisive.

Dizzy, even. Was it Lori DeKampf's movements? Her attempt to sound sexy? The inappropriateness of the context?

Cooler heads prevailed.

"I'm afraid there's been a misunderstanding," said Kenny, looking up into Lori DeKampf's waiting face. "I've just been engaged to be married."

She recoiled mechanically. It wasn't unlike how she moved when, having just put it down somewhere while addressing a subordinate, she reached to retrieve her clipboard.

"I see," she said, her voice suddenly distant. Everything had changed. "Who's the lucky lady?" she asked, walking back to her desk.

Kenny panicked. "Glanda," he said.

"That's an interesting name," said Lori DeKampf, already back in her chair. "Is she Swiss?"

"Yes, she is Swiss," he said, startled by her presence of mind. "She's from Switzerland."

"Did you guys go to school together?" she asked, looking coolly through some papers on her desk. She too was improvising now.

"Yes, school," he replied, like a television sitcom character lying about something and trying to buy time. "We went to school together. I met her at UVA. We took a couple of classes together, ha ha, and well, you know, ha ha, the rest is *history*." He realized he was backing toward the door.

"Yes, history, that's funny. Because you studied history."

"Yes, which totally prepared me for my career in catering," said Kenny, smiling weakly.

She looked back down at her paperwork. "Yes, that. Well, you should probably get back to the function. Evan is probably wondering where you went off to." She looked up and smiled, as if she were waiting for him to say something or just leave.

"Um, okay, yes," he said. "Okay, so, um, have a good evening, Lori."

"Mm-hm," she said, looking back down at her desk now.

Kenny went back downstairs as the sleep specialists were finishing up their awards banquet. He hadn't been upstairs as long as he thought; neither Evan nor the others had even noticed he was gone.

Sleepover

"Knock knock," said Kate as she opened the door into the living room at Talmadge Street. She had grown up in this house, but as an adult, she always announced her arrival this way.

"Knock knock, who's *there*!" added a smaller voice. Taylor came in next to her mom, carrying the rolled-up sleeping bag she sometimes brought when she spent the night at her grandmother's house.

"Who is that coming in my door, I wonder?" came a voice from around the corner.

"Grandma!" yelled Taylor. She ran into her grandmother's receptive half-crouch for a hug, then back out of it and into the kitchen.

Kenny was sitting on the couch watching television. The Brewers were on, County Stadium half-full or so. They were playing the Cardinals and weren't losing yet.

"Hey, sis," he said, still looking at the game.

"Don't get up, Kenny," said Kate, dryly.

He started up anyway, and they executed this weird, light hand slap they had used as a greeting since they were little kids. It looked to outsiders like a mock handshake.

"Boss," she said, which is what they sometimes called each other.

"What's that?" he asked.

Kate rubbed at the red mark across her forehead. "I was in the Woodman's parking lot, reading a *Wheeler Dealer*," she said matter-of-factly. "Walked into the end of a canoe tied on top of some hippie's car. Hey, do you know anyone who has a small kitchen table they want to get rid of?"

"Nope."

"Taylor!" Kate yelled into the kitchen around the corner. "Your bag!"

Linda came back around the corner into the living room. "Hello, daughter," she said. "She's already got the yearbook out. I'll take the bag." Taylor was obsessed with Linda's high school yearbook—Dixie Heights, Class of 1958—and had taken to poring over it during the past three or four overnights. "Why are there so many boys named Corky?" she had asked a week earlier. She had a hard time remembering how to pronounce *Colonels* but could otherwise read much of the yearbook, and with startling accuracy for a five-year-old.

"Why don't you *set a spell*?" asked Linda, in a playful country accent she would occasionally adopt. Kentuckians of her generation sometimes did this as a way of mocking what other people apparently thought of Kentuckians.

"Okay, maybe just a minute," said Kate.

"Want a Diet Coke?" asked Linda, now back in the kitchen.

"Sure."

Kate sat down on the short end of the sectional sofa that occupied much of the living room, at a close angle to her brother. She play-kicked his leg affectionately with her foot.

"Nice duds," said her brother, noticing her skirt and knee socks. Kenny couldn't tell if they matched or not, but they sort of seemed to.

"Thanks," she said, looking at her lap. "I got the skirt at St. Vinny's just this morning." She pulled her right knee sock up in a gesture Kenny recognized from their childhood.

"Big date?" he asked.

Kate shrugged. "Is there such a thing?" She pulled her right sock up again, to her knee. "He's a guy I just met. I don't know. We'll see." She pulled the second sock up to the corresponding knee.

"Nice socks there, Lori Partridge."

Kate rotated her hand, which she kept in her lap, and slowly raised her middle finger. She smiled and squinted.

"You're a nerd, man. What you misunderstand is that my style looks like I'm behind, which actually means that I'm light years ahead of all my peers. I'm a fashion leader."

Kenny raised an eyebrow.

"You should know that," she said, leaning in and dropping to a whisper, "history-major *motherfucker.*"

"Ooh," he said in the stalest voice he could muster. "Edgy."

Kate sniffed. "I'll be the judge of that," she said, then grinned a little. "Even though you're a boring asshole, thanks again for babysitting tonight. Taylor is excited that you're here."

"I kind of live here right now, at least until I can get some cash flow."

"I know, I know. But still, it's cool that it's Saturday and you're staying in to watch Taylor."

"Actually, Mom's here, too."

"True, but *you're* the one she wants to tuck her in. *You're* the man of the hour." She leaned over again and poked his chest twice in slow motion. "How's tricks downtown?"

"Catering," he answered, stealing a look at the game. He was still trying to put the two Lori DeKampfs out of his mind. One was the almost-varsity cheerleader who had been jilted in high school and then again, this time by Kenny. The other was a now-icy boss who would punish her jilters if given the chance.

"And?"

"And it's okay," he said. "It's work." The job was still new enough that he wasn't sure what to call it. *Catering* still felt like the name you'd use for what he had been doing in Charlottesville: the work and the people doing it. Kenny's current coworkers just talked about *the Pinckney* or *the hotel.* He hadn't mastered the wording yet, so he just usually said *work.*

"You making good money?"

"Pretty good," he replied.

"Cool," she said, standing up unceremoniously. She turned in the direction of the kitchen.

"Mom, I'm heading out!"

"Okay," said Linda's voice from around the corner. Then she appeared. "Okay," she said again, visibly this time. "Have fun. See you tomorrow. I'll make goetta."

Kate turned toward Kenny. "How surprising. Have you ever known anyone else, outside our house, who knows about goetta?"

"Never. Better that way."

"Dad hadn't even heard of it 'til he met Mom," said Kate, throwing her purse over her shoulder. "I've never, *ever* met anyone in Madison who knows what it is."

"Don't let the secret out," said Kenny, turning back toward the Brewers. "Northern Kentucky's secret. Cincinnati's, maybe."

"I'm out," said Kate, like she knew she wasn't hip but that she could probably pull it off.

* * * * *

"Uncle Kenny," said Taylor from the staircase. "Come *on.*" She stood holding her favorite stuffed turtle, which she called Anna, and stared at Kenny as if he were on the verge of breaking a promise.

"I'm coming, I'm coming," he said, heaving himself up off the couch. The Cardinals were now four runs ahead of Milwaukee, and he had lost interest anyway. Taylor sighed, dropped her shoulders, then bounded the rest of the way up the stairs to her grandmother's room. Her energies could turn on a dime.

When she stayed at Talmadge Street, Taylor liked to sleep next to her grandmother—but always on the floor, next to the window. She preferred to be close enough to "hear Grandma snoring" but liked the way the carpet looked "close up." Something about her pillow—loaned from Linda's bed for her use—which she wedged up into the corner. She took some pains to arrange the pillow just right before she could be read to properly. The few times Kenny had tucked her in, Taylor had scripted a very precise way she wanted him to sit against the wall.

"What do you want me to read you?" he asked, once she was settled.

"No books. Tell me a story about when Grandma was little."

Kenny was surprised, still new to this.

"You want me to get Grandma? She can tell it better."

"No, you," she said, determined. "Make it up from what you know, but how about Grandma is a little girl in it, and how about she has a bird friend, and they go on a Kentucky adventure."

"Aha," said Kenny, already adrift.

"And how about the bird is named Taylor. How about she's like a girl, but she's a bird."

Kenny had no idea where to start. How do you start a story like that? There were so many random elements.

"And how about it starts in a hut, like the huts they used to have in Kentucky."

Kenny had just recently graduated from college, but he knew enough about his parents' home state to know that there weren't huts. At least he was pretty sure there weren't.

"Well, Taylor, when Grandma was little, they lived in a house, up on a hill, and..."

"Make it a hut," said Taylor.

"Yes, a hut," he said, hesitating. *Maybe I just need to start right in,* he thought. Then, like a small motor, he opened up. "Once upon a time," he said, in as soft and varied a voice as he could muster, "in a hut up on an old hillside, there lived a girl named Linda Maesby..."

Taylor's face brightened. "That's Grandma and Grandpa Maesby's name! That's not Grandma's name."

"Well," replied Kenny, having been knocked immediately out of his narrator role and forced to footnote his own story. "That actually *was* Grandma's name when she was a little girl. It's called a *maiden name*. It's the name a girl has until..."

"Make the bird come in the window, and make the window really big," said Taylor.

Kenny felt something like a hiccup in his chest. Irritation, or a recognition of his ignorance.

"Aha," he said. "Once upon a time, little Linda Maesby..."

"And how about her bird friend Taylor comes in," said Taylor.

"And her bird friend, little Taylor," said Kenny, stifling a yawn. "They lived in a hut at the top of a hill. It was a big hill that looked down onto a creek, in which there floated many strange growths." *Growths?* he thought. Okay. Why not?

"What's a *growth*? Is that like it *grows*?"

"No, *growth*. A growth is a thing that grows," said Kenny, yawning overtly enough now that he had to talk through the yawn. But better to continue. "In this creek with the floating growths, there lived a special fish."

He paused then looked at Taylor, expecting her to interrupt him again, maybe to ask what color the fish was, or to ask him to call the fish *Kate* or *Miss T* or some other actual person she knew. But she didn't. She just sat there looking interested and very, very awake.

She was a harder audience than he had expected. He had no idea where the thing would go next. But he clearly had to keep things moving. He was growing tired.

"Aha, yes, the growths in the creek, and the fish. Well, the fish, it was a beautiful fish, but it was a *very lonely* fish."

"Like the Very Lonely Caterpillar!" said Taylor excitedly, remembering a character from one of her favorite books. Kenny envied physical books for a second, and their ability to just have a story, all finished and set in place. No improvising required. You just turned the pages.

"Yes, yes, lonely as a caterpillar," said Kenny. Taylor's eyes settled into a more tired-looking pose.

"What did the fish do?" she asked.

"Aha, the fish, yeah. One day, the fish just floated up to the surface and yelled, 'Bird! Bird! Come down here, bird!'..."

"The bird's name is Taylor." She yawned.

"Yes. 'Taylor, Taylor, come down here. I want to tell you about how bored I am.'"

"How about he wants to learn how to fly?" said Taylor, like she knew Kenny needed the help.

"Yes, yes, 'I want to learn how to fly,' said the fish."

Her eyes grew wide. How did you know when a kid was about to fall asleep?

"And how about he wants to fly up to the hut, and they all fly around all the huts, and they can see all of Kentucky from where they're flying!" Her mouth was open, as if it would just be easier for her to jump back into the storytelling process that way. Kenny paused, just for a second, still not used to this style she had—or to tucking a child in with a story at all, for that matter. It was all new. You'd have thought college would prepare you for something like this, especially when you liked stories.

"Yes, they both wanted to fly, both the fish and Taylor the bird," said Kenny. Taylor closed her mouth and relaxed a little, grinning and sitting back into her pillow.

"So they flew up and up and up." He waved his hands out away from his body, a little like a ringleader introducing the trapeze artists, and looked up toward the ceiling. Taylor followed his gaze upward. "Up toward the sky, where they could look down and see the huts."

Taylor sat straight up. "And how about Grandma is a little girl in the hut!" she almost yelled. "How about Grandma comes out of the hut and sees Taylor and the fish and says 'Let's all be friends and fly over to Lowell and see the playground!' and they all fly over to the Lowell playground!"

Kenny hadn't expected the vigor of her response. He understood that his job here was simply to put the child to sleep. He knew she was excited, but still: he was the storyteller. He was the narrator, and it could have been a better story had he maintained a semblance of editorial control over the thing. Taylor was so far ahead of him now that his head spun.

"If we're from Kentucky, why don't I go to *school* in Kentucky?" she asked.

"Well, we're not from Kentucky."

Taylor looked disappointed.

"We're from Wisconsin. From Madison. Grandma is from Kentucky, and Grandpa was from Kentucky, even though you didn't know him. And Grandma and Grandpa Maesby are from Kentucky."

"They live there!" said Taylor, no longer disappointed. "Tell me something that happened to them, when they were little." She became quiet and sat back again into the pillow, looking very directly at her uncle.

Kenny felt a new kind of discomfort. He realized he was being asked, by this child, to recount a history that he wasn't sure he had any command of. He knew Taylor had recently taken to paging obsessively through the Dixie Colonel yearbooks that Linda still periodically consulted—and which, in fact, she kept in a bookshelf in their kitchen, now that Taylor was showing interest in 1956-era Taylor Mill Kentucky, bobby socks, and crew-cutted boys named

Corky posing at the free throw line. Kenny had grown up hearing a lot about people in Kentucky, Linda's friends and members of his own family, Harlan's childhood in rural Jessamine County, and Harlan's own more distant, country family who sounded so aloof and uninterested in their own son. Kenny *knew* there were stories in all that, but he didn't really know the stories themselves all that well. His mother knew some, but not all the way through to the end—after all, he had himself asked *her* sometimes at bedtime to tell about this place they had come from. She could start stories or tell you about particular people, but she didn't have the knack Harlan had always had, to grip you early in the story and hold you rapt until the very end. That had gone away when he had died, and now Kenny wondered how he could pass that particular torch to Taylor. He wasn't sure he could. He wasn't from Kentucky; his parents were.

"Well, once when Grandma was little, she was in a spelling bee."

Taylor raised her eyebrows. "She was in a bee?" Kenny remembered the spelling bee at Lowell when he was a kid, but he must have been in at least third grade before he even knew of its existence.

"Not a real bee," he said. "It's like a contest."

Taylor yawned again, longer this time, which Kenny found promising.

"We have contests sometimes in Miss T's class," she said, her tone finally a little softer and more indicative of something like fatigue. "But usually, most people win. Miss T says everyone deserves to win."

Tell that to the Cardinals, thought Kenny, who knew that County Stadium was probably already starting to empty out right about now. *Everyone deserves to see the Brewers win once in a while,* she could have said.

Taylor yawned again. "What about *you*? What about when you were a little boy?"

The cogs in Kenny's brain wheels caught a little, for the first time. This was something he could do with a little more confidence. He also felt like, since his niece had been so interested in flying and imagination, he could lie.

"Well, Taylor," he said, his voice suddenly a little more of a baritone. "It just so turns out that when I was a child, I did a lot of traveling in outer space."

Her body looked tired, but her eyes were wide open again. Kenny didn't have enough experience as a child-tucker to know that this meant Taylor wouldn't be awake much longer. *Not long for this world,* as Linda said about children on the verge of sleep. But now he had a body of work he could draw on: all those stories he had written as a kid, imagining far-flung adventures with his friends, battles against all odds, strange and fantastic places. Tucking in wasn't so hard after all, it turned out. Now that he was free to tell the kinds of stories he had imagined as a kid, he wasn't long for this world either. Now he could finally create a whole new one.

The Planet Darthle
Written by Kenny McLuher, age 11

Black Stallion's log: Stardate 11919300:7

We have been circling Darthle for eight consecutive days. I looked over at the co-pilot Kurt and asked if he wanted to land. "I guess," he said. "Doug," I said, "set warp level at factor 2." "Aye aye, Kenny!"

I asked Darlene, the ship secretary and weapons manager, to get the basic pistol sets ready for us. "Aye aye, captain" she said with a friendly and polite smile. She wore pretty much makeup and a dress style uniform, but she knew about karate and pistol sets like nobody's business.

We landed in an open space. "It seems to be a desert, Kenny," said Doug. "It must be," I said. Then a laser shot out from nowhere and knocked Kurt and I out. Doug regained consciousness and acted like he was unconscious. Some warriors marched out of the bushes with what appeared to be their commander. Doug slowly, unnoticably, set his pistol to stun. Vrrrüuüt! He shot them and revived us from unconsciousness. "Take their weapons so they can't harm us," I said. They returned to consciousness. "We come in peace," I said. "We don't want to hurt you."

"Maquque unt!" yelled the leader. "Seize them!" A laser shot

from the sky and temporalily paralized us. "Nagoosche," said the leader, "they spunky, full of pep, make fine specimen. We take them to Redean."

Black Stallion's log: Stardate 11919301:7

We woke up this morning in what appeared to be an arena. As soon as we woke up, we heard a crowd cheering. A door opened. 10 foot tall men walked out of the door. 3 of them. Weapons were tossed to us. A sickle blade with a strap around it. "Faloarkeledork Klarbem!" the monsters yelled as they charged us.

Kurt threw his "Klarbem" and sliced off a monster's head. Two monsters went for Doug and Kurt jumped on one's back and I sliced one's arm all the way off. He angrily lunged for me. I pulled out my laser gun, set it to blast and blew him to bits. Kurt sliced his monster's back open and Doug started stabbing it continuously until it died. There was silence among the crowd.

I whispered to Kurt, "Must call for fighters and rescue party. NOW!" I pulled out my communication talkie and said, "McLuher to Black Stallion. Send rescue mission and twenty fighters to point of existance. Red alert! Out!" The door opened again. Out stepped a 20 ft. creation, half gorilla and half killer whale, but on two feet. "You mean we gotta fight that thing?!!!" said Doug, terrified.

Black Stallion's log: Stardate 11919302:7

"Set your pistols to blast!" I said to Kurt and Doug. Vrrrüuüt! "Aaaauuuuuuurgh!" it yelled. IT WASN'T EVEN HURT!

We were glad to hear the sound of Black Stallion fighters coming thru the air. BAAR BOIR DEIRR! It was shooting laser beams at the stadium. The rescue party parachuted and helped us kill the ape killer whale combination monster. They handed us jet packs and we flew to a fighter. The fighter pilot asked me, "Captain McLuher, are we going to leave the Darthle solar system now?" "Yes, we are going to the Alpha Communa beta IIX station, pilot.

Back to the mother ship." "Aye, sir!"

As we were leaving the solar system of Darthle and Darlene was putting the pistol sets back, Kurt said, "Kenny, they have much to learn on Darthle. They are a violent people. They should learn that peace is the only way by now."

You Can Take the Boy Out of Kentucky

Breakfast and voices were what woke him up. Kenny came downstairs to the smell of homemade goetta frying and the sound of Linda and Kate talking about the man she had been out with the night before. He could tell before he even reached the kitchen that there would be no more such dates with this particular guy. Taylor was in the living room, watching an episode of *The Flintstones.*

"What did you do to Taylor last night?" said Kate.

"Good morning, Kate," said Kenny, walking right to the coffeemaker. He came back over and hand-slapped her. "Okay, Boss, I'm awake now."

"She told me she wants to get a *klarbem* and fight the aliens."

"Awesome," said Kenny.

"Then she said it's 'important for peace.'" She shook her head, but in an approving way. "Next time I find a date who's not a dick, we'll have to hire you to tuck her in again."

"It was harder than one might think," said Kenny, looking up as he sipped his coffee. "And I don't recall anyone hiring me."

"Let's call it part of your rent," said Linda, with an alpha-mother glance.

"Okay, okay," said Kenny.

"*Klarbem?*" asked Linda. "What in heaven's name is a *klarbem*?"

Kenny shook his head. "I don't know. I don't remember. I made it up along the way. Just made up a fighting-aliens story like I used to write in school when I was a kid, after spelling and all that other busywork."

Linda scowled. "No knocking spelling, young man. It's the foundation." She relaxed her face, signaling the end of her fifth-grade teacher voice. "I remember those stories you used to write. I have a crate full of them up in the attic."

"No, I'm not taking them," said Kenny, into his coffee cup.

"I like the word *klarbem*, whatever it is," said Linda, ignoring his declaration. "And I like that it somehow brings peace. You remind me of your dad, dropping a strange little seed in your stories like that."

"I don't remember Dad's stories as all that weird," said Kate, getting up to start a fresh pot of coffee. "He sure told a lot of them, and they had detail, but I don't know about weird."

"Well, maybe not *weird*," said Linda, "but *specific*."

"He *was* a literature guy," said Kate, "and a full-on hill jack."

Linda smiled. "True, true. And Lincoln's biggest fan." She took a drink of her coffee. She had only recently become comfortable mentioning Lincoln, who had arguably been the cause of her husband's demise. "Yes, we certainly did hear a lot about him around here—almost as much as I did in Lexington. Your dad wanted all those Confederate Todd ghosts in the Todd family to remember that their Illinois in-law was also a Kentuckian." She looked out the window for a second. "He sure did turn up in a lot of Dad's bedtime stories."

"Did he?" asked Kenny, suddenly alert. "I don't remember that so much—I mean, I remember Dad's obsession, but not when he was tucking us in."

"Oh yes," said Linda, "When it was his turn, I'd walk by your rooms and hear him weaving these little things into whatever story he was making up. Of course, he loved reading the Uncle Remus ones, but I'm talking about the ones he was obviously inventing as he went along. He'd say things like 'rail splitter' and 'the Emancipator' and such like that, like he was maybe trying to work in some lesson there."

"History majors waiting to happen," said Kate, looking at Kenny with a big-sisterly glint.

"One of us escaped that fate," replied Kenny. Kate responded by raising her coffee cup as if she were about to give a toast.

"I've actually had a few dreams about Lincoln lately," said Kenny.

Linda nodded. "They say you sometimes pick things up from when you were a kid, then your brain remembers them and kind of replays them in dreams, later," she said. "Maybe it has something to do with change, graduating from college, moving home. Something like that."

"May be," said Kenny, pronouncing it exactly like his parents and grandparents did.

* * * * *

Kate and Kenny finished the dishes together, an event marred only briefly by a moment of friction over who would tackle the goetta pan. Kate had yielded, accepting Kenny's slap-shake as one might a bow of gratitude.

"I'm going out for a little walk," said Linda, after she had answered a question Taylor had just posed regarding the Flintstone family car. "I've just about exhausted my knowledge of prehistoric automotive technology."

"We're out," said Kate, drying the pan. "I have to get Taylor over to Jenna's house in the next hour or so. Playtime, don't you know."

"I do know. Bye, girls." She gave Kate a little hug and waved into the living room at Taylor. "Kenny, want to join me?"

"Sure," replied her son, and they went out through the side door. They walked a little, then Linda brought up Harlan again, as if she had been thinking about the whole thing some more.

"I know you miss Dad a lot."

"Of course," replied Kenny. "I get sad still. But like, this morning, you mentioned storytelling and Lincoln. I think it's pretty fascinating, the whole Southern thing."

"What do you mean?" asked Linda.

"Well, like Dad had this big dilemma all the time. How 'Southern' was he supposed to be, here in Madison, I mean? All that."

They walked down La Follette toward Winnebago Street. The East High School tower rose up behind the Sons of Norway. Kenny thought of the sycamore, which they'd walk by in just a minute or two.

"Harlan didn't really start acting all that Southern until after we 'moved North,' as he put it," she said. She rarely used his dad's given name in her children's presence. "Usually, it would start mostly when we were around Grandma and Grandpa, or around any relatives on my side, after Kate was born and our transplant had started to look like it might take."

The walk had transformed into a spontaneous family seminar on how Harlan had become preoccupied by his Kentucky roots as they settled into their lives in Madison. On their trips home, Harlan would turn into a real booster, touting the uniqueness of the Dairy State, Madison, its progressive traditions, its lakes—and especially its fishing.

"Dad's regular reports on his fishing discoveries made your grandpa more relaxed around him in those days," said Linda, as they approached Schenk's Corners. "Let's maybe turn back up Atwood."

Harlan had been a little intimidated by the Maesbys when he started seeing Linda. His own parents were dead and had always been so cold with him anyway that he had broken many of his Jessamine County connections by the time he and Linda were in their last year at UK. The Maesbys seemed such a close and coherent clan.

"I'm not sure, but I think that when Dad realized your grandpa liked the fishing updates, it was like he had unfogged the whole Upper Midwestern part of Grandpa's mental map of the country. We never really knew how many lakes there were up here. Your dad liked that he could bring that to my family, in his stories."

They passed the Barrymore Theater, the recently renamed Cinema Theater, an arthouse cinema that also showed a lot of pornography. Linda still called it "the Eastwood Theater," even though it hadn't had that name for twenty years.

"Let's cross here," she said, habituated to avoiding the place when in the company of her children. When they got to the other side of Atwood, Linda returned to her memories of Harlan's Wisconsin boosterism.

"The fishing thing, I remember it especially during our trip for Thanksgiving after Kate was born," she said. The McLuhers had driven all day through the farms of Illinois and Indiana, their four-month-old daughter alternating between stints of sleep, crying for food, needing a diaper change, and flat-out yelling. It was 1963, four days after the president had been assassinated. Sitting around the living room as they settled in, once Shirley had whisked the baby off into another room, they began trying to talk about what Kennedy's murder meant, about what kind of country they lived in. The conversation kept darkening, so soon they just fell quiet. After a few minutes, Edwin lifted his head up and said to Harlan, apropos of nothing except the need to change the subject,

"I heard that Wisconsin has more lakes with muskellunge than any other state in the Union."

"For some reason I remember that conversation," said Linda. "Your dad's reply sounded like he had just stepped off a Greyhound from Nicholasville. 'That don't surprise me,' he said." Right after she reproduced his accent and facial expression, her face brightened.

They walked back into the neighborhood along Division Street, over on the lake side of Atwood. Linda slowed down as if to linger some more on these memories, maybe even to pass them along with more clarity.

"Back here, your dad became more aware of where people thought he was from, especially as you all grew," she said. "I could have done the same, I suppose, but we were settling into life in Madison, and we both liked it. 'You gotta live *somewhere*,' he'd say. I don't know, I guess it just wasn't too important to me where I came from—you know, in how I acted around my friends or at work, things like that. I already knew where I was from."

Harlan, on the other hand, began to notice that anyone who had heard he was from Kentucky would refer to him as "Southern" or "from the South" without a moment's hesitation. At first, he would correct them—*Kentucky is not really the South, it's just Kentucky*—often adding that his wife was actually "from the Ohio River Valley" or "from near Cincinnati." But quickly it dawned on him that he *was*, in fact, from the South —relatively speaking—so he'd better get familiar with how he sounded, what kinds of expressions he used. In short, how he was representing the place he came from.

By the time Kate and Kenny were in high school, Harlan had become a natural code switcher. In middle school, Kenny started to notice when his dad was about to reach into his most Southern repertoire. Usually, it was near the end of the day, when Harlan was tired but knew that some of Kenny's or Kate's friends were coming by the house. In that case—after basketball practice, say—Harlan's accent deepened a little, sometimes aristocratic, sometimes more on the *Hee-Haw* side. Once, when Kenny was gearing up for a school dance in the ninth grade, he brought the girl by the house so his mom could take some pictures before they walked over to the school. It was his first real date. Maybe that's why he remembered his dad turning it up so hot that night.

"She's a big old girl, ain't she?" Harlan said loudly, in praise of his son's new friend. This embarrassed the date, who was in fact pretty tall for her age and had begun to really dread anyone drawing attention to it. Linda noticed the gaffe and the girl's rapidly blushing cheek.

"Harlan's not used to beautiful Norwegians!" said Linda, kindly, shooting him a corrective glance.

Kenny had not noticed the girl's discomfort because he was writhing in his own. His dad had grinned a little too hard, his mouth opened a little too unnaturally. He had mountain-up-talked the last two words, combining them in a friendly *ainchy?* like Kenny would have often heard, in a more natural form, when visiting relatives in Kentucky.

At other times, though, Harlan's country sound seemed more normal. Both he and Linda accented the first syllable in the words *insurance*, *umbrella*, and *eclipse*. Linda still did, regardless of her mood or the context. Harlan spoke most naturally when he didn't feel on stage or like he had to perform as a Kentuckian for other people. When he was working on a project in the garage, for example, fixing something or doing a woodworking project.

"Doggone it," he'd say, half-cussing. Or, in conversation, "Yeah, boy."

Linda and Kenny crossed Atwood at Ohio, on their last lap toward Talmadge.

"So, you think he ever figured out how to be a *Kentuckian* here?" asked Kenny, slowing down and looking Linda in the eyes for the first time during their walk. "I mean, you know, by the end?"

"I don't know, son," she said. "I really don't."

She almost never called him *son.*

The Chiffonier-McLuher Debates

The night after he tucked Taylor in, Kenny dreamed about Lincoln again. Actually it was more of a Lincoln-themed affair. The president himself was nowhere to be seen.

In the dream, the McLuhers were driving south on US 51, their usual route on trips to Kentucky. As they neared the Illinois River—just as he often did in real life—Harlan said, "You all know Ottawa is right near here!"

Then they were in the town itself. Having never been to Ottawa in waking life, Kenny wasn't sure what anything looked like. He just knew he was there, and that it was on the Illinois River. It was, as his dad had announced so many times in the family car, one of the places where Lincoln had debated incumbent Stephen Douglas for his seat in the US Senate. The setting had transformed, from the inside of the family car to a large, dim auditorium.

Then, behind a podium on the stage, stood not Lincoln or Douglas, but Harlan himself. He was nervously brushing something off his chest—food, maybe cookie crumbs—and looking up periodically at another podium, several feet away and empty.

Sometime thereafter, up strolled Knox Chiffonier IV, the Jefferson biographer Kenny had served at Birdwood Pavilion. Chiffonier stood ramrod-straight, lightly coughed once, then tapped the microphone. Kenny half expected to hear the boilerplate feedback sound they put in television shows and movies where someone is tapping on a microphone, but in this dream there was no sound at all. Harlan looked at Chiffonier and nodded.

"Good evening, Mr. McLuher," said Chiffonier in his deep Mississippi accent.

"Evening, Dr. Chiffonier."

"*Mister* Chiffonier," said the adversary, icily.

"My apologies, Mr. Chiffonier," said Harlan, bowing a little for some reason.

"No harm, no foul," said Chiffonier. *No way he would say that,* thought Kenny.

"We are here to debate," said Harlan, tersely.

"That we are."

At which point things began.

"My son has just left Virginia," announced Harlan, by way of introduction, "which is a Commonwealth." He sounded like Lincoln in Kenny's other recent dreams, proclaiming a thing casually as if it contained all you needed to know, but in a way that also sounded a little encyclopedic. It was the wrong voice.

Chiffonier looked more natural. He nodded, looking around for a lowball he assumed someone had placed near him. The gesture was usually the second thing he naturally did once he had come to rest in a standing position, in almost any new location after about four o'clock in the afternoon.

"As you probably know, Kentucky is also a Commonwealth," Harlan continued, "but for the sake of an easier debate, let's just call them both 'states.'" He brushed off the front of his shirt again, despite a total lack of any visible detritus. "Kenny is now a graduate of the illustrious University of Virginia, an institution of higher learning you know so well, and is back in the bosom of his family in the state of Wisconsin." Still unlike himself. Such a strange style of speaking.

He brushed off his shirt again, nervously, his eyes remaining fixed on the floor this time. "Minus me, of course."

"My condolences," said Chiffonier.

Do you say that directly to the departed person? thought Kenny. Maybe this was a "lucid dream." He was impatient to see what would come next.

"You are kind," replied Harlan.

"What is your position, sir?" asked Chiffonier, looking around one last time for the drink that wasn't there. He lost some of his ramrod-straightness and settled into a gentler posture. He rested a hand on the podium.

"Well," said Harlan, in the way Kenny had heard so many older men in Kentucky say it. "I believe I am here to make a point about the South, the Midwest, and what lies in between."

"A border?"

"It may not be as simple as a border."

"And what would that point be?"

"That it would be best if Kenny..." He looked directly at his dreaming son. "If Kenny found some kind of way to stay in Wisconsin, now that he is back there." He would have preferred to say *back here,* but of course they were all in Northern Illinois for this debate. Plus, Kenny couldn't tell where his dad really *was,* or even *if* he was, other than in memory, stories, and dreams.

"Fair enough," said Chiffonier. "I'm not sure how one could call this a debate, or why it has occasioned these podia."

"Well, I think we may have some things to clear up about my family's relationship to you, to your work, to your vision of the

South." He was starting to sound less like a nineteenth-century orator and more like himself.

Chiffonier straightened again, a mild but noticeable effort. "With what facet of my view of the South might you take issue?"

"Well," said Harlan, a third time. "You write mostly about Jefferson and Monticello. Let's just say the whole Commonwealth of Virginia. But the South, where would you say it begins?"

"Young man," replied Chiffonier, in a lecturing tone. "I believe you may be baiting me, hoping I'll let loose some claptrap like *It begins where you feel it should* or, God forbid, *In that cold Pennsylvania ground where our last boy fell.* Well, I won't."

"You're not answering my question, Mr. Chiffonier."

"All right. One could say that the South begins, for someone like you, at the Mason-Dixon Line. We can probably agree on that criterion."

"What do you mean by 'someone like me'? I am from Jessamine County, right up against Fayette County, where Lexington is. Some have called Lexington the 'northernmost Southern city.'"

"And Louisville the 'southernmost Northern city.' Yes, I have heard those chestnuts." He sighed audibly.

Harlan began to perspire. Kenny knew that his father was intimidated.

"So what is *your* point?"

"My point, Mr. McLuher, is that for a very long time, you have been looking at this whole thing from an Upper Midwestern perspective. You moved to Wisconsin and settled there, beginning in 1962."

This was right, at least partially. He and his young wife had moved to Madison in 1962, but they hadn't really thought of themselves as "settling" there until a few years later. But Harlan let that sit for a moment.

"I do see things now from Wisconsin's point of view, mostly," said Harlan, "I'll grant you that. If there is such a thing. But you know, I still have my childhood and youth in Kentucky in me. Even as... as I am now."

"You do, and that's a good thing."

"I have read your work," said Harlan, on the offensive now, "and the work of writers intent on elevating figures like Jefferson and places like Monticello above most other figures in our history."

"There are no figures like Jefferson," responded the historian, "and there is no place like Monticello. There is only Jefferson, and there is only Monticello."

"I knew you were going to say something like that. So predictable. You fit the mold."

"Of what, may I ask?"

"Of the standard apologist for the old Confederacy."

Chiffonier smiled. He had heard this before, usually during his occasional visits to universities in Northern cities.

"This attribution is not new to me." He had said *attribution,* not *accusation,* Kenny noted.

Harlan stepped out from behind his podium and walked over toward the place where Kenny was standing. Or sitting, or whatever position he was in, as the dreamer of these events. Kenny felt a rush of something, even in his sleep. Seeing his father's face as he approached, he could see Harlan had aged since the last dream. Chiffonier remained behind his podium, examining his cuticles while he waited for the next move.

"Son," Harlan whispered nervously to Kenny, "I don't think I can do this."

In a movie version of this dream, Kenny would have hugged his father and pleaded, "Yes, you can, Dad. *You can do anything you set your mind to.*" But in this dream, as it was, he just continued to behold the scene quietly, impersonally.

"He won't admit he's grandstanding. He grew up in Jackson, Mississippi! I looked it up. It was his career that brought him to Virginia. He got some lucky breaks. He lives in Staunton now, you know where that is." Kenny did know Staunton. It was on his path home from college, just beyond Waynesboro. He had also lived in Central Virginia long enough to learn that the city's name rhymed with *canton,* not *wanton,* as most English speakers from other places might guess.

Harlan looked at his watch. Maybe the dream was coming to an end, or something else was about to happen.

"I do live in Staunton, Mr. McLuher," said Chiffonier from behind his podium, in a rather loud voice. He was only trying to be heard, to check the acoustics, but it nonetheless felt a little rude for a scholar of his stature. "What does that have to do with this question of regions?"

"You're not a Virginian," said Harlan, turning toward Chiffonier. He turned back to Kenny and repeated, in a much lower and more plaintive-sounding voice, "He's no Virginian."

He is actually, thought Kenny, feeling a little guilty about it. *He put his time in. He chose Virginia. He has devoted his life's work to Virginia.*

"I heard what you said about my coming from Mississippi!" chirped Chiffonier, his neck fat jiggling slightly. He was getting angry but quickly regained his composure.

Harlan was rapidly losing his. "That's 826 miles! It's a 12-hour drive from your hometown to where you have settled."

Chiffonier smiled. "You said it, Mr. McLuher. I have in fact *settled,* long since. In Virginia."

Harlan looked like he wanted to pace a little, but he remained where he was standing. "Lexington to Madison is 515 miles. That's my drive. Less than two-thirds the distance you had to go when you came to central Virginia."

"Those are just numbers."

"But mine are much lower than yours!"

"Yet mine are all in the same country," said Chiffonier, calmly. "It's all the South."

"You don't get it, Mr. Chiffonier," said Harlan, his argument long lost by now. "I can get home to see my wife's parents, in a single day's drive, with time for supper when we get there. You can eat bratwurst at a Reds game, just like you can at a Brewers game. People love beer. We're standing on a Midwestern route right now. Ottawa is just off that path that I go back and forth on all the time. I take my kids to Kentucky faster than most Kentuckians can get to the Carolinas."

"You are talking about Northern Kentucky, the Ohio Valley." He cleared his throat. "You are talking about Germans."

"So what? It's still closer."

"That doesn't make you Southern."

"I'm not trying to be Southern. I'm trying to be a Kentuckian who has settled in Wisconsin."

"You are a Wisconsinite," proclaimed Chiffonier, as if delivering a diagnosis. "And that's fine and dandy. There are some fine things up there in Wisconsin." He struck a boyish, defiant stance, his small hands forming ironic little fists. "Fightin' Bob La Follette!"

Harlan was wringing wet. "Why do you say 'up there in Wisconsin'? Would your family say 'up there in Virginia'? They're farther away from you, way farther!"

"Quite possibly," said the historian, looking at his fingernails now, then back up at Harlan. "There's no harm in acknowledging the journey it takes to get home to family." Such control.

"There you go!" yelled Harlan, thrusting his finger up in the air, still several feet away from his podium but temporarily back in the game. "You admit that the distance between Jackson and Staunton is enormous!"

"Only in miles."

"What else is there? Some rivers, maybe." He attempted a wink at Kenny.

"All of it is my home. But there are borders. You're on the other side of one. Wisconsin is practically in Canada."

Harlan knew he was beaten. He was always hunting for simi larities that could make the area stretching from Central Kentucky to South Central Wisconsin into a single region, a place whose inhabitants would feel connected to one another. But his mental gerrymandering had never really worked. Just because he could imagine a place and tell stories about it didn't mean that place actually existed—not as the coherent, comprehensible place he wanted it to be, anyway.

Chiffonier dabbed gently at his dry temple with a monogrammed handkerchief, as if to silently mock Harlan's lack of such a tool right when he needed it most. He didn't need the handkerchief at all; he had simply chosen it, as a gesture of style. Like something you might do in fencing, after you have sent your opponent's weapon clattering to the floor.

"A minute ago, you asked me why I used the expression 'up there in Wisconsin.' I could just as easily have asked you why so many people in Kentucky use the same expression with *you* when referring to where you have chosen to live. For you it may just seem like a day's drive home, but for them, you are quite far away. These same people take for granted their natural kinship with faraway South Carolina or Florida. But not Wisconsin."

Harlan slumped further, unable to rebut.

"Take basketball," said Chiffonier. This was almost too much. Kenny wondered if there was such a thing in dreams as a mercy rule. "That's a sport you enjoy watching. Perhaps even playing, what do I know? Adolph Rupp coached Kentucky while you were still a student. Was he not a legend?"

Harlan nodded. It was true. He figured where this might be leading. He couldn't win the debate, but at least he could follow it.

Chiffonier wasn't finished. "Kentucky plays in the SEC. Occasionally—very occasionally—they play Wisconsin. Or Marquette. You like those games."

Harlan nodded again, his eyes closed.

"But when can you go see such a game in person? *Never*, that's when. The SEC, the Southeastern Conference, is a constellation of basketball arenas throughout the firmament that is the American South."

The firmament? Wasn't this kind of Southerner bigger on roots, on earthly analogies? Chiffonier took out the handkerchief again and triumphantly wiped his still-dry brow. "Wildcat fans in Northern Kentucky don't care if the drive to Madison is two hundred miles shorter than the drive to see their team play Arkansas; they're going to make that Arkansas drive. How often do Kentuckians drive to Madison, Wisconsin?"

Harlan hung his head. Chiffonier had so many points that Harlan just couldn't pursue the things he had originally intended to say about the South. It would have just been sour grapes. Plus, Harlan had just made a strong case for how large the South was—creating a trap for himself. Next, he would have had to acknowledge the diversity of thought and experience he knew lay across those vast Southern spaces. In order to lead a new charge—the original charge he had had in mind—he would have to stereotype wildly, generalize crazily, betray his own principles.

Things began to break into individual units, as they do near the end of particularly intense dreams. Who knows how or why sleep does this to us? Chiffonier remained behind his podium, but Kenny perceived him from below, lit up like a waxen ghoul. Harlan was still far from his podium but not clearly in any one particular place—muttering, looking for a foothold on a piece of ground or a stage or a riverbank. Something, anything. Somewhere, anywhere.

Chiffonier was whispering now, things like "I have left my children in Mississippi!" and "It gives me solace to know they are still in my country!" and "The South will always call her children home!"—his drawl rolling ever deeper into Hollywood Southern accent territory.

Kenny saw Harlan standing by the sycamore at Winnebago and Fourth, just a few blocks from their home. Time had stopped, the dream whirlwind now a tranquil summer day. "I never left my children," Harlan murmured.

The Stars and the Mud

They had been on this walk a thousand times: up Williamson Street, over the Yahara River by a sandstone-bricked old tavern called Mickey's, past Ace Hardware and St. Vincent de Paul, sometimes all the way downtown. They had followed this route since they were kids. *Plowing a bond*, as Kenny's dad would have said, for with the walking came the talking.

"It was so real. It was like I was in that big room. I could feel the dust, hear the squeak of the seats."

"Cool," said Kurt. "You always had wild dreams."

"Yeah, but this one... it was like my dad was right there, and I could almost imagine, I don't know, a full transcript of the debate."

"A *transcript*? That's mighty specific."

A passing Volkswagen bus slowed to a stop, and the driver waved them past. They waved back and crossed Willy Street.

"And that historian—biographer, whatever he is—some dude I met at a catering function in Charlottesville, *Knox Chiffonier IV*. That was his name, and he was right there. Crystal-clear, too."

"That name, man. It's right out of *Gone with the Wind.*"

"He was handing my dad his ass, and I had to watch the whole thing."

"Dude, your dreams are like movies. No one else I know has dreams like that."

"Once he had my dad clearly beat—the whole thing about how my dad wasn't anywhere near his own home, like he was some kind of lost refugee or something—once he had him really beat, the guy was, like, feverish, all red. I could see this one strand of hair laying across his bald head."

"Pretty specific," said Kurt.

"My dad kept trying to explain how the Ohio River connects with the Mississippi, how that whole watershed makes the place almost like a country," said Kenny.

"That might be a stretch," said Kurt.

"Is it? I was born and raised here, and I go to Kentucky all the time. I'm pretty comfortable there."

"You ever fish right here?" Kurt asked as they walked over the bridge. Kenny looked down instinctively, as if he hadn't already seen the Yahara River a thousand times before. It flowed under them as always, on its straightened little way to Lake Monona, a few blocks to their left.

"No, not really. I've never really fished as much as you. Usually, we were on a lake. Camping, seems like. My dad always preferred fishing on lakes."

"I always thought that was funny," replied Kurt. "Him coming from that southern part of Kentucky he was from, I mean."

"Central. Central Kentucky."

"Yeah, Central. But I saw this bass fishing show a couple months ago. In the South, but they had Kentucky in it. Isn't it mostly rivers down there? Although maybe man-made lakes, like TVA impoundments and stuff?"

Kenny didn't really know too much about lakes in Kentucky. Well, maybe Laurel Lake. His parents had taken them camping there once. It was hot. Kenny was probably about seven. He remembered them hiking uphill somewhere. "Lean forward!" his dad kept saying to Kenny and his sister, who kept complaining about how steep the climb was.

They passed the hardware store, then crossed the street to the St. Vinny's side. They came into the big main room through two sets of grimy glass doors taped up with posters for upcoming shows around town. Mostly local bands—Killdozer, Cattle Prod, the Gomers, Isle of Dogs—with one or two Chicago blues acts. One poster still advertised a show at the Crystal Corner, a storied bar across the street, that had been closed for a few months following an apartment fire upstairs.

"You seen the Tar Babies yet?" asked Kurt. "Very funky, man. Guitar funky. They just signed with SST."

Kenny liked going out to hear live music in Madison. Even since before he had hit the legal drinking age, Kenny had been in all the main live music clubs in Madison: the Crystal, O'Cayz Corral, the Nar Bar, the Wagon Wheel, Club de Wash. And the Willy Bear, on a smaller scale. And all that free live music at the Memorial Union down on campus. There were tons of bands in Charlottesville, too. The biggest difference was only that nobody in the crowd at the Mineshaft or Sigma Nu or the C&O had also been in Mrs. Brooking's class with Kenny at Lowell, filling out those spelling sheets or laughing at his drawings.

Kenny had heard about the Tar Babies but hadn't seen them yet. "No. They play a lot?"

"I think they're on tour now," replied Kurt. "Or they're about to be. SST is pretty big. I think they're in Seattle or San Francisco, somewhere like that."

"The details grow murky," said Kenny mischievously, as they wandered into the store. The debate dream was now safely behind him.

"Fuck you, Socrates."

"What's Socrates have to do with it?" asked Kenny, unsure of what they were talking about now but long used to this kind of back-and-forth with Kurt.

"You want to check out the records?" asked Kurt, technically still on the subject of music.

"Sure."

They walked past some mannequins dressed in dusty sweaters and caps, along the front of the store. Looking into the showcase in front of the cashier's area, Kenny noticed an abundance of rings and watches.

"Lot of cheap crap in there."

"Cheap crap is what made this country great, captain."

They came down a small flight of stairs into the books-and-music room, as it might rightly have been called, whereupon Kurt descended immediately on the records.

"Actually I'm gonna check out the books," said Kenny.

"Yeah," replied Kurt, sliding a Tony Orlando and Dawn album out of the bin for inspection.

Kenny headed for the US History section but a small bookcase full of local titles caught his eye. The handmade label taped along the top shelf said *WISCONSIN*. Whoever had made the label had spent extra time on the W, topping it with lilting little serifs, leaving the others alone but framing the whole thing in a handmade rectangle. The label-maker hadn't used a ruler, just a ballpoint pen and some tape. It looked like a labor of love. Or boredom.

"Real US History," said Kenny to himself, as if he held the feeling strongly and someone were listening.

There were some dusty volumes about cheese factories, the automotive industry, and the University of Wisconsin. Wedged into this section was a stapled pamphlet from long ago, some kind of report on forestry products and "agricultural outbuilding framing integrity." Kenny reached for the only book that didn't have a title on its spine. He was intrigued. About eight inches tall and probably a third of an inch wide, it was brown, like the cardboard the section label had been made on. He pulled it out and read the cover. *HASH,* it read, in all capital letters. Then, in smaller print,

CHOPPED, SEASONED AND WARMED UP
Marcus P. Wheeler
Windsor, Wis.
Published by the Author
Copyright 1908
Times Print, De Forest, Wis.

Surrounding the text was a stylized kitchen scene of sorts—a hand-drawn, cartoonlike design made up of a cooking pot below, a rectangular sign in the middle, some kind of kitchen knife with a curved blade, and some steam coming off the whole thing, at the top.

"Poems?" asked Kenny, still talking to himself. He didn't read poetry, really. But the book intrigued him. He opened it at random and landed on a poem with four stanzas. It was titled, "One Saw the Mud; the Other Saw the Stars (An Allegory)."

Two soldiers escaping through prison bars—
The one kept his eyes on the mud.
He cared not for Jupiter, Saturn or Mars;
His mind did not wander away to the stars;
He was hoping to land without jolting or jars
Or a horrible shocking dull thud!

The other looked up to the heavens above.
And when he had severed the bar,
He caught sight of Venus (the goddess of love);—
And thinking the value of "ideals" to prove,
He pushed his way through, with a squeeze and a shove,
Still fixing his eyes on that star!

The first safely dropped, in the mud where he aimed.
Then hied him away from the bars.—
The other collapsed and was frightfully maimed.
(The guards who recaptured him always have claimed
They treated him kindly, and could not be blamed
For his bumping against the stars!)

Now, therefore, I always aver and maintain
That mud has a practical use.
If we grasp at a star all our efforts are vain.
We belong on the earth. On this earth we remain.
Since this is our portion why should we complain
Or treat good soft mud with abuse?

He looked up for a second, as if to consider the last line.

"Treat good soft mud with abuse," he whispered, slowly, and grinned. Pretty funny sounding. Reminded him of his Grandpa Maesby, who repeated homemade poems so often that most of his grandchildren could recall them. Kenny remembered one in particular, a limerick:

The chicken went out for a ride
Round the house, on its sunny south side
When Grandma made chase
She got egg on her face
For the house-rounding chicken had died

It made little sense, but it rhymed—like every other poem Grandpa Maesby would recite, sometimes *ad infinitum,* to any grandchildren present when the spirit took him. "You pups want to hear a rhyme?" he would ask, to the delight of the audience in question.

"Edwin," Kenny's grandma would admonish, if she happened to be within earshot. "Nothing blue, please." She said this a lot and in the same way every time.

"Blue, blue," Kenny's grandpa would reply, "so said the boob!" The grandchildren present would wriggle and giggle wildly.

Kenny read a few more little poems in the book ("Who Shall Be Greater?", "Song of Stalwarts," "A Wireless Message") then saw that it only cost a quarter. So he decided to buy it.

Slipping the book under his arm, he looked back over toward the record bins and saw Kurt, holding some albums and engaged in conversation with a girl about their age. They were only twenty or so feet away, and he couldn't hear their conversation, but Kenny recognized her as their elementary-school classmate Darlene Gustafson. She had moved away from Madison when her parents divorced, in the seventh grade, then come back to live with her mom in a house on Rutledge Street during their last year of high school. Kenny seemed to think she had gone to college somewhere important, maybe Princeton or Yale.

"Hey," said Kenny as he walked up to the record bin. His *hey* sounded a little Southern to him all of a sudden.

"Kenny McLuher," said Darlene, more grinning than smiling. She was holding a Black Flag t-shirt and a blender.

"Darlene Gustafson," said Kenny, "and her appliance."

Darlene snorted amicably. "A woman needs a blender." They performed a half-hearted hug which, due to the book he was holding and Darlene's t-shirt and blender, was more like a forward lean followed by a light tap.

"I'd like you to meet Darlene's blender," said Kurt, poker-faced and looking back at Darlene. "I forgot to introduce you to the blender." Kurt would joke this way—affectionately but weirdly out of sync with the direction of the chatter. Like, you'd be standing with him at a bus stop and a stranger would ask you for the time, and Kurt would say, "Good thing we're all looking out for each other, our watches and our buses and such."

"You're weird, man," said Darlene to Kurt.

"No, *you're* weird, man," replied Kurt. "I'm *a* weird man."

"So what are you up to these days?" she asked, looking down once into the blender, then back up at Kenny.

"Right now I'm just working a bunch at the Pinckney Plaza, in their catering service."

"Oh, that's cool," she said. "Downtown."

"Yeah, downtown. It's all right." He looked over at Kurt. "It's no Willy Bear, but it'll do for now." Kurt raised his eyebrows and did a cartoonish Gallic shrug, punctuating the slowing conversation between Darlene and Kenny, probably to give it a little air.

"How was UVA?"

Kenny was pleasantly surprised. "You remembered where I was going to school."

"Oh yeah," she said, seriously. "When you got accepted, you only told about nine hundred people. Twice."

Kenny laughed. "Mea culpa."

"Seriously, though, great school. I thought about applying, too, probably one of the only Southern schools I'd have gone to."

"But you got into Princeton," said Kenny, not quite sure how or why he remembered this and suddenly unsure. "Didn't you?"

"Penn. Just graduated, too, as I'm guessing you just did." She took the blender lid off with her Black Flag t-shirt hand and began to fiddle with it nervously.

"Yeah, in May. What about you? Are you looking for a job, or do you have one, or...?"

"No, I'm back for the whole summer. Got a sublet." She pushed the t-shirt into the open blender, put the lid on it, and began nervously twirling a piece of hair behind her ear. "I just started an internship."

"Oh," said Kenny, who had begun to hear the word *internship* a lot during his last year at UVA. He still didn't really know what it meant. He knew medical students did them, but around him it seemed the people using it were mostly studying business, interested in working in big companies, or maybe engineering.

"In what?" he asked, unsure if this was the right preposition.

"In publishing, sort of. Cottage Grove Press. You've probably never heard of it."

He hadn't. But it sounded serious, like a place that would publish real books by real authors. With Kurt, or maybe even Darlene, Kenny might talk about bands "touring" or "getting signed," but he wasn't sure how far into the subject of publishing he could venture.

"What did you major in?" she asked.

"History," replied Kenny, "like all good food service workers in Madison, Wisconsin."

"And cab drivers," said Kurt, studying the cover of *Seals and Crofts' Greatest Hits* but obviously following the conversation to some degree.

Darlene grinned. "I get it. My degree is in English."

"Well, it's cool that you have an internship in that," said Kenny. "I mean, publishing—that seems like a path that makes sense."

Darlene smiled like someone's mom. "It does make sense, I hope. I got a fellowship to Michigan for grad school this fall, so it's a natural transition. The books are pretty obscure, but it's a literary press."

Everything sounded so professional and adult all of a sudden. Just a minute earlier, this same person had been nervously stuffing a Black Flag t-shirt into a used blender, and now she was talking about literary presses and grad school.

"So you want to train to be a writer?" asked Kurt, finished with his examination of Seals and Crofts.

"No, academia."

"What's the difference?"

Darlene looked down, almost a little embarrassed, like she had grown accustomed to being where no one would have asked this question.

"Well, I might write some, but mostly I want to do research and teach."

"Oh," replied Kurt. "Publish or perish, right?"

Darlene brightened up again.

Kenny looked down for a second, thinking about what he had just read about stars and mud. He didn't feel much like a soldier escaping anything, but he wasn't sure he wanted to just look at the mud every day, either.

"You guys going out to hear any bands this weekend?" she asked. She was looking right at Kenny.

Power Walk

Rounding the corner fast, Linda pumped her arms with more purpose than someone just taking an average afternoon stroll through the neighborhood. Kenny had seen his mother "power walking" many times over the years, long enough to have worked up a parody of her arm movements (which he had debuted at a family picnic when his dad was still alive), but he had never noticed the way she took a corner. The intersection at Talmadge and La Follette was the final turn on most of her walks, her home stretch. Kenny happened to be sitting out in their small front yard as she pulled into view.

When she made the turn onto their street, her hands performing their standard piston thrusts, she made a harder left than usual, her right leg crossing ever so slightly over her left toe and landing pointed inward—in the direction she was now about to take forward. This brought the rest of her person back into a straight line, but to Kenny it seemed abrupt. He started, expecting to see her fall, but she didn't. It was just a move he hadn't noticed before. She looked like a skater making a gentle inside turn. A middle-aged mom skater, going a little faster than she had expected, maybe. *Maybe there's something wrong with her knee*, he thought.

Their house was close to the corner, so that by the time her left foot had straightened out her trajectory, Linda was within talking distance of her son. She gave him a wave.

"It's a magnificent day," she proclaimed. This was a phrase Kenny's grandfather always said, with frisky irreverence, every single time it rained or looked about to rain.

"It actually *is* pretty magnificent," replied Kenny, standing up as Linda arrived at their short front walk, exaggerating the movement of her upper arms for effect. "If you're a duck-walking old lady."

"Monty Python!" she exclaimed, continuing past him theatrically, widening her eyes. Her gaze unbroken, she stopped abruptly and lifted her right leg, extending it forward awkwardly and raising her hands to the sky.

"Ta da!" she yelled, holding the pose for a second. She looked like someone being robbed in yoga class. "Woman with a purpose!" she added, dropping her arms and legs.

Kenny rolled his eyes. "I'm calling the police," he said. She patted him on the cheek, and they walked into the house.

* * * * *

The kettle began to whistle, and Linda went to get some tea bags and mugs. Kenny was sitting at the table, the afternoon light filtering into the kitchen. His mom often had tea around this time of day, when she wasn't at school.

"You want feminism or art?" she asked, displaying two of their well-worn coffee mugs. One, off-white, read, in thin blue letters, *A woman needs a man like a fish needs a bicycle*. The other, shorter and a little wider, was black, with fat white letters that spelled *art slut*.

"I want one that says *fart slut*," said Kenny.

Linda adopted the exact same poker face Kenny had just made. "How about I fill it with toilet water?"

"Point taken. Your choice." She served him the *art slut* mug.

"Oh, before I forget, there was a guy for you this morning on the answering machine," she said, spooning a little sugar into her tea. "Somebody named Wayne."

This surprised Kenny. "Wayne called me?"

"Yeah, he sounded pretty Southern. One of your UVA friends?"

"Sorta," replied Kenny, not really knowing how to describe Wayne exactly. "He's not a student, but we worked together at Catering."

"Oh. Well, it wasn't a long message. He just said he'd probably call back, and he said something about a rock concert in Wisconsin."

"Dead show," replied Kenny.

"Who?" said Linda, who had only a vague idea who the Grateful Dead were. Her awareness of popular music had grown very spotty after about 1962, other than Simon and Garfunkel, the Carpenters, and maybe Helen Reddy. Jerry Garcia was born around when Linda was, but Kenny had long assumed that pop stars were mostly known by people at least a half-generation younger than them.

"A band tons of people my age like, especially in Virginia," said Kenny. Vaguely aware of the Dead himself as a kid in Madison, he had met diehard fans his own age when he got to Charlottesville. Wayne had never said much about the Dead, though. Metal and prog rock seemed more his thing.

Linda took another sip of her tea. "I saw Darlene Gustafson at Woodman's."

"Yeah, I saw her, too, the other day. Me and Kurt ran into her at St. Vinny's."

"*Me and Kurt?*" she said, raising an eyebrow. "Interesting

subject in that sentence. How much did we pay for you to go to Virginia again?"

"Nothing, actually, except for all that insurance money."

She smiled then became unusually quiet. She took a sip of her tea. "I'm sorry, honey."

"It's okay, Mom," he said, then grinned. "We got our money's worth, though. UVA was fun, and studying history opened a promising career for me in food service."

Linda smiled. "Yes, well. Darlene. She told me she had run into you all." *You all.* Kenny's mom was the only one of the East Side parents he had grown up around who said it this way. "She hasn't really changed very much. I don't think I had seen her since you all were in middle school. She said she had moved back."

"She actually moved back senior year. We graduated together from East."

"That's right," said Linda. "I'm starting to confuse all the Lowell kids. I never had her in my class, but I did have Kendall and Liz." Kendall and Liz had been close friends with Darlene, right around the age when "close friends" meant swiftly changing alliances and dramatic betrayals of trust.

"She went out of state, too," said Kenny.

"Where'd she go?"

"Penn."

"Where *is* Penn? Penn State?" asked Linda, looking up at the ceiling like she was taking a test. Kenny's time on the East Coast had taught him that Penn was kind of a big deal, not just a state school, but his mother showed no inkling that Penn meant *Ivy League* or anything else that might set it above the name of the state that she assumed gave it care and feeding. "What city?"

"Philadelphia. The University of Pennsylvania. She's home for the summer, too. But she's going to grad school this fall. She got some kind of fellowship."

"Oh, really. Where?" asked Linda, suddenly very focused. She may not have cared what school you went to, but her ears pricked up when you said *fellowship.* She had been her class salutatorian.

"Michigan. English. She wants to do a PhD."

"Hm," said Linda, turning to take her mug over to the sink. "You certainly have an interesting group of friends," she said, carefully avoiding both praise and skepticism. Kenny felt a loop closing, as his mother returned to what he knew she cared most about: family and friends and who they were for each other.

"I don't know," said Kenny, sipping the last of his tea. "Darlene's not really a friend, more like a childhood friend." He looked out the window for a second, unsure. Linda noticed his look.

"Well," she said, in a way that sounded like both the beginning of a conclusion and the opening of a new topic, should the listener opt for that. "Sometimes you rediscover one you had, maybe they become one later."

She took another sip of her tea and began singing, "*Make new friends and keep the old...*"

"*One is silver and the other gold,*" said Kenny, completing the verse his mother had sung to them constantly when they were little kids. "Yeah, that's probably about right. But I just wonder, you know, *grad school.* And *English.*"

"What about history?" said Linda, sitting back down at the table. "Your major was kind of in that same vein, wouldn't you say?"

"Well, yes and no," said Kenny.

"I just mean *vocationally,*" said Linda, careful not to sound like she was about to ask her son what he wanted to do when he grew up.

"Different. Like, she's doing what Dad came *here* to do. And you came here with him, while he was doing it, and it didn't really turn out like he thought it would."

Linda pursed her lips, as if to punctuate what her son had just said. Kenny knew the look. It didn't signify anything, except maybe that she was about to comment as neutrally as possible on what she had just heard.

"Nothing really turns out the way you think it will, most of the time. You want to make God laugh, tell him your plans."

Kenny grinned, then got serious again. "By the time I started thinking about books and school seriously, I hadn't ever really considered Dad as a 'vocational' English guy."

"Well, I don't know about vocation. But he sure loved language. And reading. And stories."

"I know," he said, more quietly than he had intended. He decided not to mention Lincoln this time.

A plane passed overhead. Their neighborhood was so close to the airport. At least once a week, the Air Force fighter jets based at Truax Field would pass loudly over their house. Depending on the weather and time of day, sometimes you could even see their shadows race down the middle of the street, in a perfect parallel line. The passenger jets were bigger and slower. By the time they got to Talmadge Street, their landing gear was down and the name of the airline completely legible. For planes, they were low, but to Kenny, they always seemed so high and fast. And Talmadge Street so low, so quiet, shady, and unmoving.

Darlene

It had been unusually warm, but Kenny had the time, so he walked all the way downtown for his catering shift. When he came into Lori DeKampf's large office to check the schedule, no one was there. He was surprised to find his column completely blank.

Just a few seconds later, Lori DeKampf walked into the office. "Kenny," she said, walking straight to her desk. She set her clipboard down then began to read a note someone had left for her. "Today's function changed up a little. We didn't need as many caterers."

Kenny's stomach tightened a notch. "So, I..."

"You can go home," she interrupted, still not looking up.

"Okay," replied Kenny, slowly. This had never happened in Charlottesville. Once you were scheduled, you worked. "I guess I have an unexpected day off."

"Mm-hm," said Lori DeKampf, apparently still reading. "You know, seniority. Got to make the call sometimes."

"The Pinckney," she added, as if to lend authority to her pronouncement.

His stomach tightened further. "Are you still working on the schedule, or...?"

She finally looked up, then let out a little sigh. "No, Kenny, it's done. I'm afraid it's pretty sparse these next couple of weeks."

"But I have no shifts. None."

"I know. Seniority," she said, then produced a slight clicking sound. "I know you have that North Carolina degree in your pocket."

"Virginia," said Kenny, correcting her for once. "The University of Virginia."

"Yes," she said icily. "Your *university degree* from the University of Virginia." She seemed hungry for something everyone could see but which only she would be eating. "You're one of the new guys, anyway, and the new guys always have to do this. Most have another side thing, you know—for when it slows down like this. Painting houses, carpentry, whatever." She waved her hand around a little. "The new guys all get this."

Kenny looked back at the schedule. Every other caterer's column, without exception, was full of shifts. Functions every day. His column was the only one totally empty. Lori DeKampf looked back down at the clipboard and began tapping on it like it was a calculator.

"Just give us a call in a week and a half to see how it plays out. No need to come in, just call us."

Us.

Kenny turned and left without a word.

* * * * *

The walk back to the East Side was a mild blur. The sky had turned even bluer, and it was balmy, but Kenny had to walk for at least ten blocks before he could notice what a lovely day it actually was. He was halfway down Williamson Street before he fully realized he had been effectively laid off. He knew Lori DeKampf had it in for him. He hadn't even gotten to know her as a boss, other than knowing that the movements of her clipboard could be an efficient barometer for how stressed she was. But you had to know how to read those movements. The splits move a few days before had come out of nowhere, and he hadn't known how to react. Turning down her advance was what did it.

I could drink a beer, he thought, as he passed the Crystal Corner. It was still eleven o'clock in the morning, though, and everything seemed closed up. The Crystal was still closed "until further notice" anyway, while they fixed up the damage from the fire earlier that spring. The Tar Babies' name was still on the little marquee above the door—probably left over from a mid-winter show.

"Hey McLuher," came a voice from the crosswalk. Darlene Gustafson was crossing Willy Street to Kenny's side. She was holding a lumpy plastic bag.

"Hey Darlene," said Kenny, some energy returning. "What's up? What are you up to?"

"St. Vinny's, of course," she said. "I don't work on Saturdays." She reached into the bag and pulled out a shirt to show Kenny. In 1970s iron-on letters, it read, *CAMP KENNEBURL '76 KEEP ON TRUCKIN.* The letters were misaligned, having clearly been applied by hand.

"How 'bout this?" she said, holding it up to her chest as if she were modeling it for a photographer.

"It is pretty classic. Five bucks says the counselor leading the arts and crafts activity that day was on 'ludes."

Darlene smiled brightly, as if to say *Oh you!* or *Come on, now!* but just laughed instead.

"Actually, I think I just got fired," said Kenny.

"What? How long were you even there?"

"Four weeks, I suppose. Just."

"What did you do, hit on somebody?" she said, coyly.

"They suck. Seniority stuff. No job security at all when there's a dropped event on the schedule." This sounded better than admitting you were being punished for something.

"Oh," said Darlene.

"Actually, I was hoping to drown my sorrows with a morning beer."

She lit up.

"It's less morning than it is nearly lunchtime, which makes that idea totally legitimate. Maybe Mickey's?" she asked casually.

They walked the couple of blocks down the street to the tavern and walked through its banged-up entrance. The room was dark and smelled like old beer. Several stools apart from each other sat two older-looking men, nursing drinks that looked like they contained a good deal of rail brandy.

"A beverage at the bar?" asked Kenny.

"A little depressing," whispered Darlene, then raised her voice back to a normal volume. "Sure. It's our only choice for sitting."

They walked up to where the bar curved, so that they could each take a stool facing the other. A little more robotically than he would have preferred, Kenny pulled Darlene's stool out for her.

"Getting fired sure brings out the gentleman in a guy."

"My pleasure," Kenny replied stiffly.

They settled onto their stools and surveyed the dark room, to avoid suddenly feeling like they were on a date. They ordered Hubers, which the bartender delivered in bottles.

"Cheers," said Kenny, clinking Darlene's glass. The bottle-tinkle acted like a bell, granting them permission for slightly longer eye contact and unlocking smoother, if still light, conversation. One of the two lone men let loose an uncovered sneeze. You could hear the liquid spray out of him, wetting a medium-sized area of bar surface. The bartender, his back to the sneezer, continued washing and drying dishes.

"Gross," said Darlene, frowning and crinkling her nose at the same time.

"Juicy," said Kenny.

Darlene's expression returned to normal. "It's actually pretty normal, I guess." She leaned forward and lowered her voice. "*If* more than a little rude, to do it that particular way."

She leaned back again, suddenly very poised. "I actually have a story about sneezing. Want to hear it?"

"Sure."

"When I was about seven," said Darlene, leaning forward again a little, "I was watching Phil Donahue by myself in the living room, and all these middle-aged women were talking about orgasms."

Kenny tried to avoid making any kind of facial expression.

"It being the early seventies, I'm pretty sure it's because none of them had ever *had* one," she said, matter-of-factly. "Anyway, I thought the word was cool. *Orgasm.* The *s* and the *m* together. But I was seven—I had no idea what they were talking about. So sometime after that, probably that same day, we were in the car going to Woodman's or somewhere, and I asked my mom what an orgasm was."

"All right," said Kenny, a little looser now. He took a sip of his Huber. "The seventies."

"Totally. And since my mom was always bragging about how 'liberated' she was, of course she was going to answer me."

"What did she say?"

"She takes a second, stays looking straight ahead, then just goes, 'It's like a *sneeze*, honey'."

"Maybe that's why that guy over there just lit a cigarette."

"Nice. But seriously, it turns out to be true," said Darlene, "neurologically, I mean. I told that story at a party in Philly, and some pre-med majors told me it was the same impulse, chain of events, whatever." She waved her hand humanistically, unscientifically, yet certain of what she had heard. "Also, you know how you really *want* to sneeze? It's like the virus knows you are its vehicle, its way forward, so it creates this agreeable experience you can have, so it can spread its seed."

She said *seed* a little more slowly than expected, emphasizing it.

"Like when a horse eats an apple off a tree. One of those pre-med students made this point about fruit—that it's just a tree's way of spreading its young. It's like the apple tree wants to have sex with the horse." She took a drink of her beer. "I think he just said that because he was kind of hitting on me."

"An apple tree 'trying to have sex with a horse?' Yes, I think he was hitting on you."

Darlene laughed.

They fell quiet for a few seconds, then Kenny changed the subject. "When you were on the East Coast, did you ever visit Virginia?"

"I did, actually," said Darlene. "I went down once with a Penn friend, who was from Richmond. We stayed with her high school friends and went out swimming in a stream somewhere, in May. Pretty nice to be able to swim then."

"Yes, spring is long down there, and it's pretty warm."

"But, still. The South... I have to say it: Virginia felt a little *slavey* to me."

What? Even if he understood what she meant and even respected how casually she had used a clever word to denote centuries of horror, Kenny felt a little defensive. He felt this way himself, suspected a lot of white Southerners were racist, the kind of people who would have done nothing about actual slavery in the old days but who would say, now, of course, that they would have. But if their conversation followed up too much on this thought, might Darlene toss Kentucky into the same bag? Kenny wasn't from Kentucky, but a lot of people he loved were, and in conversations about the South, Kentucky would most certainly be included. So he changed the subject again.

"So at Penn, do they talk about 'Mr. Franklin'? At UVA it was all 'Mr. Jefferson' this and 'Mr. Jefferson' that."

Darlene laughed. "No, Ben Franklin wouldn't have allowed that."

"I'm pretty sure Thomas Jefferson did. In fact, I bet he left *detailed instructions* for all faculty and students to refer to him this way. Maybe even all Americans, in perpetuity."

"Ooh, *perpetuity*," said Darlene. "I like it."

"Thank you, madam," said Kenny, nodding in a way he hoped signaled he was mocking how monarchs move their heads. The eleven o'clock beer—by now the eleven-forty-five beer—was kicking in a little. "You English majors aren't the only ones using big words."

Darlene had relaxed considerably. "So you're saying, basically, that you're Jefferson and I'm Franklin?"

"We could get outfits."

"A show at the Crystal Corner, with a band. 'Founding Fathers Night.' To get in, you have to dress up."

"The Crystal is closed, my dear," said Kenny, in an English butler voice.

"Ooh yes," said Darlene, "fire!"

"Wherever it happens, I'm definitely dressing like Jefferson."

Kenny hailed the bartender, who already had two new Hubers when he came over, bored-looking. He opened them and left the old ones, then went back to his sink.

"I'm going as Benjamin, but not the one you're thinking of." She finished the first Huber and pushed it away. "Benjamin *Rush*, that is. *Doctor* Benjamin Rush."

"Ah, also a signer."

"And a close correspondent of your friend Thomas Jefferson," she added, looking at him a little longer this time.

Kenny was impressed that Darlene knew these historical figures, and he liked the idea of Founding Fathers Night in a local bar. Most of the streets around there were named after those people, anyway: Baldwin, Spaight, Franklin, Dickinson, Jenifer. But the ideas in Darlene's playful banter, the words, meant less now. It was really her voice, and the suddenly smoky look in her eyes, that interested him. Kenny's attention had shifted quickly to those aspects of the interaction.

"We could practice by dressing up first in private, Mr. Jefferson," she said coquettishly. "You know, just to check the authenticity of our garments."

There was a silence, but she continued to watch Kenny for a response. She picked up her new Huber and took a long drink out of it.

A number of things happened shortly thereafter. They flirted a little longer, Kenny giddy but trying to sound cool and older than he really was. Darlene didn't seem to care. She made a few more low-voiced references to clothing, never directly mentioning removing it but alluding a couple of times to the fact that it was there, ultimately, to cover something more essential. *Liberated,* Kenny thought, recalling that old term and remembering that two different women, over the past few weeks, had made unexpected passes at him. Springtime was upon him, even in this dank bar in the late morning, and it seemed time to make a pass back. So he tried one.

"As Mr. Jefferson once said," he whispered, "your place or mine?"

Darlene's eyes flashed, as if she were one of those *Donahue* guests, her goal finally in view. "Mine," she said. "I'm on South Paterson, and my roommate is away all weekend. I don't know that we have to necessarily finish these Hubers."

Galaxie 500

"Mary," Glenn Gruszka yelled back through the side door he had just walked out of, "where did you put that inflator pump?"

It was only ten o'clock or so, but it was warm again and pretty dry. Kenny sat drinking coffee on the front stoop of his mother's house, pondering the fact that he had lost his job. It was a mixed bag. On the one hand, where was the money going to come from now? On the other hand, no more Lori DeKampf. He had only quit one other job in his life—at a franchise pizzeria in high school—but he remembered the feeling of freedom that came in that first day or two after you tossed off the yoke.

He still glowed from the night before. He and Darlene had lounged for a little while in bed. "You can stay" was all she had said. In addition to the pleasure it brought, physical intimacy seemed like a form of hospitality, and he didn't want to spoil that—so he left. A full overnight could seem like overkill.

"Hello there, young man," said Glenn as he rounded the big red Ford Galaxie 500 sedan he kept parked by the side door of his house. The car was almost twenty years old, but Glenn was always doing something to it, in it, or near it. Three bumper stickers festooned its rear: a blue-and-white one that read *Union carpenters are lean, mean building machines*, a bright red rectangle that said *Watch my rear, not hers!*, and an American flag made to look like it was waving in the wind. Just above the fender were the words *NO JAP CRAP*, arranged by hand in those adhesive reflective letters you sometimes see on mailboxes.

A veteran of the Second World War, Glenn had grown up in Green Bay but stayed in Madison after meeting Mary at a baseball game, then marrying her only a few weeks later. He worked as a carpenter for the Wisconsin Department of Corrections. A career housewife, Mary had grown up on the East Side, and the couple had taken the McLuhers under their wing, selling them Mary's brother's old house next door to their own. At something of a loss. They had been especially attentive to the family after Harlan died so suddenly. They had no children.

"Hi Glenn, how's tricks?"

"Tricks is tricks, don't ya know," replied Glenn, in his inimitable up-north baritone. He often ended sentences with this tag-on, which Kenny's Kentucky-eared parents always heard as *dole-cha nole.* Kenny could hear it too, but to him it was just the sound of the place, like a cardinal's song or the bell at St. Bernard's, tolling the hour. It was a home sound, fashioned by time and proximity.

"What you got there?" asked Kenny, looking at the red plastic box Glenn held. Glenn turned it around and looked at it, as if for the first time.

"Flea market. It's for pumping up an air mattress."

"You going camping?" joked Kenny.

"It'd be good for that. No, it's nifty, though." He held up a cord attached to the rear. "You just plug it into the cigarette lighter, and it charges right up, don't ya know. Here, watch this." He went to open the driver's-side door, but Kenny stayed on the stoop. "Come on, let me show you."

Kenny got up, stretched, and walked over to the sedan. There wasn't anything to be learned by it—Glenn would just point to the cigarette lighter, describe literally how you would plug the charger into it, then probably do it in front of Kenny, by way of demonstration. All of which he did.

"Whoa, that *is* pretty nifty."

"Wait 'til you see this now," said Glenn. He opened the box and flipped a small switch, after which the box began emitting a scratchy, low hum. Air blew noncommittally out of a small port on the side.

"See? It's inflating right now. You need a hose, though. I think I have one that fits." He flipped a switch on the box, but the sound continued.

"Aha," Kenny said. "A good flea market find there."

"Dammit," cursed Glenn, flipping the switch back and forth with more vigor. "Oh shit," he added, and Kenny saw a puff of light blue smoke rising up from beneath the dashboard. Glenn yanked the cord out of the cigarette lighter, and the smoke dissipated.

"Yep," said Glenn, closing the car door, as if the only problem had been the lack of a hose. "I'm going to go down in the basement and see if I can find one." *A hose, he means,* thought Kenny, who saw that whatever fire had started appeared now to have gone out.

"Okay, thanks for showing me that," said Kenny.

Glenn was already through the door by now, his purposeful gait propelling him forward. The screen door slammed shut behind him. Kenny heard the words *Mary* and *hose* from inside the house, followed by the familiar acoustics of another door closing somewhere beyond the kitchen.

"Hey Mr. Jefferson," came a voice from behind him. He turned around to see Darlene standing quite close. She was holding a dandelion, which she held out to Kenny. "Look what I brought you."

He wondered if he should give her a kiss or a hug, given the previous evening's interlacings, but ended up deciding just to accept the dandelion. "What have we here?" he said, trying to sound older than he was. Darlene looked happy but no different than she had at Mickey's, before things had turned kittenish.

"You want to go for a little walk with me?"

"Sure," said Kenny, trying to sound casual. Her appearance had heartened him. "Let me just put this down." He laid his coffee cup on the stoop.

"*Art slut*? Your family is cool."

"Aren't you working today at your internship?" he asked.

"Yeah, but they don't need me until this afternoon. We're waiting for some stuff to be delivered for a thing with some authors—at the Pinckney Plaza, actually, in a couple of weeks, a meeting thing."

"I'm not likely to be working that particular event."

"I guess not," said Darlene, looking serious. "Anyway, they just told me to take the morning off. Thought I'd swing by." She said this in a friendly way. They both waited a second, to see where the conversation might go next, and looked around while they awaited the next turn.

Darlene peered over at the Gruszkas' small front yard, which was cluttered with old decorations: two flowerbeds made from old whiskey barrels cut in half, three bowling balls partially burrowed into the grass, four concrete pelicans, a foot-high statuette of the Virgin Mary with a little grotto around it. The Blessed Mother was a compromise: Glenn was Polish and raised Catholic, but Mary was Methodist, so when they got engaged, as she put it, he "went over." Glenn's mother wasn't happy about that, so after they got married, Glenn put the Virgin in the yard and that had healed things up, more or less. The four-foot length of homemade picket fence at the corner of the yard, unpainted but festooned with a plastic Christmas wreath, had come later. A compromise, it underlined the generic Christianity of the yard.

"Whoa," said Darlene, beholding the display.

"My mom loves the Gruszkas' yard. There aren't any others in the neighborhood that... *egregious*, I guess. She says it reminds her of Taylor Mill."

"What's Taylor Mill?"

Kenny realized the missing context, the need to bridge those four hundred and fifty-some miles.

"It's where she grew up, in Northern Kentucky." In Madison, the word *Kentucky* was usually sufficient, so saying *Northern Kentucky* to Darlene was like inviting her into his house. Kenny had acknowledged this nuance without thinking. "It's the main road there, too."

"Lots of stuff in the yards on old Taylor Mill?" asked Darlene, the word *old* sounding a little ironic, like some of his friends at UVA might have said it.

"People do put things in their yards, I guess. I suppose it's a form of expression for a lot of people." Aware he had just said *people* twice within a couple of seconds, he girded himself for teasing from Darlene, who was quick on her feet around words. When Kenny was talking about people in their place, he felt a little protective of the words he chose. But no teasing came.

"Expression like *that*?" she asked instead, looking at the Galaxie 500's rear bumper. Her voice had a new and not very agreeable edge to it.

Kenny made a cartoonish fist and moved it back and forth, like a singing sailor gesticulating with a full mug of grog. "There is power in a Union!" he sang in a bad British accent, aping Billy Bragg's recent re-do of "The Battle Cry of Freedom."

"Yeah, well, I'm for *that* part," said Darlene, unmoved.

"Labor unions. They brought us the weekend."

"Are you joking?"

What Kenny had taken for young-love gaiety was quickly ebbing away. "No, I'm not. That is actually true about unions." He scratched his head, a nervous tic. "Hey, I'm a Democrat, you know. You don't need to worry about that. And so are my neighbors." Noting party affiliation had seemed like a good idea, for bringing Darlene back around.

Her hard look did not soften.

"Yeah, union, but it's kinda like an Archie Bunker union guy thing. Rah rah, sis boom bah, wave that flag."

A very recent image of Glenn crossed Kenny's mind. Determined and elderly, leaning into his car to share his electric air pump. For Kenny, Glenn was somebody.

"He did fight in the Second World War, Darlene."

"You mean the war that ended in killing millions of people with an atomic bomb?"

"Two hundred thousand or so," said Kenny, more rigidly than he had meant to and less for precision's sake than just to slow her down. "Is *this* what we are talking about?"

Darlene's looked back at the bumper stickers. Her frown firmed up a little more.

"I suspect that it's the 'Jap crap' part you object to, Darlene." He had meant to say it this way, risky as it was, but adding Darlene's name at the end of the sentence immediately felt like a mistake. She glared at him.

He tried levity. "Come on, *Cheap Trick at Budokan.* Those fans were Japanese, screaming like girls at an Elvis concert." He grabbed an imaginary microphone. "I want... you... to want *me!*"

"American hegemony is what that man is celebrating."

He saw Glenn again in his mind's eye, this time inside the McLuhers' house, a couple of nights after Harlan died. Linda had been crying hard all afternoon, and Glenn had knocked gently and called into the house, "Special delivery, everybody"—a little lightly, just because he hadn't known what to say. He may have never had to deliver food to a woman in her early forties who had just lost her husband. Kenny was in the kitchen then, and he saw Glenn walk in gingerly, leave the casserole on the table, then droop visibly when he saw Linda there on the couch. He just said, "It's a little frozen, you might want to defrost it a little," then slipped out quietly.

This memory made Kenny a little angry. He had just spent a tender night with Darlene; why did she have to jump all over Glenn this way? He felt like calling her a name, insulting her, maybe even telling her to leave.

"Let's walk a little, you want to?" he said instead. Darlene turned away from the Galaxie 500. She moved as if she were digesting a grudge.

"Okay, yeah," she said, her calm returning a little. "They probably say the Pledge of Allegiance in their house."

Kenny laughed politely, but his ears had reddened visibly. They walked some more, quietly. A plane passed overhead. Darlene watched it fly out of view, like she was gazing at a star.

"Okay, whatever, they're your neighbors," she said, after a few long seconds. "He's a veteran, whatever. But it's just so provincial, that kind of shit. I get so sick of it."

How can we be sick of things yet? thought Kenny. *We're children compared to them. We're just getting started.*

"Provincial," she repeated, pleased with her choice. "It's the kind of thing I can't wait to be rid of. This place is so fucking small."

Compared to where? Kenny thought. *Ann Arbor?* He had never been there, but he figured Michigan might not be your top choice if your goal was to avoid bumper stickers praising American automakers.

"Well, by the end of the summer, this will all have been a dream," said Kenny. "You'll be onto your grad school projects."

Darlene smiled weirdly and grabbed his hand. "You're sweet," she said, as if he had just given her a gift but wasn't someone she had known all that long.

Letter

The mail came early that afternoon. Kenny had been back from his walk with Darlene for maybe an hour when he heard the *thunk* in their mailbox. As usual, it was mostly junk, every envelope addressed to *Linda McLuher or Resident.* Except for the last one: a handwritten letter from Tracy the Vegetarian.

> *Dear Kenny,*
>
> *It's been a few weeks now since we wrapped up our little adventures as students of THE UNIVERSITY (as those famous arrogant window stickers say, especially in the parking lot of Birdwood and around the Law School), and I thought I'd drop you a line. How are you?*
>
> *Maybe you want an update—because you are sad and lonely and miss your old Catering pals in C-ville! Seriously, I don't know about that, b/c that era is done now, Steelmark Services made sure of that. Or maybe it was some UVA bigwigs, I don't know.*
>
> *Anyway, I'm really enjoying Etta's, it's VERY relaxed and they have an equal number of male and female servers. I guess that*

matters less than it would have a couple of years ago, but nonetheless I notice how egalitarian it feels, and I think you'd probably like it here—if, that is, you ended up staying in some kind of food service job.

Not much else is going on. Chris stayed in C-ville, too, but he's talking about moving to Alaska. Alaska! Fishing boat work, I think. I'm not sure he's ready for it. I have a friend from Torydon (where I went to high school) who did that, and he was pretty macho, but he came back to NOVA with his tail between his legs after about a month. Turns out the actual seafaring types are pretty rough and make you work pretty hard. No London Broil after one of those shifts.

Blah blah blah. English majors, you say! You history majors always say that.

Seriously, though, I guess I was just thinking about you today and wanted to say hello. It's cool that you gave me your home address last year when all us letter writing nerds were updating our address books in the servery. Do you remember that day? That wedding or whatever it was that fell through b/c the bride (the UVA sorority princess alumna or whatever) got cold feet at the last minute and her whole Massachusetts family just decided to throw a standard cocktail function instead? There were way too many of us booked, but Catering kept us on anyway, since they had promised us the shift (no way that's happening anymore in the Steelmark Age, you can be sure of that bucko), and the New Englanders kept calling the almost-groom "that Virginia bas-tahd" (Kennedy family pronunciation), even though the almost-groom was ready to go and was the one that ended up getting jilted by the sorority girl alumna that was their little angel, apparently!

I'm going on and on here, not sure why. English majors! I guess I was just thinking about you—of course our little "moment" in the servery just before commencement remains in my mind, what the &%#@?... But seriously, I really liked hanging out with you and wish we could have done more of that (even maybe the servery moment, nudge nudge!). But seriously, I'm just feeling nostalgic, I guess. And we just graduated!

My parents came down last weekend, and we had a kind of gentle "talk" about the "future." My dad is an Episcopal priest. I probably told you this, but I can't remember, and so every "talk" we have feels a little bit like Mr. Rogers. I love him a lot, of course. I just mean that I don't want you to imagine my dad is some kind of boorish bourbon-swilling pompous real estate baron or whatever else you probably (sometimes rightly) imagined about the people I've been around most of my life. I know you are a little suspicious of the "bourgeoisie" (my word, which won't surprise you), and I suppose we're part of that gang, although I went to Torydon on scholarship, and because of my dad, we've always been kind of on the sidelines of that group, like servants a little bit maybe but all in the same confirmation class or on the same field hockey team. I'm not complaining, just saying that my parents' apparent discomfort with my "waitressing job" put me on edge a little. They are sweet but just don't understand that time right after college nowadays. They were married by now, and my dad had his own little church (= a stable job). Ironically, he was also an English major—wait, I guess he had just finished seminary, and my mom was finishing her B.A., but I digress. My plans remain to see this thing out at Etta's. C-ville is mellower than I thought, certainly more than good old uptight NOVA.

I don't know why I'm going on like this, and I don't want you to get the wrong idea. I miss all you guys from Catering, you in particular maybe, and I just wanted to say hello. Write me a letter sometime if you want to, although I know you're back home now and probably settling in, maybe with your family and a new job and whatever, maybe a girlfriend, I don't know.

Take care and let me know if you come through C-ville anytime soon!

Love,

Tracy xoxo

American Gothic

The *Capital Times* lay open on the coffee table. Harlan's preference for the afternoon paper had predated his children's arrival in the world, and it was how Linda still got her news. A fresh paper was always out in the open somewhere. Nobody ever seemed to get more than a few feet into the McLuher house before glancing at a headline.

Today, though, Kenny was too distracted for that. Darlene's dissertation on the smallness of his neighbors had left an acrid taste in his mouth, and he had just read Tracy's unexpected letter. Nothing earth-shattering, but it had come as a surprise—especially on the heels of the walk with Darlene, which had ended with that oddly blank goodbye.

It wasn't so much Tracy's tone that surprised him. It was the revelation that there was more to her than he had realized just a few weeks earlier, and for the whole time they had known each other in college. The voice he heard in the handwritten words had challenged his memory of her. By the time he had finished reading, the nickname *Tracy the Vegetarian* had lost its sheen. Logan had dubbed her this after one of their inconsequential catering arguments, his bravado always most vigorous when the object of his ire had left the premises. Kenny felt a little ashamed that he had gone along with the nickname. They had mocked a person who was sweeter and less ironic than anyone had thought. *Love, Tracy.*

Her letter also pointed to other conclusions he had jumped to, among them the certainty that she was a spoiled rich kid who could never understand real people or ideas because of her class. Kenny had pegged her, then seen her throughout his time at UVA, as the personification of an entire region—"the East Coast" or "the South" or "Virginia" or whatever other entity he could name to represent the worn-out, cynical opposite of the Midwest or East Side or Talmadge Street he had been yearning to hold up as a down-to-earth, honest paragon of American authenticity and wholeness. The way she talked about her family in the letter had complicated his certainty. They were church mice. What a moron he had been.

Ten or fifteen minutes after he had sat down, Taylor walked in through the kitchen.

"Hi, Uncle Kenny," she said, flopping onto the couch next to him in a clumsy, Kate-like move. She saw the newspaper on the table. "Is that the *Dealer Dealer*?"

"Gimme five," said Kenny, slapping hands with his niece. Kenny was just starting to get used to how a five-year-old might see things, but what struck him most was how they heard things and said them. *Dealer Dealer.* A year before, a fireman visiting Taylor's preschool class illustrated his support for smoke detectors with a cautionary tale about an "old grandma who had half her face melted off." Taylor was so terrified that she wet the bed every night for two weeks, but Kenny's favorite part of the story was that Taylor called the guy a *fighter fighter.*

"No, it's not the *Wheeler Dealer,*" he replied, slipping the letter into his pocket and picking up the newspaper. "Just the plain old *Cap Times*."

"Oh," she said, "I see."

Kenny looked at her. "I see, said the blind man... as he picked up his hammer and saw!"

Taylor twisted her face up a little. "*What*? What did he see?"

"Never mind." Grandma Maesby used to say this to him when he was little. Kids were so literal.

"Are you going to tuck me in again tonight?" She was staying over again. No date for Kate, as far as Kenny knew; sending Taylor for overnights just gave her some breathing time, and Linda liked the company.

"I don't know, Taylor. I don't know if I'm going to be here." He recalled how exhausting it had been.

"Aww," said Taylor, twisting her little torso suddenly then punching the sofa pillow in protest. Linda called this kind of move *kid body*, which only adults found amusing. For kids, it was just a natural way to punctuate the vocal part of a story.

"Well," said Kenny, thinking he probably wouldn't see Darlene that night anyway. "It's possible."

"Yay!" said Taylor, performing a second torso-twist, this one more exuberant than the first.

* * * * *

After dinner, Linda turned on the television, her habitual company most evenings since Harlan had died. "Hey, you pup," she said. Taylor looked up from something she was making with scissors, paper, and masking tape, over at the kitchen table. "It's just about time to brush those teeth. Five minutes."

"Aw, Grandma. Will that be *absolutely necessary*? I'm working on something."

Kenny noticed the wording. Linda just answered the question. "Yes, it will."

"Okay," replied Taylor, her kid body now fluently signaling resignation. "Uncle Kenny's tucking me in, so that's all right."

Kenny looked up. "I guess I've been hired."

"I guess you have," said Linda, turning back toward the TV. "You can't get good help anymore."

As Taylor led her uncle up the stairs, he could already tell she had way more energy than he did. Was tucking children in always like this? How did parents, or guardians, or whoever, do this every single night?

"Time for the lady chair," said Taylor. This is what she sometimes called the pillow, once she had wedged it into the corner. "Grandma calls this my *pallet*."

"I know. That's what Grandma and Grandpa Maesby always call beds they make for us on the floor."

"Nobody in my class ever heard of that," said Taylor.

"Maybe their grandmas and grandpas don't say it that way."

Taylor shrugged. "Okay," she said, bringing closure to the matter. "Uncle Kenny, do you know about Ryan?"

"Ryan?"

"Yeah, Ryan. Miss T told us a story about him. He lives in the sky in the winter."

"Oh, you mean *Orion.* Sure, I know about him. He's an imaginary hunter in the sky, but he's really a constellation. They used to imagine constellations were people in stories, in the good old days."

Harlan and Linda had both kept their own parents' habits of referring to the past as *the good old days.* This was one of the few country expressions that all the McLuhers continued to use without a trace of self-consciousness.

"Miss T told us about consolations. She said they're like little families of stars."

"Yes, constellations"—he repeated the word, as if correcting gently would help it congeal over time. "They're like that. They're kind of like families, like groups."

"Miss T says you should pick your favorite star."

Something jiggled in Kenny's mind. "Oh really?" he asked, allowing her to keep the floor a little longer. The kid said some entertaining things at bedtime, but Kenny was also genuinely interested in what she might have to say about "picking a star."

"Yeah, you're supposed to pick one, like it's your own star, and you should think about it and think about your goals for it."

"Aha," said Kenny, a loose thought still rattling around in his mind. Then it landed: that poem he had discovered at St. Vinnie's! The book by the guy in Wisconsin in 1908, that little poem about the two soldiers trying to escape from jail. Maybe this was what his mom sometimes called *a good teaching moment.*

"Well, Taylor, it sounds like Miss T is teaching you all about goals."

"That's what I just said."

"Aha, yes." He cleared his throat. "Well, it's probably *good* to set your sights on a goal, to follow through..."

"Through *what*, Uncle Kenny?"

He had forgotten to avoid figures of speech. "*Follow through* just means stay the course."

"What's that?"

He closed his eyes for a second, then reopened them.

"What I mean is Miss T is teaching you that it's important to plan for something you are doing in the future. You know, like say you are going to Northern Kentucky, and you know Grandma is going to take you to Johnny's Toys."

"Johnny's Toys! They have a castle inside, and you can go in it!"

"Yes, yes, they have a castle. And let's say Grandma is going to take you there so..."

"Grandma McLuher or Grandma Maesby?"

Kenny rubbed the bridge of his nose. "Grandma Maesby, whose house you are visiting."

"We're going to Grandma and Grandpa *Maesby's* house?" exclaimed Taylor, sitting fully upright with a bolt, "We're going to *Johnny's Toys!*"

Kenny put up his hand and pumped it twice, like a crossing guard signaling to a driver that a passel of schoolchildren was about to pour into the street. "No, no, I'm just saying *imagine* you were going to Grandma and Grandpa's, and you knew they were taking you to Johnny's Toys. You'd want to save up a little money to bring, so you could buy something, right?"

Taylor raised an eyebrow. "When Grandma Maesby took me to Johnny's Toys last time, she *bought* me a toy. I didn't have to use any money."

Kenny sighed. "Yes, you're right. Well, anyway..." He wanted to get to the mud and the stars, but he had lost his momentum.

"The thing about what Miss T said about the stars, I mean, they are great—and *beautiful*—and in the good old days people used to imagine they were hunters."

Taylor looked impatient. "What's your point, Uncle Kenny?"

His "point"? Could he ever catch up?

"Well, Taylor, sometimes," he said, his coup de grâce suddenly in sight, "sometimes, it's not the star that counts, it's the mud."

Taylor raised the other eyebrow. "The *mud*? What mud? Mud's on the *ground*, Uncle Kenny!"

Back to the starting board. Kenny began wandering through the images and events that had recently crossed his mind. He would mine them for ideas for the next part of whatever story he might invent, with the mud and the stars somehow front and center. But thoughts of Darlene distracted him. She had sounded pretty prejudiced when she went off on the Gruszkas, yet she was so smart. How ambitious and talented she was with words, writing, and reading. Grad school, literature—a career. Or teaching or researching or whatever professors did. Wherever they did it.

As distractions often do at night, one thought led to another, and his dad came to mind. Was Darlene *like him* somehow?

Harlan had moved to Wisconsin, an accidental migrant, thinking language and literature might yield a stock in trade, but he had quickly abandoned those things before he could even get onto the track that might lead him there. He had *settled,* as Kenny's other ambitious friends sometimes said derisively and which Darlene was bound to say one day soon—if they continued to see one another, anyway.

A memory from Lowell School floated into view—something about shooting for a star, aiming for your dreams. Maybe a poster. He imagined the image of a star shining brightly up to the left somewhere, and the dreamer—some cartoon animal or child?—poised on the precipice of some cliff or mountain, his gaze directed up at the star. Kenny could feel danger in what lay below the character's idealistic little feet. This gave him an idea for something that might finally resemble a story.

"*Once upon a time,*" said Kenny slowly, feeling the crystalline power of those four little words, "there were two soldiers languishing in prison."

Taylor said nothing. She was watching and listening.

"Yes, they languished," repeated Kenny, enjoying that he was no longer about to be interrupted. "They languished and languished, until they could languish no more."

"What's that?"

He ignored her. "Well, one of them said to the other, 'Hey Bill'—that was the name of the other soldier, the first one was called Henry—'Hey Bill,' says Henry, 'I think you and me should *bust outta* this dump.'"

Taylor giggled. During the *bust outta,* Kenny had made his voice excessively slow and deep.

"'Yep, I aims to bust us outta here,'" Kenny continued. Then, afraid he had gone too cowboy too fast, he reined in the drawl. "So Bill says, 'Yes, Henry, you are correct.'" (Bill's accent was slightly British.) "'I reckon, in *busting outta* here, we should pay close attention to the grounds and surroundings.'"

"'Nonsense!' thundered Henry," (whose voice had reclaimed its Gene Autry sound). "'We must think of our goals, Bill! We must find our star and follow it! For if we don't follow our star, who are we, really, but bungling clowns?'"

"Clowns!" said Taylor, bursting with excitement.

Remembering that winding the child up wasn't the best way forward, he cranked it down a couple of notches. His British-sounding hero, Bill, would be the soldier with an eye on the mud.

Kenny kept the story going for a few more minutes, developing little details here and there to keep Taylor rapt and wear her down at the same time—beginning to understand that tiring out a child this way, with a good tale, as the curtain of day begins to fall and the child's brain yearns for rest, is one of the best ways to settle a kid down. Plus, he was finally leading, and she was following her uncle and the tale, into a quieter country that bordered on sleep. By the time the soldiers had caught Henry, and Bill had gotten away, Taylor's whole body was drooping into the lady chair.

"You know, Taylor," said Kenny, arriving at the moral of the story, "the stars are fixed in place, actually. We are the ones moving around them. Where we are is moving, all the time, but it can still be small and muddy."

No, wait, this wasn't it at all. Kenny thought of Darlene bemoaning how "provincial" things were in this place, this neighborhood and town, as he was crafting his little conclusion. He wondered, did *he* also feel this way about his hometown, about the East Side? Sure, he could really focus on the "mud," but did that have to be a literal place? Didn't "mud" mean the details, the moment, the little things that happened on your way to a satisfying adult life, wherever you finally settled or whatever you settled for? Did it matter that much where he ended up?

"Well, not muddy, really," said Kenny, stumbling now. "I mean, sure, you can focus on your star, but, um, you have to watch where you walk, so you can, you know, get away and not fall down or get caught..."

Taylor drooped but was looking a little sad. Maybe it was only that she was about to fall asleep. Her lower lip wasn't quivering, like it did when she was about to cry, but her eyebrows were reddening a little, and her mouth looked sad.

"I want to see a star, but I want you to stay here, Uncle Kenny," she said. "I want you to stay with us. I don't want you to get caught like Henry did."

She yawned. Then, three seconds later, she was out like a light.

Still on the floor, Kenny uncrossed his legs and stretched them out, taking care not to jostle the sleeping child. He stood up, trying to decide if he wanted to go downstairs and watch some television, take a little walk around the block to wake up some, or just go to bed.

Once he had been standing for a few seconds, he chose the walk, then headed down the stairs and out the side door.

* * * * *

It was eight-thirty or so when Kenny came out onto Talmadge Street. It was early summer, and the days were long; the sun had gone down but still lit up the sky. Its fading light had left a pinkish hue on the world.

He kept on walking up Talmadge, toward Atwood Avenue. "I'll go to the lake," he thought, finally relaxing after the rapid-fire efforts required by coming home, finding an okay job, getting good at it quickly, then promptly losing it.

He came up to Atwood at Corry Street, using one of those triangular neighborhood routes that force you to hop over and backtrack a few yards before you can resume any meaningful path leading you to Lake Monona. Atwood Avenue had been a rite of passage for both Kenny and Kate: the first major street they were allowed to cross without adult supervision. Crossing Atwood Avenue alone had unlocked Kenny's view of the larger

East Side, illuminating the many larger routes leading outward from Talmadge. Atwood Avenue had been for Kenny what the high dive had been for his mother at Pleasure Isle, that big unchlorinated concrete swimming pool where she spent her summer days. Becoming a teenager had nothing to do with numbers, she had once told Kenny—it was just what happened once you had learned to execute a swan dive without a splash.

As he walked down Hudson Street, an aroma of some flower wafted by him, and he noticed how the trees had leafed out. June in his neighborhood reminded him a little like April in Charlottesville. An older couple on a porch waved at him, and he waved back. They looked familiar, but he wasn't sure he knew them. Did they go to church with the Gruszkas? Did they have bigoted messages hand-painted or stickered onto their cars? Did they think foreign countries were worse than their own?

Darlene reappeared in Kenny's thoughts. He was still angry, but her physical charm was probably what had brought her into the daydream—it was a gentle June night, after all, and he had just been noticing gentle flowery scents and leafed-out trees. Yet this Darlene was just a bodiless name, an idea. Another especially important thing was missing, too: her voice, which he had begun to appreciate for its roughish feminine edge, especially when she joked playfully about something they both knew about or might share.

This daydream Darlene may have been invisible and voiceless, but she did have some words. Words that the real Darlene had used earlier that day: *rah rah, hegemony, atomic bomb.* For a second, the kindness of Tracy's letter washed up against him, but Darlene and her sore words kept returning.

No cars in sight. He crossed Sommers Avenue.

Now he imagined Glenn Gruszka's face. A younger version of it, leathered and staring straight ahead—a G.I. maybe, like an unnamed actor in a War Department training film. This was maudlin and embarrassing. Why was Kenny turning a real person into a propaganda poster for himself? What did he know about G.I.s, or war, or the past at all, really?

But then again, he thought, what does Darlene know about any of that, either? As he often did during Socratic-method debates with himself, he reached into his family to illustrate his point. His grandparents were Democrats, what Logan would have called *Northern liberals*, who spoke openly about things like sex, divorce, drugs, hippies, and menstruation, even around their grandchildren. But their lives were as down-home conservative as you can get; they always seemed to Kenny to be in or around their house and yard, working on things or cooking or hosting family gatherings. They were country people. They went to church. You could be both. Darlene clearly had not yet learned this.

But wait. Did his grandparents have some bigoted thoughts, about certain things, from time to time? The Gruszkas did, which Kenny had allowed in his argument with Darlene. So his own grandparents probably did, too. Maybe he did, himself. Had his rush to defend the Gruszkas' integrity been too simple, too childlike?

A big lilac bush caught his eye, its flowers dried up now. Its neighbor, a rambling honeysuckle, was flourishing. He picked one of its little flowers and bit off the end, leaving the little trumpet on his tongue for a few seconds. A hint of sweetness, but no real nectar. He spit the detritus into a yard and walked across Center Avenue.

He thought of the Gruszkas—standing next to each other, like the old farmer couple in that famous Midwestern painting "American Gothic." Kenny had learned in an art history class that this painting was satirical, and that Grant Wood had resented his Iowa hometown and conservative upbringing. Kenny was no farm kid, but "American Gothic" somehow reassured him. Any quiet image of a Midwestern thing usually did. What's more, the famous painting had provided a template for Kenny to imagine the Gruszkas, at least during this walk through the neighborhood. Like some plywood cutout farm couple they could stand behind, to protect their aging bodies from whatever Darlene or Kenny's other upwardly mobile friends felt like throwing at them. Tomatoes? Molotov cocktails? Mud?

Mud seemed like a good choice. It would be an ironic thing the movers and shakers Kenny imagined could throw at the half-shielded Gruszkas, standing in front of their home and their Galaxie 500 with its jingoistic pride and exhortations against Japanese cars. Ironic because, at least according to the poem Kenny had recently discovered, the ones throwing mud at the Glenns and the Marys of the world, or at least of this neighborhood, would naturally be looking up at stars the whole time, at least at the stars they had chosen. The ones looking at the stars would lose their freedom first.

Kenny knew he had to slow down. None of these villains he was imagining were real, and no one was actually throwing anything at anyone. Thinking and walking wound him up, but walking long enough would make him calmer. He came down the hill and crossed Oakridge Avenue, Lake Monona now looming downhill. Maybe he would go for a swim tomorrow. He thought about how wading into cold early-summer lake water tingled and required you to choose. Keep wading or just get it over with and submerge?

He turned down Lakeland Avenue and thought of Taylor now. What was her job in this daydream? What did she have to do with Darlene and the Gruszkas? She was just a little kid.

Wait a minute, though. Maybe Taylor was also starting to wonder what story *she* was in, where everything was supposed to be, to go. When did she belong in her grandmother's room and what did the lady chair make her think about? When would she be able to walk alone from her own apartment to her grandma's house, without her mother? Right now she was probably dreaming about a place called Johnny's Toys, a shop full of trinkets and a plywood castle that, to her, was fully real. And somewhere else.

Taylor could see a story and knew you could live in it. Maybe most kids could do this. What about the rest of us, though? As he looked out over Lake Monona, Kenny wondered what he had gone to school for. He read all the time, studied history for a reason, not because it led to a paycheck for doing it, but just because he couldn't stop doing it. He was always trying to see himself in history, looking for the story around him, to make places more real.

Maybe storytellers could do this. A historian could *talk a place into being*, could make sense of it like no painter could, like no politician could. If they were good enough, maybe anyone who saw the story of a place could be the narrator, could make the place exist, even—in the ways they explained its origins, its style, its ways. Every place needed its storyteller, its narrator, to be a place at all. Kenny just couldn't figure out which story to follow. He wasn't a historian; he was just an East Sider who had gone to college in another state.

Just then, a strange breeze picked up, and the sixteenth president joined Kenny's daydream. His name did, too: the words *Abraham Lincoln,* followed by a sour taste, a surge of acid reflux. Kenny's belly twitched, and he remembered how hard it had been to tell that bedtime story just a half-hour earlier.

Lincoln's face stayed hard, front and center, then disappeared. Then, as so often happened in the Lincoln dreams, Harlan's face came into view. Kenny thought of how hard his storytelling father, in real life, had tried to link stone horse-farm fences and Ohio River water to Talmadge Street flight paths and railroad tracks and bottled Huber. Then how he had made that simple mistake of crossing that street when he did, carrying all those books about the Great Emancipator.

Kenny had just story-told Taylor to sleep. Lincoln had just guided Kenny back into the anxiety and wonder of waking life. Harlan had jumped in, reminding Kenny how hard it is to make one place have meaning in another. Who got to tell the real story of his East Side neighborhood, Kenny wondered, and who would they tell it to? Maybe if he just kept walking for a while, in the twilight along the lake, without wondering about anything at all. That way, it would matter less that the only stories he had to tell were when he was tired, tucking in his five-year-old niece and just making things up as he went along.

Fish and Chicken

A week and a half later, Kenny walked all the way to the Pinckney again, on the off chance his column on the shift schedule had begun to fill up again. He had assumed that job was over, but why not give it one last look? When he got there, it was still the only column on the schedule without a single shift. Neither Lori DeKampf nor her clipboard were in the office, making the place feel even emptier than usual. Now certain that this would be the last time he would set foot in the Pinckney Plaza, at least as an employee, he left the building and began the long walk back to the East Side.

He was passing Mickey's when he heard what sounded like a shout from below the bridge. It came from a spot where people often came to fish in the Yahara, in a shady current where bigger fish came to hunt smaller ones.

"A little help, somebody!" a voice yelled again. It sounded dire. Kenny sprinted to the edge of the little bridge, scanning the area for someone in distress. Twenty or so feet downstream, a middle-aged man stood on the bank, struggling with a fishing pole. A broken-in Montreal Expos cap shaded most of his face. He had something big and apparently surprising on the end of his line.

"Get my net!" he yelled, spotting Kenny above him. "It's in the truck!" He gestured rearward with his head, both hands on the rod, his spinner locked. "*Maskinongé!*" he yelled, "*Je vais t'avoir, mon estie!*"

Running off and around the bridge now, toward the only vehicle parked along the river, Kenny thought the man had just said something in French. Or was it Portuguese? In spite of the few years of Spanish and French he had taken, Kenny's knack for words remained solidly within the confines of his mother tongue.

"In the back! In the back!" yelled the man, still fighting the fish.

Kenny grabbed the aluminum handle protruding from the back of the Toyota pick-up and brought the stranger his net.

"Hold it, get ready! I had a little striper and a big musky just clamped onto the guy," he said. "He's on there right now!" His English was flawless, but Kenny noticed an accent. *Onto da guy, on dere right now.* Not really a French accent, so maybe Brazilian? He looked biracial, but there were black people in both countries. But way more in Brazil, guessed Kenny.

"The net, the net!" yelled the man.

"Sorry, yeah," said Kenny, focusing again on the action at hand.

"Here he comes, *tabarnak*, come on!"

His spinner came around a half-turn, but the fisherman was moving carefully. The big fish wasn't hooked, just clamped onto the little striped bass at the end of the line.

"I want to get him in before he has time to change his mind," said the man, his gaze focused like a laser on where the line penetrated the surface. The dot it formed danced around on the water as the musky took the prey right, then left, then right again.

Then the line went slack.

"Shit, he's gone," said the man, lowering his rod. "The striper's gone, too, else he'd be moving the end around." He looked at Kenny and chortled. "Or maybe he just had a heart attack. Thanks, man."

"Sure," said Kenny, "better luck next time."

The man nodded, reeling in his empty hook now and looking at his bait box. Kenny walked back up onto Williamson Street and headed back toward Talmadge.

* * * * *

Grocery bags sat full on the kitchen table and most of the counter by the sink when Kenny came in through the side door.

"Hello," came his mother's voice from around the corner. "I'm in the basement!"

"It's me," yelled Kenny. Linda emerged a few seconds later, a big roll of masking tape in her hand. "Taylor made a potions cabinet out of my last roll, used the whole thing. Give me a hand putting these groceries away, would you?"

"What's a 'potions cabinet'?"

"I don't know," said Linda, "Ask her. Here." She handed him a bunch of celery, and they began moving the rest of the food from the bags to the fridge and pantry. There was a lot of chicken.

"I thought we'd have a little barbecue tonight. Maybe you could use some of your chef skills while you wait for that scheduling problem to sort itself out."

"Not a chef, Mom, just a caterer. That's a waiter who doesn't have to write anything down."

Linda shook her head and raised a didactic finger. "I stand corrected, but *au contraire!* A waiter with supervisory skills, and a history degree, to boot! Now *you* stand corrected."

"Aha," said Kenny.

"And," added Linda, "as you're reading up on grilling this chicken, thereby gainfully employing yourself, you might invite a few of your friends over. If you wanted to."

"You did get a whole lot of chicken for a run-of-the-mill grocery trip."

"Always thinking ahead." Linda tapped her temple. She had always tried to keep her helpfulness discreet, so that Kenny or Kate would feel the thing had been their own initiative.

Someone knocked on the front door. Two knocks, the second one more hesitant.

"Can you get that, hon?"

Kenny walked through the living room to the front door and saw Darlene standing outside on the stoop. She was holding a small bunch of dandelions and was wearing a baseball cap that read *PENN*.

"Hey there," he said, opening the door to her.

"Hello again," she said, holding out the dandelions. "Our little tradition."

He took the dandelions and stood aside, waving her into the room with his free hand.

"A graduate of the prestigious University of Pennsylvania!" said Linda, walking into the room to see who had arrived.

"Yes, Mrs. McLuher, that's right," said Darlene, smiling mischievously. "It's no UVA, but I liked it."

"You should be very proud of yourself. *And* Kenny told me you got into the graduate program in English at Michigan. Congratulations!"

"Thank you," said Darlene, looking down for a second. "I'm pretty excited about it."

"That's wonderful! You all visit. I'll put the rest of the groceries away," said Linda, looking at Kenny. "There's an awful lot of chicken in there!" She walked back into the kitchen, humming the melody of *Fly Me to the Moon*.

"Somebody's in a good mood," said Darlene. "Does that mean we're having dinner?"

* * * * *

"Step aside, captain," said Kurt as he toddled through the front door, a six-pack of brown Huber bottles in one hand and a big metal salad bowl in the other, a taut lens of plastic film protecting some kind of coleslaw inside. "Sides courtesy of the Ursus Williamus." He was wearing a black t-shirt reading *PREFERS RAW MATERIALS* and was trailed by their old friend Doug Stacy.

"Whoa, check out all these college kids," said Doug with a grin, directly to Darlene. She smiled and hugged him. He kissed her back on the cheek.

"Hey Doug Stacy!" she said, her enthusiasm at least two dandelion bouquets deep. "Long time, no see, man."

Doug leaned into Kenny and hugged him with one free hand, the other holding a bag of tortilla chips. He always brought a bag of tortilla chips, usually picking them up at a gas station or grocery store at the last minute. For him, a *dish to pass* was always chips.

"More college kids!" he said to Kenny, who returned his little hug with a quick pat on the back. "You guys are all over the place now." Kenny had known Doug since kindergarten. They had been in all the same sports, cafeteria debates, and afterschool adventures around the East Side together, but Doug had a very precise idea about what work was for. Kurt had recently gotten Doug a job at the Willy Bear, but everyone knew that a "real job at Oscar" was what he wanted. That big meat factory on the North Side, with its blinking black smokestack ringed in red and white, the Mecca of American lunch meat, the home of the Wienermobile. Everyone knew the famous "Oscar Mayer Wiener" jingle, but Doug's intentions had nothing to do with the delicacy itself. Ever since he was fifteen or sixteen, Doug had talked about owning property—and in surprisingly concrete terms. "Once I get that job at Oscar," he'd say, "the parties are all gonna be at my house." Or "After I've been at Oscar a few years, I'll probably build a garage with a little apartment upstairs." He knew that a lot of people in the neighborhood around "Oscar" worked there, had good jobs, regardless of whatever people were doing over around the Capitol or down at the university.

"So, what's this chicken we're all so excited about?" asked Kurt.

"Come on, I'll show you," replied Kenny. All four walked like a little train into the small kitchen around the corner, where Linda sat looking at her old copy of *The Joy of Cooking*.

"Put that away, Mrs. McLuher. The chicken heroes have arrived."

"Hello there, Kurt," said Linda, giving him a friendly hug. "And Doug, good to see you. It's been a little while."

"Hi, Mrs. McLuher," said Doug, with a nod.

Kenny looked at Kurt. "Okay, Willy Bear head chef. I've never actually grilled chicken before. Just brats and hot dogs and stuff like that. What's the secret?"

"*Head chef*? Surely you jest. Put meat on the heat. Heat the meat. Eat the heated meat." There ensued a mild round of polite snickering. "Really, it's pretty simple. Maybe brush it every once in a while with some kind of salad dressing or something. You can just test it by tapping it."

"I already started the charcoal," said Linda, putting away the recipe book. "Kurt's technique sounds pretty good. Your dad used to marinate the meat sometimes. I guess that's probably about the same as brushing it with oil."

Kurt touched his nose. "Exactly. Come on, captain. Let's see if you have the chef in you." They went out onto the deck in back, where Linda had set up the grill.

The smell of lighter fluid wafted across the deck like a ghost. Kenny noticed the afternoon light falling on the side of the house, then shifted his attention to the flaming coals. He had, in fact, cooked any number of hot dogs and even a few hamburgers on this very grill, but none until after his dad had died. Harlan always worked the grill, and Kenny had just been the kid who ate what his parents made. Not until he had a couple of years of college under his belt had he tried cooking in any real capacity, and even then, most of it was of the Oscar Mayer variety anyway.

They watched the charcoal slow its glow. "It's got to ash over before you start," said Kurt. "Then it will be ready."

"Yeah," said Kenny, who remembered his parents saying this. Or maybe he had read it on the bag. Educated man that he was.

Once the charcoal was ready, Linda brought the chicken out and slid all those breasts and thighs and legs out onto the grill. Kurt and Kenny began tending the meat—tapping it with metal tongs as the meat underwent its foretold transformation.

Doug lit a cigarette. "Funny," he said, blowing smoke off to one side. "We're, like, eating the same kind of way the cavemen did."

"Grilled chicken?" asked Darlene, an eyebrow half-up. Kenny knew she was preparing a remark.

"Well," said Doug, taking a nervous draw, "grilled *something*. Like mammoth or sabertooth and stuff like that."

Surprisingly, Darlene said nothing. "Mammoth, but on a spit," she finally added. Doug laughed a little.

"Seriously," said Kurt, turning a breast over with the tongs. "Figuring out how to heat the meat you just killed, that must have been something."

"Especially for the animal," said Darlene, sipping her Huber.

"Okay, smart ass," said Kurt, the readiest of all of them to engage Darlene. "The animal wouldn't have felt a thing. He'd have already been speared or run off a cliff or whatever."

"Ah yes, and when do we go out spearing and cliff-pushing?" asked Darlene.

"No need," said Kurt, "Kenny's mom did all the spearing for us."

She had, in a way. In the sense that, by buying all that extra chicken, she had encouraged Kenny to invite his old friends over, thereby making it inevitable that their convening take place over the food.

"Hey Kenny," said Doug, who had broken open the bag of chips and was still chewing on one. "You're always reading history and stuff like that. When *did* cavemen figure out how to cook meat, anyway?"

"No idea. We never got back to prehistoric cooking."

"College," said Kurt, slapping Kenny good-naturedly. "What the hell is it good for if you can't learn the basic timeline of when we learned how to grill out? As a *species,* man?"

He tapped at a thigh then turned it around.

"Hey, I did learn something last week from a guy at the Willy Bear," said Kurt. "You know that all the street names, just about all of them around here, are signers of the U.S. Constitution?"

"Signed two hundred years ago last year," said Linda, who had just come out of the kitchen. "Didn't you all learn this when you were at Lowell?"

"Two hundred years," said Doug mildly. "Huh."

"Hamilton, Sherman, Rutledge," said Kurt, "and Franklin, Madison, of course, all the obvious ones."

"All the dead patriarchs you can name," said Darlene. "Whose servants cooked their meat over an open flame!" Kenny couldn't tell if she was joking—the first part sounded like the beginning of a diatribe, but then she seemed to let up in a self-deprecating way that allowed her to stand by the first thing without being too serious about it.

"I'm *glad* all those guys are dead right now so we don't have to share any of this chicken," said Doug, rubbing his stomach. "Or this beer."

Kenny was surprised that it had only really occurred to him recently that all those streets were named after Constitution signers. He and Darlene had just joked about it at Mickey's. His mom was surely right: he had probably learned this fact in elementary school, but the historical stuff that started to get his attention back then was more related to conflict, danger, war, things like battles, even the really unjust ones he would learn the nuances of much later. All those little stories he used to write always had him as the protagonist, as most children's stories do, but he always seemed to surround his own character with those of his friends—including at least one or two of those standing around the grill with him now, drinking Hubers and tapping thighs for doneness. Was this where most stories came from?

"I ran into a guy this morning who I think may have been French," said Kenny, his mind mingling history and geography as a result of all the dead-white-men talk. "On the river, fishing." He told them about the walk home from the Pinckney, the yelling from down by the water, the musky who joined the smaller fish on the end of the guy's line.

"Whoa," said Kurt. "That happened to me once, with my uncle, on Monona. Well, *to* my uncle, but I was with him. He had a bluegill on his hook and this big-ass musky just chomped on."

"That's exactly what happened to this French guy," said Kenny.

"But think about it—the hook is already inside the bluegill, or at least wedged pretty fully in his mouth"—he made a sudden twisting gesture with the tongs, to illustrate—"so the musky pretty much has a choice. Getting hooked himself would be pretty random. He could just let go if things got dicey."

The chicken was done, and Kurt began to tong the meat onto a platter Linda had brought over and left on a little metal table next to the grill. Kurt didn't signal he was going to tell what happened to the musky in the end. Having established that the fish had a choice, the story was over.

"Yeah," said Doug, not an angler as far as Kenny knew but suddenly impassioned by the hypothetical dilemma of the musky, "but like, if it twisted around and stuff"—still holding his beer, he nonetheless moved his hands quickly clockwise a few degrees, like he was driving and steering to avoid something that had just popped out in the road—"the fish's mouth would be, like, in a position to where it would get partly hooked, then *blam!* You got him."

"Yeah," said Kurt, irritated someone had kept the musky prospect alive, "but now you have a musky on your four-pound test or whatever little line you have, and you have to bring him in. A *musky*."

"I don't know about the pounds, but the thing for *me* is, if you yanked, you could probably bring him up out of the water." *Yanked.* If Doug was going to get the job at Oscar Mayer for any length of time, he'd probably have to sound a little more like he knew about fishing. Still, Kenny could see how engaged Doug was in this little tale they were all now sharing, like a French guy about to capture a musky on the Yahara River.

The food was ready, but Kenny still wondered: what if the French guy had caught that unexpected, valiant fish?

The FRENCH attack!

A WAR THRILLER written by Kenny McLuher, age 11

CHAPTER I

My squad was in the mess hall when the intercom sounded. "These men please report to my office: Kenny McLuher, Kurt Lemke, Brad Vogel, Rob Henning, Doug Stacy, and Brian Berry." "That's us. Maybe it's another mission!" said Kurt excitedly. "Let's go guys," I said.

When we got there the captain said, "Men, I have an assignment for you. The French have my son prisoner on an Island in the Atlantic ocean. Your mission is to find him, rescue him, and bring him to me." "Yes sir!" I said. We boarded the plane at 2:00 that day.

Our pilot flew over the island at 3:00 and we parachuted out. When we landed we took off our parachutes and walked deeper into the jungle. We would later find out the mistake we had made leaving our parachutes out in the open.

A French battalion was patrolling the island when they found our parachutes. "Americans. Some where on this island. We must find them" said the French sargeant, licking his lips. We were hiking along the east side of the island when we saw the French soldiers. "Hands up, Americans!" they pointed their guns at us. "Now!" I yelled. We all pulled out our submachine guns and all you could hear was RAT-A-TAT-TAT!

CHAPTER II

It was their blood that spilled. "All right, men. We've got to get to the captain's son, and fast. Undress the dead soldiers and change clothes with them. That way we'll get to Bob (the captain's son)," I said. As soon as we were changed to look like French soldiers, we started toward the barricks.

When we got to the gate, the guard said, "State your business." "Special orders to see the prisoner." "Enter." When we got inside, Bob looked at us. "You're not French soldiers, you're Americans," he said. I said, "We've come to rescue you. Now let's get out of here before they discover us." "Hold on," said Bob, "I know something. It's a secret tunnel leading to the Jungle." "Let's go!" I said.

When we started to come out of the tunnel there were French soldiers waiting for us. The sargeant said, "You Americans are very persistent. Too bad we knew about this tunnel. It was all a trap. You see, if we hadn't of been here you would have been home free. But we're tired of wasting time with you. So you are to be executed tomorrow at dawn! To the prison with you!"

CHAPTER III

"A fine mess we've got ourselves into," said Doug. "Have any more explosives, Brian?" said Kurt. "Why yes! We'll lure the guard over, knock him out, light my explosive, and throw it on him, then split!" "Far out!" I said.

We plotted the escape. "Okay, Brad, do your stuff!" I said. "Aauughaaghaa! Help guard, come quick!" yelled Rob. Brian ran to the door. "Come quick! He's having an attack!"

The guard rushed to the door and ran inside. "Now!" Brian thought. He hit the guard with a stick and knocked him out cold.

"Take his gun, Brad!" I yelled. "Let's go!"

We escaped from the enemy camp and Bob said, "The safest place would be the north beach. Let's go!" We radioed for a chopper and got one. When we were home we got purple hearts and special thanks from the captain, Bob and Bob's mom and Bob's girlfriend Darlene. It was finally over. The adventure was finally over.

Dorcely Catering

Kenny sat up in bed. The dream had been just like one of those stories he had written so many of as a boy. The *French*? What was that all about? The heroic soldiers he and his friends played in the dream were the kinds of adults he had imagined in the fifth or sixth grade. What Kenny remembered most—and what he took most seriously—was the very end: the battalion's return home following their daring rescue mission. For months now, all of Kenny's dreams seemed to be about home.

The French as villainous captors, the cast of inner-child characters, and home: only a dream could concoct a mix this odd. Digesting it all at once, just a few seconds after waking up, had put Kenny a little on edge. Maybe to confirm that he was out of that world and back in the real one, he checked his alarm clock. 10:02 a.m. Remembering the total lack of responsibility he currently enjoyed, he relaxed a little and began to ponder the clock itself. It had always had just two jobs to do: display the time and wake Kenny up for school or work. It had done this for years, its glowing red numbers unvarying and vigilant. It had been by his side through college and come back to Talmadge Street with him.

It was only a tool, really. A small brown box, sitting rigidly on the table as it displayed an ever-advancing set of figures meaning different things at different times. Seven-ten: *time to get dressed!* Two-thirty: *pick-up basketball in Wirth Court Park, in just ten minutes!* Three-thirty: *shit, I can't believe I'm going to bed this late. I have a shift in four hours!* Popping out periodically like this, time nonetheless lived grounded in its small rectangle.

Kenny felt a shiver of ambivalence. Maybe he should start looking at the smaller things for guidance. Things like this clock. Was this the stars-versus-mud thing again? He considered it further. In a way, time itself roamed free, while the little electric or wind-up bodies of actual clocks littered the world, more or less aligned with each other but each one trapped on its own local table or wall. The wandering of time was locked in too, in a way, programmed to move in the same way, yet it followed a path one could locate from everywhere. *Like Orion,* thought Kenny. Not always visible from everywhere, but vast and true. Like stars.

But indentured as it was, Kenny's little brown electric alarm clock was always immediately visible when he woke up. Always right there, time incarnate.

The mud, he thought, and this gave him a boost. That funny little poem again.

He got up and pulled on his jeans. It was mid-morning and already pretty warm. He felt a little better about being back in his house, if even just for the time being. If the little clock was like the mud, thought Kenny—time itself, in a form you could handle—then so were all these people he had known for so long, back around him now. His own mother, alone now in her own house, sometimes sharing it with Kate and Taylor. Of course, Linda also had friends and did plenty of other things, at home and well beyond Talmadge Street. Yet Kenny still thought of her primarily in relation to his father, sister, and niece, and to the house itself. It was the story they held most in common.

His friends were part of his story, too. Even his recent adventure with Darlene was like a chapter in a book that had begun when they were kids. So was Tracy's letter now, even though she had no idea who Darlene or his other friends were. Like his family, these were the real people he could most focus on, close up, to understand where he was supposed to be and what he was supposed to do. These were the people who could guide him next. Like the mud in the poem.

Yet Taylor's part in the story was less neat, less analogous. Sure, for some reason he had told her that the stars were fixed and that *we* were the ones always moving. But sometimes the star you thought you could see was just leftover light, the memory of a star no longer there—he had forgotten to mention this detail during his storytelling improvisations. They were as changing as they were fixed. Because she was five years old, Taylor was changing fast, too, faster than anyone else, growing like a sprout and full of new words and ideas. The others seemed to notice this much less, maybe because they had grown up and were around her the whole time, just going through their days together.

What surprised Kenny more about being around Taylor, as opposed to the others, was her keen imaginative interest in the people and places she knew. Especially when she was falling asleep, or when Kenny was trying to get her to. Maybe all little kids did this. His mom and Kate liked to reminisce about his dad, but Taylor's imagination lit up brighter than ever right when it should have been shutting down. And it was the stories that took her *away from home* that lit her up so much, thought Kenny, even if she wanted those stories to be about people she knew and loved.

Kenny walked out of his room. The aroma of coffee hit him in the hallway, and it occurred to him that Taylor would keep growing and might even get a fellowship of her own one day, as Darlene had. Or that she might find some way to leave her home for a university in some other state, as he did. It was startling that such a normal idea would bother him. Wasn't a smart person supposed to take paths like these? Of course, a proud uncle would want this. Heading off toward the horizon could lead Taylor to learn more stories and maybe even do something important with them, sweeping her into other, more exciting places. She had grown up with mud around her. What was the matter with stars leading you away, as long as they were the right ones?

* * * * *

When he came into the Willy Bear that afternoon, Kenny was surprised to see the fisherman sitting at the bar talking with Kurt. He knew it was the fisherman because of the worn Expos cap, which the guy was now wearing backwards.

"Captain," said Kurt, greeting Kenny. "What can I get you?"

Kenny moved up to the bar and looked at his watch: it was only four-thirty, and he had just come in to say hello. But maybe a beer, why not?

"A Huber, I guess. Just a quick one." He was standing next to the fisherman.

"Kenny, meet Laurent. He's from Quebec."

The fisherman turned to Kenny and cocked his head. "Hello. Aren't you the guy that got me my net the other day?"

"Ah, yeah, that was me." *Quebec.* Not France, not Brazil. "How's it going?"

"Laurent and I were just talking a little history here, captain." Kurt didn't seem busy yet.

"Hey Kenny," said Doug, washing glasses over at the sink.

Kenny hailed Doug then turned back to Kurt. "What kind of history?"

"The history of the fucking English," said Kurt, which earned him a lifted beer from the fisherman. "And the history of you looking for a catering job."

"I have a catering company," said Laurent, making a Gallic move with his mouth and cheek for a second, to announce an imminent modification. "Just a little one." Kenny remembered hearing his accent the first time and trying to pinpoint where it was from.

"Aha," said Kenny. "I guess our bartender here told you I've been working in catering."

"And that you're on hiatus at the moment," said Laurent, looking at his beer, "which could be an interesting fact for me."

"Is that so?"

Laurent smiled and loosened some more. "My wife and I run the thing, we're called Dorcely Catering. My last name is Dorcely. Original, yeah?"

Kenny smiled politely.

"Well, as I was just telling your barman friend here, we're small but trying to grow a little. Just a little." He flashed an inch of air between his thumb and forefinger. "But enough that we need somebody who knows how to serve and set up and clean and all those kinds of things."

It *was* an interesting fact. Across the bar, Kurt made an expression that said *I told you so.*

"So have you advertised the position?"

Laurent laughed. "No, no. No advertising. We've only been here a little over a year. I thought I'd go out and have a beer in a nearby bar first." He nodded toward Kurt. "Bartenders know."

"We know," echoed Kurt. "And we know *caterers*, too. Who happen to be out of work."

"Maybe we could hear a little more about what you did last?" said Laurent, rotating on his stool toward Kenny a few more degrees.

"Is this an interview?"

"Not really. Not formally."

Kurt went to the walk-in, and Kenny and Laurent continued to talk. Business began picking up: a few more customers filtered in, mostly for a beer, but a couple ordered burgers. The last burger order was a little loud, temporarily pausing the conversation. Kenny took a sip of his Huber and looked toward the rear of the bar and saw the redhaired woman at her table again. Laurent noticed.

"Somebody you know?"

Kenny scratched his chin. "No, not really. I don't think so. She was here last time I came by to see Kurt. He didn't know her, either." He looked at her for a full second more. Something about her seemed familiar. "Anyway," he said.

They resumed their previous conversation, which turned from Kenny's work at UVA and the Pinckney Plaza to Montreal, Laurent's hometown. Laurent had studied history, too, at UQAM—one of Montreal's largest universities—before dropping out to work in his father's restaurant. His dad had come from Haiti, sent by his affluent parents in the mid-fifties to study at the University of Montreal. After the dictator François Duvalier came to power in Port-au-Prince, fresh and more economically diverse waves of Haitian immigrants began rolling up the Saint Lawrence. Laurent's grandparents left their country and ended up in France, where they spent the rest of their lives quite poor. Laurent's dad quit school and used his remaining money to open a little restaurant, where increasing numbers of younger countrymen began to assemble and discuss Montreal's "Haitian community." Laurent's mother got a job waiting tables there. She was what he called a *Québécoise pure laine*—a "pure wool Quebecker," a descendant of original settlers from Picardy.

"Farmer-lumberjack-priest hybrid, the strongest and weirdest predominant settler strain in North America," said Laurent, ordering a second beer. He was enjoying the mix of job interview and history-nerd chat as much as Kenny was. Probably because, for Laurent, "history" wasn't just dates and names. It was where you came from. And who.

"We don't have to go all the way back to the fur trade," said Kenny, "but I did have one question for you about Montreal."

"Let's hear it."

"Well, it's about John Wilkes Booth," said Kenny, his eyebrows knitted into a serious line now. He decided not to share his recurring dreams about Lincoln. "I was reading about him last year, and I always remembered the part about the assassination and him being chased and finally caught, all that."

"Yes," said Laurent, "*Sic semper tyrannis!*"

Kenny pictured Lincoln's dashing killer yelling Virginia's state motto, after he shot the president, then leapt down onto the stage. Laurent's full-bodied Booth quote should have felt more disturbing, given Kenny's unusual relationship with the sixteenth president, but it was impressive that he knew it at all. Plus, all the talk about the passing of time, Haitian dictators, muskies, and the possibility of a job had taken the edge off.

"That's right," said Kenny. "But he had been meeting with co-conspirators in Montreal. How did people pass through that border so easily in 1864? I mean, he was a famous actor."

"I know, it's wild," said Laurent, noncommittal but apparently aware of the basics.

"But why *Montreal*?" asked Kenny, comfortable admitting a historical fact he probably should have known and which bothered him. "I know it's Canada, but we think of Canada as a haven for escaped slaves. Like, it's the *North*. Why Montreal?"

"Fucking English," said Laurent, smiling even bigger.

Kurt came back from his latest trip to the walk-in, lowering his voice dramatically.

"Hey Kenny, Red's back, did you see?" he asked, thumbing surreptitiously toward the rear of the bar.

Kenny waved him off. "Kurt thinks that girl back there likes me," he said. Laurent laughed.

"Not *thinks*. Just *senses*," said Kurt. He lowered his voice again.

"Last time she was writing some *mighty strange poems* in that notebook of hers."

All three men looked back at the redhaired woman, all of them simultaneously pretending to be looking at other objects in the vicinity. Oblivious, she was writing feverishly in her spiral notebook, stopping to claw at her neck and chest every few seconds, like she had a terrible itch.

"Hm," said Laurent, curious and possibly a little disturbed.

"*Forgive me,*" said Kurt in a near-whisper. "It's what she was writing, line after line, in her notebook, that last time."

"And," added Kenny conspiratorially, "she fell asleep, right at the table."

Laurent gave a low whistle. "Bartenders know," he said, simply.

"Hello, chummy-chums," said a woman who had suddenly appeared next to Kenny. She and Laurent exchanged a European-style kiss on each cheek.

"Boys, meet my wife Kim."

"Hello," said Kim, her eyes and Kenny's meeting for the first real time. "Hey, didn't you go to East?"

Kenny recognized her. "Yeah. Kenny McLuher. You're Kim Fratelle, aren't you?"

"Kim Dorcely now. When did you graduate? Weren't you, like, two or three years after me?"

"Two," said Kenny, who had nursed a crush on Kim Fratelle for a full semester before two important cruelties of male adolescence occurred to him: first, that she was two years older than him, and second, that girls matured so much faster than boys. This had made Kim Fratelle the equivalent of five or six years his senior, adjusting for maturity inflation. He felt a latent rush of pride that she had not only just recognized him but addressed him as an equal.

"Nice to meet you, Kenny. Or meet you *again,* or whatever."

"Kenny's trying out for the job," said Laurent.

Kim brightened. "You cater? Food service? Cook?"

"The ordinary catering stuff," he said, diffident but also suddenly professional.

"He studied history, too," said Laurent. Then, looking at Kenny, he added, "and he was this close to helping me land that *maskinongé*." He clapped Kenny on the shoulder.

I'm in like Flynn, thought Kenny. He looked back toward the redhaired woman and saw that she was scratching at her neck and chest again, still writing quickly in her notebook.

"Well, Kenny," said Kim. "When do you start?"

"Wait a second," said Laurent. "He hasn't said yes yet! Or seen the kitchen."

"I'm game," said Kenny.

"Well, let's get you set up to see the place first," said Laurent. "Our kitchen is just around the corner. Do you want to come by tomorrow? You could start the day after tomorrow if you were ready—we have a small wedding and could *really, really, really* use a hand by then."

"Yes," said Kenny.

"Forgive me," said a flat-sounding voice from behind them. Kenny wheeled around and saw the redhaired woman, standing a foot away from him, clutching her notebook and purse to her chest. Four thin scratches, slightly pink, ran in parallel across the front of her neck. She reminded him of a woman in one of his early Lincoln dreams. She was staring right at him.

"Forgive me," she said again, louder this time, then turned and walked quickly out the front door of the bar.

That was weird is what someone would have said if they hadn't been so taken by surprise. Instead, there was silence, then a collective exhale and a series of glances, of solidarity or shared witness.

"That was weird," said Laurent.

Drought

"When exactly is this heat wave going to break?"

Kate sat back on the couch, mopping her brow with a washcloth she had just pulled out of the fridge. Taylor was sitting at the little table Linda had installed by the front windows, next to the television. Preoccupied by the drawing she was working on, she didn't seem to care about the lack of air conditioning in her grandmother's house.

"It is hot," said Linda, in the kitchen doing dishes. "But at least with this drought it's not so humid. Could be worse."

"How's that, Mom?"

"What?"

Kate sat up and yelled, "Never mind." She re-balled up the washcloth and tamped down her temples, one at a time. "I'm ready for a cold front," she said to no one in particular.

Kenny walked through the front door and dropped his backpack next to the cabinet where everybody put their keys and wallets and sunglasses.

"Hey boss," he said to Kate. She held her hand up, and he slapped it.

"The catering kitchen is pretty nice," he said, thinking someone might ask. "It's little, compared with the servery in Charlottesville, and a lot smaller than the Pinckney, but I kinda like that."

"It's just a family thing, or...?"

"Well, it's their own company, pretty pro, but yes. It's just them. And now, me."

"Cool. I thought you were interviewing still."

"I think they hired me during that conversation at the bar. I just didn't know it yet."

"Lucky duck," said Kate, genuinely happy for her brother but also a little jealous about how positive he sounded talking about something having to do with work. "Let me know if another position opens up."

"Sure. They were just talking about how they were hoping to rent a few more rooms in the next building and start a nursing home on the side."

Kate threw a couch pillow at him. "Seriously, I'd work at a place like that. When do you start?"

"Day after tomorrow, there's a wedding. Small, or kinda small, but a wedding. I expect I'll be out of here by seven at the latest. It won't go late, but I'm thinking it'll be a ten-hour shift." He was, as his grandparents would have said, full of vim and vigor.

"Speaking of work," said Kate, getting up slowly. "I'm out. See you tomorrow. Taylor, have fun with Grandma."

"I will," said Taylor, still working diligently on her drawing. "I'm going upstairs to tape this to the wall." She got up immediately and took her work up the stairs.

"Hey hon," said Linda, appearing in the kitchen doorway, rubbing some oil into one of her cast iron skillets. "Your friend Wayne called again. They're on their way."

"That's right, the Dead shows," muttered Kenny, who hadn't heard from Wayne for a couple of weeks. The new job development had erased the memories, fairly weak already, of talking to Wayne about how he might swing by after the shows at Alpine Valley. He was looking forward to seeing Wayne again. They had shared a slice of their lives together somewhere, if not all that closely. He just didn't know yet how much time this new job would allow for visiting.

Kenny took a shower to cool down, then came back downstairs and started reading the *Capital Times* that had just landed on their stoop. The big news was depressing as always but felt even heavier, given the heat: some scientist at NASA had noted that "the greenhouse effect" had made the first five months of 1988 the hottest stretch since anyone had been keeping records of those trends and announced that "global warming" had officially begun. "You can say that again," said Kenny to himself, already perspiring enough to wipe off his forehead. The article warned that the Southern and Midwestern regions of the United States were likely to start experiencing droughts and heat waves more often than before.

A half-hour or so later, Wayne knocked at the front door.

"Hey man!" he said, standing by the front door stoop and wearing an Uncle Sam-style hat with a pin of Jerry Garcia on the front. He made a peace sign. "No comment!"

Next to him, in a bootleg Molly Hatchet concert t-shirt, stood Fats Trustell, Wayne's childhood friend Kenny had played Dungeon Lord with. On Wayne's other side was a skinny brown-haired guy Kenny had never seen, wearing a dashiki that fit a little too tightly, tennis shorts, and loafers, without socks. He looked a little high—which, given where these guys had just spent the past few days, was no surprise—but he also smelled like gin. His shorts were on backwards.

"You know Fats," said Wayne, still grinning open-mouthed.

"Hey Fats," said Kenny.

"This is Stanley from Minnesota," said Wayne, nodding at the new guy, who stared ahead stoically. "We met him at the shows. He's along for the ride, wants to crash with us here tonight, if that's all right."

"Sure. What's up, Stanley? You all just staying for one night?"

"May I urinate behind those bushes?" replied Stanley, in a monotone.

"Aha, yeah, well—come on in, you can use the..."

"No, it's fine, I'd prefer those bushes if it's all the same to you."

Kenny found the stranger's insistence a little unusual. But, as his dad used to say, *when nature calls, she calls*. He wasn't one to stand between a peeing Minnesotan and a couple of conifers.

"Yes, we got to roll on back tomorrow, hoss," said Wayne, scratching a nascent beard. "It's a long-ass drive to Virginia."

Stanley stepped quickly to the bushes and began to wrestle with his shorts, taking a full minute to wrangle them down far enough to free himself to pee, unfettered. The group took casual note then turned back to look nonchalantly at one another, out of respect for Stanley's privacy. Not that he seemed concerned about that.

Wayne grinned. "Behind the bushes? He seems to be getting *behind* mixed up with *in front* a lot."

"Ha ha, yeah," said Kenny, hoping the transition to a new conversation would lead them into the house. "Why don't we go inside?"

"Whew, yeah. You got AC? It's sure hot up here in Wes-consin."

"Sorry, no."

"Still," said Wayne, looking around the living room as if he had just parachuted into a farm field in Normandy. He looked at all four walls and then the ceiling. "It's pretty cool in here, nice and comfortable."

"These must be your Dead Fan friends," said Linda, coming down the stairs.

"Dead *heads*, Mom," said Kenny, sounding like an embarrassed teenager.

"Well, welcome to our house, you all."

"I'm Wayne," said Wayne, removing his Uncle Sam hat. He held his hand out courteously to Linda, who took it and smiled.

"I'm Linda McLuher." She almost always said both her names when introducing herself to her kids' adult friends, observing formality but leaving open the possibility that one might use her first name.

"A pleasure to meet you, Mrs. McLuher."

Fats stepped up and put out his hand, too. "Hello, Mrs. McLuher. I'm Ronnie."

"Nice to meet you, too, Ronnie." She shook his hand, too, and smiled again.

Surprised that Fats had used a given name Kenny had never heard, Kenny realized that Stanley had not come into the house yet.

"Hey, where's your friend?" he asked.

"Aw, he's not really my friend, he's more like a Dead show, um, *co-traveler*," said Wayne, looking at Kenny then Linda.

"Well," said Linda. "Bring him on in. You all hungry?"

"Um, sure, I could eat," said Fats, looking at Wayne.

"Yes, that'd be great, Mrs. McLuher," said Wayne. "Let me go get Stanley. I'll be right back."

Fats stood in place while Wayne, then Kenny, went back out the front door.

Outside, Stanley had finished his business in the bushes and had pulled his backward tennis shorts back up into what passed for their normal position. He hadn't moved otherwise, staring up into the silver maple tree that towered over them from behind the Gruszkas' yard.

"Um, hey, Stanley, you want to get your stuff and come on in here with the rest of us?" said Wayne, a little louder and slower than usual. He reminded Kenny of how his Uncle Bill once addressed a blind concession stand worker at a Reds game.

Stanley waited a couple of seconds then turned around and walked past Wayne and Kenny, directly into the house. As Kenny stood aside to motion Wayne back in before him, he could already hear the newcomer in the living room.

"Hello, I am Stanley from Minnesota," said the voice.

"Hello Stanley," said Linda, as Wayne and Kenny came back into the room. "Welcome to our house."

"Thank you heartily for your welcoming words," said Stanley, with an unironic bow. Linda smiled. As a seasoned fifth-grade teacher, she was pretty unfazed by less conventional styles of communication.

* * * * *

Sitting around the living room sipping Diet Cokes or glasses of water, they talked. Wayne and Fats described the Dead shows at Alpine Valley, a farm hillside that had been converted into a major outdoor concert venue. Some of the concerts in the weeklong series had been stronger than others, but after a few days, the relentless heat and dust had taken much of the joy out of the experience.

"You had to get your water from these trucks they brought in," said Fats. "And after a couple days those Port-a-Potties were, well, let's just say, *no longer a option.*"

"Aw, Fats, is that really necessary?" asked Wayne, looking like he had smelled something unpleasant. "There's ladies present."

"That's kind of you, Wayne," said Linda. "But Ronnie, you go by *Fats?*"

Fats grinned as Kenny began to squirm slightly in his seat. His mother could seem unabashedly country sometimes—direct, maybe, not shy about referring to parts of bodies or words that might otherwise have seemed impolite in their particular society. Class, region, whatever.

"Yeah, my friends always called me that, Mrs. McLuher. But usually with adults, I mean parents and so on, I use my real name."

"I like *Fats,*" said Linda. "I had a friend at Dixie—that was my high school—who went by that nickname. A boy, of course. A girl would never choose that name. Not only did he not *mind,* to the rest of us it never felt, I don't know, like a put-down."

"Either way," said Fats, who seemed to have had this conversation before.

Someone knocked at the door.

"You got more friends coming over?" asked Linda, energy in her voice. She was up before you knew it, headed for the door.

"Not that I know of," said Kenny, staying put.

"Darlene!" said Linda, still sounding caffeinated. "Come on in." Darlene walked into the living room and waved shyly at those assembled.

"Hey Kenny, I didn't know you had company. I was just going to see if you wanted to go for a walk. My cousins are coming over in a little while."

"Hey Darlene," said Kenny, a little hesitant about taking any more walks with Darlene just yet. "These are friends from Virginia. Guys, this is my friend Darlene." She glanced at Kenny for a half-second, maybe because he had used the word *friend.*

He made fuller introductions. Hands were shaken, more Diet Cokes poured in the kitchen. Fats introduced himself to Darlene as *Ronnie.* She seemed a little nervous, but Kenny couldn't put his finger on it. Maybe a little uncertain about joining this group for an unspecified period of time, still unsure of what kind of gathering it was.

"Darlene," said Linda, who had stayed longer in the room than she usually did when Kenny's friends came over, "do you have funny nicknames in your family?"

"No, not really," said Darlene, dutifully. "I mean, my mom is named Bridget, but my aunt sometimes calls her *Birdie*."

"See?" said Linda. "I'm not surprised, but I *am*, kind of. That's one thing I've noticed since we moved here, when I first got married: not as many people have nicknames like where I grew up. You know, like *Fats*." She gestured toward Fats, who lifted his Diet Coke in mock tribute. Kenny could tell he liked Linda. "Ronnie here goes by *Fats*, which was what a fellow I knew growing up used to call himself." She took a hearty swig of her Diet Coke.

"Oh, I see, yeah," said Darlene, now more uncomfortable than anyone else in the room. Strangely, Linda didn't seem to pick up on this.

"I just like when people keep their nicknames in adulthood," she said. "It's so rare in Madison, anyway. It reminds me a little bit of Kentucky. I mean, some of the people we knew at UK, and *especially* the people they talked about in their families, and especially people from the mountains. *Whistle Cat, Celery, Gazzie, Gilly, Diddy...*"

"Okay, Mom, enough old home week," said Kenny.

"Naw, I think that's great," said Wayne. "Central Virginia's like that, too. Course we're on the *other* side of the mountains I believe you're talking about, Mrs. McLuher." Linda laughed along with Wayne. Kenny noticed Fats had relaxed significantly into his chair. Stanley was tenting his fingers, leaning strangely to one side and apparently absent from most of what was happening. Kenny and Darlene seemed to be the only ones not yet attuned to the direction the conversation was taking.

"So what do you guys do?" asked Darlene, who had just taken a surreptitious peek back at the front door.

"I work for the university," said Wayne. "Maybe Kenny already told you. Catering."

"I'm working a part-time thing right now in my stepdad's furniture store," said Fats.

Darlene fidgeted in her chair, like she was either not yet finished with something or not yet satisfied by it. She looked at the mounted fantasy warrior on Fats' t-shirt and kept a neutral facial expression. "One of my African American friends from college just called me," she finally said. "She also has a parent with a furniture store. She's working in it right now."

Fats nodded his head. Darlene took a nervous drink from her Diet Coke.

"She's so sick of the way she gets treated. She's African American."

"Yes, you said that already," said Fats, smiling obliquely.

"Do you happen to have any cranberries and oat bran?" asked Stanley. "I have a very specific eating method."

Linda stood up. "Let me see, I probably have some dried cranberries. I don't know about the oat bran."

"It has to be raw cranberries, but frozen will do, if you have some of those." Wayne and Fats swapped a glance.

"Uh, well, hey—I can just run to Woodman's and pick some up. What kind of oat bran do you like?" she asked perkily.

"Organic," he said, looking back out the window at the front yard.

"Don't worry, Mrs. McLuher," said Wayne, shooting Stanley a stern look. "We can do with whatever you have."

"It's no worry, I just need to make a little run. I won't be half an hour." She let herself out the side door.

"Man, what the hell?" said Wayne to Stanley, who looked back, a little dazed.

"What?"

"Wayne, Wayne," said Fats. "It's fine, man, it's just for tonight."

Darlene looked at her watch. "So, Ronnie, how do you like, you know, living in the South?"

"I'm *from* the South. What do you mean?"

Wayne sat forward, more socially agile in this last half-hour than Kenny had ever seen him. "Y'all know I grew up in the South, but really I'm from Minnesota."

Stanley looked at Wayne as if a fresh plate of cranberries and oat bran had magically appeared before him. "How can you be from Minnesota? *I'm* from Minnesota. You're from somewhere else."

"That's true, if you get technical," said Wayne. "I'm from Waynesboro, no comment!"

"There you have it," said Stanley, turning back to ponder whatever he could see out the front window.

"*But*—" Wayne continued, raising a finger, "my grandpa was from Minnesota!"

Kenny had to admit this surprised him. "Did your dad grow up there, too?" he asked. Jim Halard hadn't come off as particularly Midwestern.

"No, Dad grew up in Waynesboro, like I did. My grandma was also from Waynesboro. She just passed five years ago."

"I'm sorry about that," said Kenny.

"It's all right," replied Wayne. "No, my grandpa was in World War Two, and he met my grandma at a dance. That's about all I know, really. He married her after only a month. They lived on a army base for a year somewhere, I can't remember where exactly, then they came to Waynesboro to settle down. My grandma's hometown and all."

"Aha," said Kenny, who often became more interested in people when they started talking about their families. "My neighbors met at a dance. He was in the Army, too. Second World War, too."

Darlene looked at her watch but didn't say anything.

"That's cool," said Wayne.

"Yeah, my grandpa was in the war, too," said Kenny. "And Glenn next door—he's that neighbor I was talking about—he's kinda like a grandpa type. He's from Green Bay."

"Green Bay Packers!" said Wayne. "No comment, though. I'm for the Vikings. My dad is, too."

"Wait, what?" said Kenny.

Visibly nervous about what was beginning to resemble a fraternity reunion in the genealogy department of a public library, Darlene leaned purposefully toward Fats.

"So, like, how does Madison *seem* to you?" she asked.

Now it was Fats who was uncomfortable. "I'm not really sure what you mean," he said. Now he was the one looking at his watch.

"Being from the *South.* You know," she said, as if they had a shared secret.

"I'll actually be up 'north' later this fall," he said, air-quoting the word *north.*

"Oh," said Darlene. "Some kind of work?"

"Naw, not really. Got to go up and stay with my aunt, help her move. She's my stepdad's sister, she don't have kids, so, you know."

Darlene nodded politely. "Oh, where does she live?"

"Philadelphia. Never been there yet, so."

"I went to Penn!"

"Is that a school?" asked Fats.

"The University of Pennsylvania," said Kenny, slower than normal, as if to justify his place in this conversation. "It's where Darlene went to school. And she's going to grad school, too, this fall. She's doing a PhD in English, at Michigan."

Darlene ignored him. "You're going to *love* Philadelphia," she said, as if she were about to answer the winning question in a math contest. "You know it was the site of the country's first abolitionist society."

"That might interest your friend Kenny," said Fats. "He's the history guy."

"I know, I know," said Darlene, who had still not looked at Kenny. "I just think you'll really like the city. Speaking of *history,*" she said, finally looking at Kenny, if only for a second and with a bland smile, "there is a *ton* of African American history in Philadelphia. It's a very open place, and a *very big* city, too." She sat back in her seat.

"A big city like Ann Arbor?" asked Wayne, with a mischievous grin. Fats winked at him conspiratorially.

"Ann Arbor isn't a big city," replied Darlene, "but it's bigger than here."

"Maybe," added Kenny, starting to feel a little sour. Ann Arbor wasn't bigger, it was just somewhere else.

"And it's only grad school," she said.

"I'm only going up there for about a week," said Fats.

Darlene looked confused.

So did Kenny, a moment later, when Wayne fixed his gaze on Darlene and suddenly began speaking in a completely different voice.

"Let me tell *you* a little story, there, kiddo," he said, out of nowhere. He sounded like he was playing Santa Claus.

Kenny heard Linda come into the kitchen. "Hey you all, I just forgot my pocketbook. I'll probably need that." She came around the corner and into view. "So... what's going on?"

"Shh," said Kenny, his eyes still on Wayne. All eyes, including Stanley's, were now on Wayne. The occasional blink was Darlene's only movement at all.

"You probably know it," said Wayne. "I may have told it to you, about the Great Up North. Maybe we were paddlin' up in the Boundary Waters." He sounded a little like Laurent. *Up in da Boundary Wadders.* "It's the story of big Paul Bunyan, that great lumberjack of the North, who changed everything for us out here in the camps, don't ya know." *Dole-cha nole.*

Darlene blinked several times in a row, then her eyes drooped. Her torso loosened. Wayne was embodying the storytelling ghost of his Minnesota grandfather, or something, and whatever drug now coursed through the story was putting Darlene to sleep fast. It was like he was tucking her in.

Everyone in the room sat spellbound. Fats's eyes were wide, but he didn't feel sleepy at all. His mouth hung open a little. He was about to get to see the thing he had heard about. Stanley had the same facial expression he had had since they arrived, but his gaze was fixed on Wayne, who was describing how Babe the Blue Ox stomped down so hard in that earth that he created the Great Lakes. Darlene was obviously no longer trying to show her solidarity with abolitionists, or Black people in the American South, or Fats, or whoever she had been laboring so hard to display her support for. She was simply, suddenly, very tired.

Kenny beheld the thing, this phenomenon, with clarity, for the first time in his life. His head felt light but fresh, like a breeze was blowing against his mind, and he remembered feeling this in the kitchen at Birdwood Pavilion. He remembered telling "The Tar Baby" to Logan and watching him go gently to sleep. He remembered telling a story in the Catering servery, or at least starting one, about an old man and a mountain, just so he could use a particular voice to show his own connection to the deepest parts of the place he was in—to *natives*, in that same servery—and watching both of them go to sleep.

Logan and Tracy, but not Wayne. In both cases, Wayne had remained conspicuously awake. And he had grown up in Central Virginia. Kenny couldn't figure this out. Or why, now, Darlene was the only one in the room who could feel the sedative. Fats couldn't. Linda couldn't. Stanley couldn't. And now, here in his home, Kenny couldn't, either. Wayne, meanwhile, was in the trance of the storyteller, and Darlene had somehow inspired that. Why Darlene?

Kenny thought about bedtime, about trying to tuck Taylor in, make up stories, the fact that the kid wanted that to happen before she went to sleep. Watching Wayne speak in Upper Midwestern tongues like this and now lucidly recalling his own attempt at Uncle Remus—or, more specifically, his attempt to bring his own father's voice into his own, by "doing" Uncle Remus—Kenny suddenly wondered what made storytelling so different from other kinds of talking. Was it a form of poetry? Therapy?

As Wayne spoke in this new voice—or this old one, depending on how you looked at it—something else occurred to Kenny. Somehow, this thing happening right now, and that had happened to Kenny in Virginia, had to do with *places*: the one they were in, the others they had been imagining or talking about. Something about a place becoming real, concrete. Kenny had not gone to Virginia to go to college, as it turned out. He had gone there to inhabit a new place, to see what it was about—a little like his parents had, when they left Kentucky for Wisconsin. To come into a place from the outside, to understand what it meant.

Unlike his parents, though, Kenny expected full access when he landed. After all, hadn't his family come from the South? He could never really understand Virginia, which must have been why the history major had made sense. Wasn't history, in the end, the story of a place? Couldn't learning history teach you to story-tell your way into the truth of a place, even if it turned out the roots you thought you had there had been fashioned by *other* stories, ones that were popular, yet inaccurate in so many ways?

The storyteller misses some listeners, obviously. Fats wasn't sleeping, Linda wasn't sleeping, even Stanley wasn't sleeping. Yet Darlene was just about to fall over. Did this have something to do with *place* again, about resisting a place in the world? Darlene had seemed as insistent for Fats to reveal something about "the South" as she was to show she had transcended the smallness of her hometown. For her, taking wing was proof you had learned something special about injustice, about the smallness of others, something others at home with where they lived just couldn't see. That would free you.

Wayne finished his tale about Paul Bunyan and Babe—a nondescript, bedtime-story-variety improvisation in which the audience learned who Paul Bunyan was, that he had special strength and was impressive to all the regular-sized lumberjacks, that Babe was huge and awkward but really kind, and that they ultimately

wandered off together, as Wayne put it, "into the western sunset." What had struck Kenny, made him feel especially alert, was the accent, the strange voice Wayne had used to deliver the tale. He had seemed possessed.

When it was over, Darlene lay slumped over in the big armchair she had been in the whole time. Wayne just got up and walked into the kitchen, where he found a glass and poured himself some water from the faucet. Everyone else got up and, working together, moved Darlene gently to the couch, where she continued to snore, deeply asleep.

"Wow," said Stanley, who went back to looking out the front window as he had before. Fats just blinked his eyes repeatedly, then rubbed them, quiet as a mouse.

Wayne walked back into the room as if nothing had happened, the glass of water half-full in his hand. "Hey y'all," he said, oblivious. "What's going on? Looks like Darlene's had a big day." He drank the rest of the water in a single gulp.

Taylor came down the stairs, her drawing in her hand. "It looks like a sleepover!" she said, awed by the collection of people relaxing in her grandmother's house.

* * * * *

Later that night, after Darlene had left and everyone else had gone to bed, Kenny sat up in the kitchen with his mother, drinking black tea with sugar and mint brought in from the yard. They were both wide awake anyway and seemed to want to talk. This was something Kenny had done all the time with his dad, especially as a teenager. His mom, too—something they did even more of after Harlan died. Probably as a way to share their grief.

"That thing tonight, I've seen it once before," said Linda.

Kenny looked up from his tea. "What do you mean?"

Linda looked out the window. It was dark. "It was after we moved to Madison. Your dad was just about to leave the graduate program. He had been poring over the pros and cons. Your sister was born, and we were in that little apartment. He just didn't know what to do. That whole English academic career idea was just a whim anyway. I had asked him if he wanted to move back, maybe to Northern Kentucky, at least be near Grandma and Grandpa. He thought we shouldn't rush into anything."

Sometimes Linda called them *Mother and Daddy*, but it comforted him that she still mostly referred to them around Kate and him as *Grandma and Grandpa.*

"We were at this party with a bunch of grad students. None of them ended up really becoming friends of ours. That was such a short little time span down there." She liked Madison's college-town amenities but usually referred to the area around the campus as *down there.*

"People were drinking, of course, and we were listening to records. This one fellow, I think he was from California. He was kind of a golden boy in the program, too. He starts talking about the Midwest. *Midwest* this, *Midwest* that. He was talking about writers, and why all the good ones always leave for the coasts."

She drained her cup. "To this day, I don't know what your father saw in that program. I always wondered *why not history?*"

She looked out the window at the dark for a second, then returned to her memory of the party. "He started going on about painters, too. Grant Wood, in particular, although I believe he was from Iowa. I guess that's still the Midwest." Linda was still under the illusion that the Ohio Valley was the heart of the Midwest, even though most of her friends thought of her as a Southerner.

"I noticed your dad looking upset. Or nervous. Something." She looked into her cup, as if she thought there might still be tea in it. "I knew he was feeling a little off."

Kenny was enthralled. He could picture his father in photographs from that era, just before Kenny was born. He imagined Harlan leaving the master's program, taking the job at the

apartment management company, working around the house, getting ready to have another child. A brief story, natural and completely true.

"The other students were talking kind of competitively with each other. It seemed like they were all trying to impress somebody. The boy from California kept coming back to his dislike for the Midwest as a place for artists, or talented people, or whatever he was trying to say. He was just showing off. The conversation veered into job market territory, publish or perish, the ivory tower, that sort of thing. All of a sudden, in the middle of all this, your dad just stands up."

"Stands up?" asked Kenny, spellbound but nowhere near sleep.

"Right up, like that," she said, nodding her head. "He looked like your friend Wayne did this afternoon, when he took on that strange voice and started talking about Paul Bunyan."

Kenny couldn't think of anything to say. He just watched and waited.

"And out of the middle of nowhere, he starts reciting the Gettysburg Address!"

"Whoa."

"That's right. The Gettysburg Address. It's not too long, really. *Four score and seven years ago*, and so forth. It's only about three paragraphs in total. Your father had it memorized, of course." She got up and put her cup in the sink. She gestured to Kenny, to ask if he wanted her to take his, too.

"No, I still have some," he said.

She continued. "He's reciting, reciting, slowly and looking off kind of in the distance, like. It's like he's competing in a forensics competition, or speech and drama, that sort of thing. His voice even changes, gets higher, like he always said Lincoln's was, in real life."

She paused, as if she were reliving the surprise of it.

"Most of the other graduate students fell right asleep. Everyone but this one fellow's wife—who was not a student, now that I think about it. She was like me, and they had a child, I think. She maybe had some kind of job. She just watched, really focused in. I thought maybe she was a history buff or something. The others—*all of them*—well, I thought they had just passed out."

She made a face to show how startled she had felt at that exact moment.

"We were starting to hear about drugs, and I knew nothing about them. The funny thing is that your dad hadn't had anything, not even a drink, but by the time we got to the car and were headed home, it's like nothing had happened. He didn't remember a thing."

Kenny sat and thought for a second, as Linda got up to wash her cup and the few remaining dishes in the sink. "Not a thing," she said, still in the memory.

What would he make of this? A lot of things had rushed into his mind as he watched Wayne, entranced, put Darlene to sleep. He thought he had figured it out. He had understood that, in these cases, the teller, the *entrancer* or whatever one might call him, was storytelling his way into a place, in a way he thought the listener needed to hear it, to bind him or them more to that fact. What he didn't quite get was how often *the story itself* could be an illusion, conceived from as far outside the place of its telling as the teller was himself, and how it so often missed its mark as a way of bringing all the listeners into the place. Storytellers were often estranged from reality. How many young fathers or mothers, exhausted and trying to put a child to sleep, understood the first thing about a flying car or a wizard or a mountaintop or a talking sheep? Stories were, by definition, out of place, if not also out of time. When Kenny's grandma said someone was *telling stories*, she usually just meant that the person was lying.

His dad's episode (which his mother had just related as a story itself) seemed of a piece with the others Kenny had witnessed or

even caused. The difference in his father's case, of course, was that he had gone right to Lincoln, his beacon, the mostly truthful Kentuckian who had also moved northwest as a young man, defying most conventions along the way. That night, Harlan's Gettysburg Address had been a public announcement of a new life. What the sixteenth president had scribbled on the back of that envelope was the first verse of a swan song.

Fire

When the travelers roused the following morning, Linda had been cooking for a half hour.

"I hope you like biscuits," she said as Kenny ushered Wayne and Fats into the kitchen and set them up with cups of coffee. Stanley was nowhere to be found.

"Can't imagine breakfast without 'em," said Wayne. "I don't think I've had more than ten biscuit-free breakfasts since I was in high school. Not counting my two years in the service, which was the worst food of my life."

"Goetta!" said Taylor, who had come in from the living room holding a drawing of two houses next to what appeared to be some kind of animal. It had a long piece of masking tape affixed to the top of the page. "Look at my cloud," she said to Fats. "It's a tape cloud."

"Nice tape cloud," he replied matter-of-factly.

"What *is* goetta, if I may ask?" inquired Wayne. "It sure smells good. Some kind of sausage? A Madison specialty?"

"Not at all," replied Linda. "It's a breakfast meat from where I grew up, in Northern Kentucky. Pork, beef, some spices, a special kind of oatmeal. Then you fry it up and serve it with eggs. We make it sometimes in our house."

They all began eating. The goetta garnered positive critiques, which were polite and may have also been honest.

"So, what's on your agenda?" asked Linda.

"Well, as much as we'd like to stay and visit, we just about used up all our away time at the shows, and it's a long drive back."

"Aw," said Taylor, working on her drawing at the table. No one realized she had been listening.

"Yep, I'm afraid we've got to get on the road back to old Virginny, ASAP."

"Where'd your friend go off to?" asked Linda. Wayne and Fats looked at each other across the table.

"Well, not so much a *friend* as mostly we just gave him a ride. I imagine he moved on, back to Minnesota or wherever. Thank y'all for putting us up."

"Happy to do it," said Linda, walking over to the stove to surveil the last batch of goetta.

"I'm going to the Gruszkas' in a little while," announced Taylor.

"That's right, Taylor. You're going to help Mary with some things later this morning, aren't you?"

"Yep," said Taylor, without looking up from her work. "Mary is a pretty close friend of mine."

* * * * *

It was still hot, but Kenny decided to ride his old Schwinn ten-speed to work. He had cleaned and oiled the chain after the Virginians' departure and tightened up the brakes a little. It would be a good machine for getting him to and from this new job, and a little breeze there and back could be good in this weather.

Laurent and Kim were spending the whole day at the servery and had scheduled Kenny for a good part of that time, so that they could finish the training he needed and also get help gearing up for the next day's wedding event. Kenny was already set to work five more events following the wedding, two of them booked over the last day alone. It seemed like this could be an okay job after all.

He got to Dorcely Catering around ten and spent just over four hours learning the ropes, prepping and sorting and cleaning, so that, in the morning, they could start fresh and ready for the wedding. He left just after three.

The Schwinn's gears shifted nice and clean as he rode down Williamson Street toward the river. He stopped for the light at Rogers Street and looked down to check his chain. He hadn't ridden the Schwinn regularly since the fall, back in Charlottesville, but nervous habits die hard. When he looked back up, he noticed a thin column of black smoke floating up from the horizon. It hung in the air, crisp and tight like the smoke produced by an extinguished candle, but he could tell it was pretty far off.

By the time he got to Atwood Avenue, the column of smoke was nearer and looked more like a cloud. Kenny thought he could taste something on the air. As he rode past the Barrymore Theater, he realized the smoke was coming from his own neighborhood. *Maybe the Ray-o-Vac factory,* he thought. *Not my house.*

He sped through the remaining few blocks, cut into the neighborhood on Jackson Street, then right onto St. Paul, looking up at the blossoming smoke every couple of seconds to gauge where its source might be. By the time he crossed Ohio, a block or so from home, he knew it was coming from his side of the railroad tracks.

He flew down Talmadge, still a full block from his house, the smoke hanging in the air like morning fog. It was on his tongue, and he coughed as he rode. He could see fire trucks straight ahead, roughly where his own house was. Parts of the sky in front of him were jet black. When he got to the corner, he dropped his bike and ran toward the house he was sure was on fire.

He had guessed wrong, but only by about twenty-five feet.

Thick smoke billowed out of the holes where the Gruszkas' first-floor windows had been. Shards of glass lay glittering across the lawn below them, a few out on the sidewalk. Angry flames licked out through the brume, like little bolts of lightning yearning to strike anything near them. The heat and smoke had blackened triangular swaths of siding above the window holes. Now and then, little flames would snake up through points in the roof, hunting oxygen as the inferno puffed and swelled. Beneath the chorus of rattlings and cracklings, Kenny thought he heard a deep, uninterrupted hum. The house was a dying giant whose last breaths would form not a gasp or a plea but a lullaby.

Neighbors stood in their yards, quietly watching. An ambulance sat in the middle of the street, two uniformed EMTs leaning against the vehicle. A fire truck was parked in the street, another halfway up into the driveway, partly in the yard. The Virgin Mary lay on its side, but the driver had taken care not to disturb the little fence or its wreath. Otherwise, the driveway was empty. Firefighters trained three separate hoses on the house, powerful jets of water curving down into the conflagration.

Linda stood on the sidewalk in front of the Gruszkas' house, screaming *"Taylor Taylor Taylor Taylor Taylor!"* A firefighter restrained her. His helmet lay several feet away; it looked like it had been knocked off in a scuffle.

Kenny noticed the naturalness of this array of things and events, everything in its place at the right time: a split-second of reflection, unbidden and safely removed. *I can see what's happening to something I love,* he thought, *and I can't do a thing about it but watch.* And totally empty of words. The shame he felt was garden-variety, but its smallness horrified him.

Kenny's vision began to blur. Unable to move forward, he stumbled back a few feet then caught himself, pondering the imploding universe that had been his neighbors' home for his entire life.

The Galaxie 500 wheeled around the corner and screeched to a halt in the street. Mary Gruszka got out of the driver's side, both hands to her face for a second or two, then reached back into the car for something. She unlocked the back door. Taylor came out, looking puzzled.

"Taylor! Taylor!" yelled Linda, breaking free of the fireman. He had politely released her. All Kenny could think at that moment was *Maybe that's the firefighter who visited Taylor's school last year*; then he broke into a run toward his mother and Taylor, about to meet on the sidewalk. His mother was still crying, and now Taylor was, too. He joined them, and they all held each other on the sidewalk for a few minutes.

Mary leaned against the fireman who had kept Linda from rushing into the house. "Glenn," she said, her hands still to her cheeks. "Glenn." The fireman put an arm around her to prop her up, and they watched the blaze finish its work, depraved and irrevocable.

Union

Linda's house was unscathed, except for a little smoke damage on the side facing the Gruszkas', and here they all were. Kate had arrived just a few minutes after Kenny, and they had all moved inside. Mary had come with them, then some of her church friends had arrived to check on her. The firefighters got the fire out before nightfall. A police detective and someone from the fire department came in to ask Linda a few questions, which she answered with some difficulty but apparently to the satisfaction of the officials. Mary spoke with them for a few minutes, then excused herself, walked up to Linda's bedroom, and closed the door. Taylor studied the firefighters and the EMTs out the window, as they worked carefully to enter the smoking heap. Kate let her watch until they were in the building, then closed the curtains and turned on the television so she wouldn't see the stretcher that would emerge, inevitably, within twenty or thirty more minutes. It was a long night.

The next morning, Taylor ate her eggs silently, staring off into the distance like a much older child. When she had finished eating, she looked up at her grandmother. "I want to have a family sleepover tonight," she said.

"Of course," replied Linda.

"At my own house."

They got all their things together after breakfast, then spent the rest of the day at Kate's. Kenny worked part of the wedding, having been talked into it by his mother, but came home as soon as the guests had left.

Kate's apartment wasn't big or all that clean, but it was comfortable. Looking out over Milwaukee Street, it was up on the second floor of a two-flat, with a porch across the front. Everyone else was finally asleep, Taylor in bed with her mom, Linda in Taylor's room on an air mattress. Kenny lay on the couch, staring at the ceiling. Everything he'd need for the next day's catering shift was jammed into his backpack, which sat upright against the side of the couch.

He reached over to look at that morning's paper again. The *Capital Times* didn't come on Sundays, so Linda had picked up a thick *Wisconsin State Journal,* which had already published news of the fire.

> ***MAN WHO DIED IN EAST SIDE FIRE CARPENTER AND WAR VETERAN***
>
> *Madison, WI—Glenn Gruszka, 68, died in his home Saturday afternoon. "The place was very cluttered," said Madison Fire Department spokesperson Joe Klingham. "We don't yet know the cause of the fire, but the shop contained a number of flammable solvent materials." Gruszka, a master carpenter for the State of Wisconsin, was also a decorated veteran of the Second World War and fought in the Battle of Okinawa.*

The notice seemed sickeningly brief. Was this all the newspaper had to say about Glenn, the Gruszkas, or their house? Their lives?

The short text reminded Kenny of the basement workshop, though. He had probably been there as many times as he had been to his own grandparents' basement. He had even been to work with Glenn once, in high school, after Harlan died; Glenn had insisted Kenny "get a look-see at the trades." They drove downtown together in the Galaxie 500, to the government building Glenn reported to every morning. He shared the shop with a loosely affiliated team of other carpenters, all of them working for various state offices and sites around Dane County. He shared the shop but had his own workbench. It was neat as a pin, maybe because a good deal of his work was happening somewhere else.

"You got to take care of the place," he had said to Kenny. "Even if you're going to retire from it. Which I'm about to do, in five years. Got to get your pension nice and full though, don't ya know."

Glenn's own workshop was a different story. He had shown Kenny how to use a band saw there, when Kenny was about eleven. They had made a small toy truck together, for a young family who lived behind them on Corry Street. By the time Kenny finally relinquished his shift at the power sander, the toy was smooth as silk—if unrecognizable as a truck. Having come of age during the Great Depression, Glenn saved everything. The place was a skein of piles and drawers and stacks and extension cords.

To avoid reviewing the jarring images of the inferno itself, Kenny revisited the events as a list. A story he could narrate, if only for himself. What had happened that day, and what were the conditions? Mary had left with Taylor to pick up some material for a sewing project they were going to work on together that afternoon. Kenny had gone to work. His mom was home. Kate was gone.

Then his mind returned to Glenn. It wasn't hard to imagine him alone in the shop, hyper-focused on some repair idea. Home, totally free of regular workplace constraints. Extension cords, too many of them, hanging everywhere, too many tools asking for too much current through a wire too thin to accommodate it all. Something burning through a housing. A spark of some kind. The can of solvent, open on the workbench. Glenn's eyes wide open in surprise as he beheld the first small explosion.

Kenny couldn't stop the story. He pictured Glenn alone, knocked back against the wall, entangled momentarily in a shop apron hanging on a hook. In his mind, Kenny could see exactly what Glenn would look like, turning to release his arm, undo the string, as a second container ignited, knocking him to the floor. Kenny envisioned the whole shop wall lit up, the wall where Glenn hung most of the tools, up against forms he had outlined in black marker to designate which tool went where. Kenny kept imagining the violence of the flash in that cramped little trap, everything tasting like metal. Grayish smoke mushrooming out of itself, filling the basement within seconds as the fire raced upward for more kindling.

Kenny couldn't stop. He had to finish. He made himself imagine Glenn, his tortured face, his mouth open—losing consciousness, no longer breathing. Dead.

It was one-thirty in the morning. The hellish vision ceased at once, then he felt a light gust of something come over him and saw a word: *Stay.* It was like he saw it floating. Then he imagined its sound, in different voices: his mother's, his father's, his sister's, his grandparents', Mary's, Glenn's. *Stay.* Each time, a separate voice. *Stay.* He felt his members loosen, his mind collect itself.

He yawned, feeling sleep alight. His muscles relaxed further, in waves—first, his shoulders, then his arms and feet. Next, his legs, which can so famously hold their spark while the rest of you waits patiently for the metamorphosis. Finally, the muscles in his chest and throughout his torso, his stomach in particular.

At first, limpid fragments of thoughts held on. Madison, the East Side, Charlottesville, Talmadge Street. Darlene. Kenny thought again of the fiery house and imagined it in the sky instead of on the ground, where it had always been. Fire yearned for the sky. He imagined the burning building slowly crossing the sky like a constellation, like Orion in winter.

Then the shifting and softening faces of each of the people around him, one after another. Where they were right now, and where they would each go during the day tomorrow. How they spoke to one another and to him, ever returning to each other until they were called, sometimes by surprise, to disappear from the world. Those who died would return in dreams, in stories, in memories shared, over breakfast, in a letter, in a flea-market find. Perhaps even, one day, in a handful of dandelions.

Kenny drifted into sleep.

"This is the last time we shall see one another," said a voice. It was the president, sitting on his enormous stone pedestal. Kenny was standing at his feet, in the Memorial, next to his father. Lincoln was addressing them, even though his stone lips weren't moving at all.

"I understand," said Lincoln. "I have long understood, and I have struggled, even after everything that transpired, after the sought-after conclusions and the histories had put so many things to rest."

Kenny and Harlan looked at one another, then back up at the statue.

"I had no choice in leaving Kentucky," said the president. He was talking to Harlan. "Unlike you, I was only a child. Others took that decision for me—yes, my parents, but also opportunity, the century I was in, perhaps a destiny larger than any of us could imagine." In the dream, a pregnant pause. "That's how so many speak of me now, anyway. I have grown accustomed to exaggeration."

Kenny and Harlan looked around, feeling alone in this place that had seen so much national drama. No one else was there. It was twilight.

Then there *was* someone there, partly obscured by one of the columns that blocked the president's view of the reflecting pool. The person stepped into view. It was a man wearing a cape. He made a theatrical bow then went down on one knee, more contrite than courteous.

"Come closer," said the president to the figure, who stood back up.

It was John Wilkes Booth. He resembled the only photo Kenny believed ever to have seen of the assassin, taken when he was merely a famous actor. Booth strode up next to where Kenny and Harlan were standing, without noticing either of them. He got down on one knee again.

"Mister President," he said, respectfully.

"That's more like it," said the president. "I forgive you."

Booth looked up but maintained his humble stance.

"I know about Montreal," said Lincoln. Booth was listening to every word. "The French have long reclaimed control of most things there, but the English remain." Kenny thought he could see Laurent behind one of the other columns, holding a cast-iron pan and a fishing rod.

"We have been reconciled for some time now, all of us," he said, as if lecturing. "But ah, yes: coexistence. This has been my hope. Union." Still kneeling, Booth recoiled, like a child getting a tetanus shot in the shoulder. "Union," repeated Lincoln.

"What are we doing here, Mr. President?" asked Harlan.

"I often ask myself the same thing," replied Lincoln. "We so badly want to stay, don't we? We belong, we stay, we know. And yet things happen, and some of us leave. We just have to go." *Stay,* thought Kenny.

Lincoln's lips still hadn't moved, but his speech had been lyrical and concise. Harlan looked young, calm, even serene. It crossed Kenny's mind, as he dreamed, that he might not need to meet his father anymore in this way, that he could visit him in other ways, in other places, but that in the meantime there were more important things to do.

"Like get those chafing dishes ready," said Laurent loudly, from behind a distant column.

"That's the spirit," said the statue.

They looked over at Booth, who had stood back up and turned around, his back to them. The edges felt fuzzy now; Kenny wasn't sure if they were still at the Lincoln Memorial, or if the president was even there anymore. Before the pardoned assassin turned back around, Kenny glimpsed long, curly, red hair. Booth had become the woman from the Willy Bear.

"Are you the librarian?" asked Harlan. Kenny was sure she was.

The woman nodded. She held a notebook and a purse. The flute solo from Jethro Tull's "North Sea Oil" wafted through the building.

"I understand," said Harlan.

"Forgive me," said the woman.

"I understand," Harlan repeated.

Epilogue

Kenny had only worked three hours that morning, doing inventory. Laurent and Kim were in Milwaukee to "see a produce guy" but mostly just to get away from Madison for a couple of days. No events at all for a week. It was the first break for any of them since Kenny had started working at Dorcely Catering. He was glad for this little pause before the next cluster of events began in earnest: three weddings and four big meetings in the space of two weeks. Late August was suddenly upon them.

The regular catering job had provided him with enough income to move out of his childhood home. He and Kurt had signed a lease on a basement apartment on Spaight Street—there weren't a lot of windows, but their little backyard had what you could almost call a view of Lake Monona. He had never lived with Kurt, but it seemed promising. Childhood friends and all.

As he biked down State Street, Kenny daydreamed about his imminent lodgings. Nothing cogent, just some scattered, ambient images: a futon against a wall, a table with some things on it, him or Kurt or one of their other friends walking through doorways, into and out of rooms. Imagining the place he would be moving into in just a few days confirmed that he had begun to settle down. Now he was no longer dreaming about *if* he would stay, just *how.*

Darlene had finished her summer internship. The Cottage Grove Press operation was run by a middle-aged married couple, out of their house. They had come from Ithaca, New York, twelve years earlier, for graduate school. Rather than pursue academic careers, they had decided to stay in Madison, to try their hand at publishing obscure works of fiction and poetry.

The internship had ended uncomfortably, though. According to Darlene, the husband "hadn't made any moves" but had taken a shine to her, which was more than evident to his wife. The week before Darlene was set to finish, the wife had left her a note, written in fountain pen, in an elegant envelope. Darlene found it on her desk when she arrived for work that morning. *You may be younger than me*, read the note, *but I know him far better than you ever will.*

It wasn't signed, and no one said a thing about it during the last week of the internship. But the gesture—an envelope left on a desk, the fountain pen, the restrained language—seemed spooky, even vaguely threatening. Darlene invented a family emergency so that she could quit early. She therefore had an extra week of time on her hands, part of which she had spent with Kenny. They had sex a few times, heard some bands, spent time with mutual friends and a few new ones, but the whole thing seemed pretty anticlimactic to Kenny. Agreeable, but a foregone conclusion. Just passing time.

Kenny pedaled through a nearly empty Library Mall and over toward Lake Mendota and Memorial Union. He and Darlene had made plans to grab coffee together on the Union Terrace, the sprawling outdoor café that so many found synonymous with this university that Kenny and Darlene knew, in a neighborly way, but had never attended.

Kenny was supposed to meet Darlene at two, at "any table near the water." As he rounded the fountain in the middle of the plaza, he looked at his watch. It was only one o'clock, so he decided to ride up Observatory Drive and look down at Lake Mendota for a while.

He rode around the serpentine curve that climbed from the Union to the buildings at the top of the hill, and to a couple of spots where he could look down on that huge lake. He felt the altitude change as he rounded the main curve, looking down to his right at some sailboats that were probably a mile from the shore. *How different this is,* he thought, remembering UVA, its red-bricked, white-columned order and uniformities, its fragrant springtime pavilions, its blue mountains in the background at so many turns. Here was the University of Wisconsin, its gravitas on comfortable display among glacier-formed hills and boulders and trees and lake views, its sandstone brick buildings settled unapologetically among this cacophony of other materials surely chosen for their proximity, cost, and, to a certain extent, their beauty.

The climb left Kenny breathless but pensive. He had grown up on the other side of the Capitol Square, closer to that other lake that lapped onto the southeastern shores of the isthmus. Then he had gone southeast, well beyond his parents' native Kentucky, to cut his adult teeth in the Birthplace of Presidents. Virginia was also for lovers, as the license plate reminded everyone, making it a natural spawning ground not only for future refugees but for whole new places, like the Commonwealth of Kentucky. Which spawned Kentuckians like Linda and Harlan—like Daniel Boone, like Lincoln, like countless others—many of whom themselves had been bound to leave, to settle somewhere else. It had been a restless couple of centuries.

He got to the top of Bascom Hill and pulled up onto the sidewalk to catch his breath. There were very few people—a student or two, a professor, a couple of tourists. Fall classes were still at least two full weeks away. In front of Bascom Hall, at the top of the hill, a statue of the sixteenth president presided over a university but was positioned so as to ponder the city itself: its streets, the Capitol building's white rotunda, and whatever lay beyond. Oddly enough for his time, this particular Lincoln was made to face forever east.

Kenny got off the Schwinn and walked over to the statue. He leaned the bike on its kickstand and sat down on the semi-circular stone bench.

"Hey McLuher," said a familiar voice. Kenny looked around and saw Darlene. She looked like she had just come out of Bascom Hall, or maybe from around its side.

"Fancy meeting you here," he said, sounding like both his mother and his father.

"Not our designated location, I know. I was talking with this grad student," she said, waving her hand dismissively. "Just a woman I met through a Cottage Grove lit project. She was finishing some summer class and is working on some stuff I'm interested in." She forced a smile that announced a new topic. "Want to *set a spell*?" she said, in her best imitation of Linda doing her exaggerated hillbilly-hostess voice. Kenny appreciated this trace of something they had briefly held in common.

"Sure," he said, patting the stone next to him. Darlene swept the bench lightly with her hand then sat down a couple of feet from Kenny, more primly than usual. She looked down the hill.

"Sure glad I didn't have to walk up this thing every day."

"Me too. Biking up was enough for me." They sat in silence for a minute or two.

"Listen, Kenny," said Darlene, in a way that underlined a certain intimacy but also seemed a little more explicit than usual. "I'm afraid I have to stand you up for that Terrace date today. I'm sorry. My mom needs me this afternoon for some organizing. We're going to K-Mart and stuff." She shook her head as if to start over. "Anyway, just getting ready for me to leave and stuff."

And stuff. She sounded a lot like Doug Stacy all of a sudden.

"It's all right," said Kenny. Any sudden jealousy he might have felt was already dissipating.

"I've really liked reconnecting with you," she said, suddenly, then kissed him briefly, definitively. He kissed her back, the same way. They stayed in their original sitting positions.

"My mom is excited that I'm going to Ann Arbor. She keeps talking about the 'wider world' and stuff, and I get it, I agree. But it's a little scary, still. Penn was just college. But now grad school... I don't know where this leads. I never thought I'd feel that way."

Kenny nodded. He kept forgetting that others of his age and station might also be having second thoughts about staying or going.

"I'm not leaving 'til Thursday," she said, getting up and putting her backpack on one shoulder. "Maybe we can have a rain check?"

"Sure."

"Let's do it," she said. "Call me in the morning?"

"Yeah," he replied. She waved and walked down the hill.

It was warm but pretty mild for the middle of August. *I'll just stay here a little while,* thought Kenny. He watched Darlene as she moved into the distance, growing smaller with each step, then looked up at Lincoln again. "Neither one of us went to school here," he said aloud, unused to conversing with Lincoln outside of his dreams. "But here we are."

He looked back down the sidewalk and could see Darlene's black backpack against her light blue t-shirt. She was almost all the way to Science Hall now, near the bottom of the hill. It occurred to Kenny that she was not unlike his own parents in some ways—striking out at this age, finished with college, and starting to explore a professional life but not exactly sure what it would be. She was a little like his classmates and fellow caterers at UVA in that way, too—except maybe for Tracy, whose remarkable letter Kenny had not replied to yet but which, two months on, he still kept folded up in his backpack.

He had read somewhere that during most of the nineteenth century, eighty percent of free adult men in Kentucky were landless. Big families willed their property, if they had any, to the eldest son, with maybe a sack of coins for the others, sending them outward to meet their own fates. Maybe this had been true in Wisconsin, too.

Kenny had gone to Virginia because his father had died, and he had chosen to major in history because stories could help him understand where he was. But what had he actually learned about history? Those boys on farms, or wherever, moving around the country—and the girls, too—were part of some bigger American story he had studied in class. He knew that there were a lot more stories out there, too, all kinds of books about the Civil War, invisible frontiers, boundaries, diaries, paintings. Full of contradictions, like all stories. And he wouldn't even be able to learn about most of the undiscovered parts of the story, the ones that had been lost or destroyed. Fires. Slavery. Family rifts.

Or the unwritten ones. Indigenous people in Wisconsin kept their most important secrets for themselves. He knew there were stories, generations of them, somewhere, housed in those memories, so many of them unspoken outside their community. And what about recent immigrants? There were just too many stories to explain this place of his.

"Kenny McLuher? Is that you?"

Mrs. Brooking, his third-grade teacher, had appeared on the sidewalk, coming from somewhere nearby. He hadn't seen her for years, other than the occasional sighting at the grocery store or on the street, but he recognized her immediately. Probably in her early forties now, she moved with a little more conscious rigor than most women her age, but with an ease Kenny hadn't noticed as a third-grader. Strung loosely over her shoulder was the same kind of backpack Darlene had been wearing.

"How are you, Mrs. Brooking?"

She laughed. "Pretty well. I'm not teaching anymore, though."

"Oh yeah?" said Kenny, suddenly aware of his posture.

"Yep. Grad school. Went back for my master's. I'm just up here gathering some things from the TA office. Finished the degree yesterday. Big oral exam!" She laughed.

"Aha. The teacher has become the student!" he said gregariously but still standing straight as a parking meter. "What did you study?"

"Public history. I start a new job next month, in Oconomowoc." She adjusted her backpack. "I'll actually be working for the historical society there. A museum job, partly."

"So you're leaving Madison?"

"Yes, but really I'm going home. I grew up in Delafield. My husband is from Waukesha. My parents live in the area. His, too. You know, we don't have children, and our parents are kind of... in need of some attention. It's the right time."

Kenny glanced at Lincoln again and thought of his father.

"Aha," he said, looking back at Mrs. Brooking. "Well, that's cool. History. I love history." She checked the time again, so he decided not to elaborate.

"I'd love to hear more sometime, but I'm running late. Jim—that's my husband—is coming to pick me up. I'm supposed to meet him down on Park Street right now." She put the loose backpack strap up around her other shoulder and held her hand out to Kenny. "It was good to see you again. I hope we can catch up sometime. Come to the museum and see me!"

"Sounds great, Mrs. Brooking. Good luck." He shook her hand.

"Goodbye, Kenny." She walked down the hill, the same way Darlene had.

The sun had gone behind a cloud, but Kenny was still a little drowsy. He looked up at Lincoln again, remembering that around commencement weekend, UW graduates often posed in their regalia up on the statue's lap, smiling for family cameras, holding their diplomas or their caps or a bottle of champagne, to celebrate their passage through this place.

No one was around, or almost no one. A middle-aged couple, alumni maybe, walked over by South Hall, across from the sidewalk Darlene and Mrs. Brooking had taken down the hill. A couple of people walked out of the Law School, further down on that same side. Everyone going somewhere, coming from somewhere, no one loitering but Kenny.

He looked at Lincoln again, at his silent but rough-looking features. *You came from Kentucky,* thought Kenny, even sleepier now. Lincoln, a statue, did not move. *You are in a lot of places, and yet you are here,* thought Kenny. He sat down at the base of the statue and touched the stone. It felt warm, but just a little. Kenny felt the urge to lie down, which he did but kept his hand on the plinth. The sky was still a little cloudy, but it felt good. He lay completely down, against the warm stone, and rested his head on his arm.

A line from the poem he had found at St. Vinny's earlier in the summer floated into his head. *We belong on this earth, on this earth we remain.* A few seconds later, he was completely asleep.

Over by the entrance to Bascom Hall, a woman wandered slowly along the sidewalk. Her hair was curly and brownish-red. It wasn't clear where she had come from—maybe another classroom building, maybe down the hill. Kenny could neither see nor hear her, asleep as he was.

She ambled up to the middle-aged couple, who seemed a little alarmed, as if she were going to ask them for money. They had never seen her before.

"Forgive me," she whispered to them, her notebook clutched to her chest.

Discussion Questions

1. There are several important women in Kenny McLuher's life. Which female character do you find most interesting?
2. Who is your favorite character overall?
3. Does this novel make you think of a place you have lived? How?
4. What could be the benefits, for a young person, of settling down in a community? What could be the drawbacks?
5. What does the hypnotic power that befalls Kenny in his last year of college have to do with his search for a place in the world?
6. What role does sleep play in this story?
7. How do preconceived ideas about race affect the characters?
8. Is *Settle Down* a story about immigration?
9. Do you believe Kenny has matured by the end of the story?
10. Would you recommend *Settle Down* to friends? Why or why not?

Acknowledgments

As a high school student in Northern Kentucky, I did a lot of public speaking. It was instructive and a lot of fun, but the most important thing I learned was that, in the "storytelling" category at the state speech and drama competition, the winners always came from the mountains. Writing can be solitary, but storytelling cannot. It is probably the most ancient form of community, after family, so here I would like to thank mine.

My wife Victoria Ellington-Deitz has inspired me with her own work and way of seeing things. Honest, insightful, and resilient, she has encouraged me for so long and in so many ways that I never know how to thank her properly. I usually just do so by repeating myself. My love for writing, teaching, and playing music is something she has always seemed to understand, and her curiosity and enthusiasm about my projects are more important to me than she can ever know.

My son Mitch Deitz, a lifelong storyteller and now screenwriter, read my first early drafts during a period of time when many of us in the family were reading through one of his first big projects, aloud and in character. His feedback on the beginnings of *Settle Down* helped me enormously, and the writers' group he runs in Chicago with his wife Ryley is a living reminder of the thoughtful and energetic generation of storytellers coming up behind my own.

My hardworking literary daughter Ella Deitz, a published writer herself, gave me other invaluable ideas on drafts of early chapters—with the precision only working poets can produce on the spot. I am particularly grateful, in this case, for her questions about children's stories. Overall, though, I feel lucky to be around her often enough to catch regular glimpses of her endlessly creative world of ideas.

An accomplished writer and musician himself, my oldest son Wilder Deitz read the first complete draft of *Settle Down* all the way through while we all hunkered down in a Northwoods cabin, taking his much-deserved vacation time to read, take notes, and discuss the manuscript with me. It was a memorable and productive conversation. I could not remember ever experiencing such depth when discussing my own work, even in professional settings. This made me proud but should not have surprised me; this is the man who, as a four-year-old child, once asked me to retell a bedtime story I had devised the night before "but with a different narrator."

Thanks also to my longtime friend John Galligan, whose own novels have inspired me for three decades now. John's thorough read-throughs, questions, and advice on writing have also reminded me why his own boys, longtime musical collaborators of my own kids, are both so talented.

I am grateful for Michael T. Braun, owner and editor-in-chief of Orange Hat Publishing and my editor for this book, a workhorse with a keen eye and an inspiring wit. He is one of those rare readers who can keep his eyes on the forest and the trees at the same time. I thank him heartily for his attention to the final drafts of this novel and for the unique conversation—on family, place, writing, and Madison—that our work together has occasioned.

One of the central places I reimagined in this novel was a real bar on Williamson Street, for a long time the heart and soul of Madison's Near East Side. I spent a good deal of time in the Willy Bear as a young man, mostly setting up and taking down amplifiers, drum kits, and microphone stands with my bandmates in the Isle of Dogs, the trio I had moved to Madison with. We played the Willy Bear many times. My late friend Steve "Truk" Cunningham (1962-2016), to whom I dedicate this book, worked the grill behind the bar there when he wasn't running sound for bands or bouncing drunks out of the Crystal Corner. We met Truk at the first show we landed in Madison. We opened for Boston indie rockers Dumptruck in the fall of 1988 at the Nar Bar, and Truk was the sound guy. Within a few months, he was so enthusiastic about our music that he offered to fund an album-length recording session of our original music at Madison's Smart Studios. He co-engineered the recording with his friend Butch Vig, who would later produce Nirvana and the Smashing Pumpkins and play drums in a band called Garbage. Our little band broke up a year later and never pursued any public life for that recording, but Truk didn't seem bothered by this. "I just wanted you to get it down," he said, a memory which warms my heart to this day. He lived in Alaska for a few years before returning to Wisconsin. He left us for good in 2016, and there has been a Truk-sized hole in Madison ever since. May he rest in peace.

My bandmates from the Isle of Dogs, Craig Totten and Kliff Hopson, are dearer than ever to me, even though we all live so far apart now. I thought of them every day I sat down to work on this story. I also want to thank my subsequent bandmates, with whom I have made much live and recorded music in the intervening years, and with whom I hope to make much more: Joe Meisel, Steve Burke, Dave Foss, Wilder Deitz, Mitch Deitz, and Ella Deitz. And those previous musical collaborators, too: Dave and Jacqui Killen, Jim Faris, David Rothman, Dave Purcell. And, to an important extent, anyone who has ever played in my East Side Acoustic Ensemble, ESAE for short. Go East Side.

Thanks to my good friend and master wordsmith John Robinson, whose critical eye and ear have boosted my own creative efforts for decades now and whose buoyant enthusiasm for music and literature of all kinds has never ceased to amaze me.

A rousing appreciative cheer to members of my old softball team, the Dark Hillbilly Novelists. The best nine-year run of my very modest athletic career so far. Did we have one of the worst records in the city? Yes. Were we once taunted by a rival Madison team, who playfully shouted insults about Southern authors just before our game? It had not occurred to me that an opposing pitcher might suggest that William Faulkner "didn't use punctuation because he had no control over it" or that "Tennessee Williams was a little too close to his mother."

Big thanks to Louisville pals Jonathan, Maggie, Whitney, Chris and Langan, for all the hosting, visiting, correspondence and friendship—and for seeing the borders around the region we all share so much more generously than the maps or culture usually do.

Merci/grazie to my students, former students and colleagues in the Department of French and Italian at the University of Wisconsin-Madison, where I make my living. I am grateful for their support, their ideas, and for the community we make together in times that have sometimes been outright hostile to the humanities as we have long understood them.

Thanks to longtime collaborator and fellow language nerd, Quebec writer and TV/film director Christian Laurence, an indefatigable and thoroughly bilingual role model who once sang my country's national anthem with me at a Montreal Canadiens game without error. I hope he'll remember that *Je vais t'avoir, mon estie!* will always rhyme with *Mille mercis, mon ami.*

Thank you to the group we call the Pals: Johnny, Didi, Cheryl, Zeke, Michelle, Joe, Cath, Andy, Jenny, Eric, Nina, Brendan, Meera, and the children and grandchildren of all those people, who I love like my own nieces and nephews.

Thanks to Thomas Jefferson for founding the University of Virginia. It must have been no small task. I learned a ton there.

Thank you to Abraham Lincoln for showing us how vision and compromise can keep us together. It cost him his life, of course. It also appears to have drained him considerably along the way. Mr. Lincoln, we are forever indebted to you.

Thank you to my whole extended family, including my cousins, aunts and uncles, all nieces and nephews, my in-laws, and the in-laws of those in-laws now, too. We are sad when one of us must leave, and happy when new members arrive, but let there always be reunions, food, singing, games, help with the cooking and dishes, and a kids' table open to children and adults alike.

Finally, I am especially indebted to the family that raised me—all of them, but my parents, Sandra Tattershall and Merritt S. Deitz, Jr., my stepparents, Dick Hataway and Sandy Freeburger, my grandparents, Paul and Stella Tattershall and Merritt and Irene Deitz, and my sister Hillary Delaney in particular. My childhood place remains dear to me. A grandparent myself now, I return to Kentucky several times a year and always take long walks past our old houses or spots where houses I once lived in used to stand. I was born in Louisville, a city I love and where I have spent much time (much of it in the East End, which readers of this book may find fateful), but the lion's share of my youthful days was spent in Florence. Twelve years of public school, with friends and family at every turn. Not unlike the typical family home, Florence is a place of constant, tremendous, and sometimes strange transformations, and rural Kenton County—where my mother grew up and where we lived later, next door to my grandparents' house—is no longer as rural as it was when I was a boy there. I feel a unique love for these places, which are just a few miles from each other and interrelated in so many ways. In spite of all the change they have undergone and which I sometimes complain so loudly about, they remain with me. I hope that those I have known and loved who live there, struggling or thriving, understand that, by settling in Wisconsin long ago, I have beaten that path across Illinois and Indiana into an irrevocable trail leading two ways home. I will never leave Northern Kentucky behind.

About the Author

Ritt Deitz has taught French at the University of Wisconsin-Madison since 2000. A Kentucky Colonel and a Knight in France's Order of Academic Palms, Deitz is also a songwriter and musician. Born and raised in Kentucky, he lives in Madison—where he has long since settled down.

www.ingramcontent.com/pod-product-compliance
Lightning Source LLC
Chambersburg PA
CBHW011746010726
47498CB00012B/2954
* 9 7 8 1 6 4 5 3 8 6 0 9 4 *